The Music of Unexpected Things

JAMIE DEACON

Ink Lane
Publishing

The Music of Unexpected Things

Published 2024 by Ink Lane Publishing
Copyright © 2024 Jamie Deacon

Paperback ISBN: 978 1 0686249 6 4
eBook ISBN: 978 1 0686249 7 1

Cover Design: Natasha Snow
www.natashasnow.com

Editing and Formatting: Debbie McGowan
www.inroadpublishing.com

Ink Lane
Publishing

CONTENTS

ORIENTATION WEEKEND

We are the music makers,
and we are the dreamers of dreams.

– Arthur O'Shaughnessy

1. GEORGIE

"STOP THE CAR. I can't do this."

Panic beats like a bass drum in my throat. Hunched in the passenger seat of Jake's Fiesta, I clutch my knees to my chest and force the words down. This is normally one of my fave things to do, ride in the car with the windows down, nineties rock pulsing while the breeze snatches at my hair.

Not today.

Today, nerves rough-and-tumble in my stomach. I must've been mad to sign up for this. Me, Georgie Wilde, the girl with no mates. I've never spent so much as a night without my family. Now I'm facing four weeks away from home, away from everything I know. Nuts, pure and simple.

But how can I say any of it? For months, ever since I got my acceptance letter, it's been *Dukes this, Dukes that*. Must've bored my family rigid. After all my big talk, there's no way I can admit the truth—that the idea of camp, of interacting with my campmates, scares the crap out of me.

Besides, this is my dream, right? Hours of guitar practice that've left my fingers tough as an armadillo's arse. Homework handed in late because I was tinkering with a new song. Feels like my whole life—all seventeen years, two months and fourteen days—has been leading up to this.

Time for a distraction.

I reach behind me to check on Star, strapped into her travel harness. She nudges a cold nose into my palm, an obvious plea to be unshackled. Poor girl. Being forced to sit for the entire journey isn't her idea of fun. My guide dog never stands when lying down's an option and submits to walks with the enthusiasm of a sugar addict on their way to the dentist's.

Lazy animal.

I scratch her under the chin. In the months we've been together, Star's become far more than my eyes. Apart from my brother, she's my best mate. Dunno what I'd do without her.

I turn to face front once more and rest my head back against the seat. Traffic thunders past on the motorway, the noise competing with Def Leppard's *Adrenalize*. The slipstream blasts July heat and the smell of sun-roasted tarmac into my nose. It should be the smell of anticipation, of promise. Instead, it makes my insides roil.

Everyone's heard of Dukes. The academy of contemporary music has churned out more stars than the Brit School. I've dreamt of going there since I was seven and watched my first Brit Awards. Curled on our living room sofa, I sat entranced by Sarel's brown-sugar vocals as she strummed her way through 'All I Want is You'. Later, when she went up to collect the award for Best British Female Artist and thanked Dukes for helping her get where she was, I thought...*that could be me.*

Ten years later, here I am, on my way to Dukes' famous summer camp. This is my chance to finally make friends, my chance to land the scholarship that'll change my future. Is it any wonder I'm bloody terrified?

It's a few seconds before I twig the album's finished. I let my cheek loll against the seat belt, listening to the wind and the rumble of the engine. Then growling guitars and an explosion of drums rip through the car.

I shoot upright, feet thudding to the floor. "Jake!"

"What?" he asks, tone innocent. "Thought you'd like to hear the new Crowbar album."

I snort. Me and my twin might enjoy plenty of the same stuff—Sunday lie-ins, classic sitcoms, sweet and salty popcorn—but heavy metal isn't one of them. "Turn this racket off."

"Racket? This is a work of genius." He gasps in mock outrage but snags his phone from behind the handbrake. Beautiful quiet descends. "How about some Slipknot?"

"God, even worse."

"Cannibal Corpse?"

I punch him on the leg. "Hey, no murdering my ears. Not when you won't see me for ages."

"Fine." He sighs. "But can we at least have something from this side of the millennium?"

Unlike me, Jake hasn't inherited Dad's passion for nineties rock. Some people have no taste. I roll my eyes and open the music app on my phone. Voiceover reads the list of artists aloud as I scroll. I hit play on 'The Resistance' and Matt Bellamy's powerful vocals wash over me.

How long have we been driving? An hour and a half? It can't be much further. I dig a sherbet lemon from the glove box and suck on it, trying to dull the nausea.

"Thanks for the lift," I tell Jake. He's doing me a huge favour, especially as he's supposed to be at his girlfriend's birthday dinner later.

Mum couldn't bring me, since she's on one of her conferences. Networking opportunities, she calls them. Glorified piss-ups,

Dad claims. Dad did offer, but he's a soppy git, would've got all blubbery and ended up setting me off, too. Plus, this way, he doesn't have to leave the record store on a Saturday. Nope, having my brother drop me off will be much more low key.

"No probs," Jake says. "I'll need to shoot off as soon as you're settled, though. Kirsten'll kill me if I'm late."

I swallow, forgetting about my sweet, and almost choke. *Don't think about it. You'll be fine. Just don't think about it.*

Dukes has four houses. Lennon and Warwick flank the right-hand edge of campus and have been shut up for the holidays. We head across to the opposite side, past Fitzgerald and on to Osborne. My house. The one to be in, according to my brother, the Sabbath fan. Me? I'm just glad the flat I'm sharing with four others is on the ground floor. That'll make taking Star out much easier.

"I'm gonna make a move," Jake says, returning to my new room from the tiny en suite. "If that's all right."

It isn't all right. I almost throw myself on him, cling to his legs like a toddler and bawl. *Please, don't go. Don't leave me here.*

I force a grin. "Course. You don't want to incur the wrath of Kirsten."

I'm impressed how nonchalant I sound, but I've reckoned without my stupid face. It betrays every embarrassing emotion, whether I want it to or not.

"Hey." Jake wraps me in a hug. I breathe in his scent; washing powder and Hugo Boss. He's a huge softy, my twin. Not that you'd think it to look at him, with his buzzcut and skull tattoos. He gives great hugs, too, comforting as hot tomato soup.

"You'll have a blast." He slaps me on the back. "Go show everyone what you're made of."

I huff out a shaky laugh. What? A quivering blob of jelly? Because that's what I'm made of right now.

When Jake's gone, I take a deep breath. *Don't panic. You can do this. One step at a time.* Task one…unpack.

I kneel on the floor, instrument case cradled to my body. The way I handle it, you'd think the Fender inside was the crown jewels. May as well be, seeing as how long I had to save up for it. Best guitar I've ever owned. I slide the electro-acoustic under the bed and have to stop myself crawling in after it like the world's most cowardly dust mite.

I sit back on my heels, brushing the chin-length tangle off my face, and squish my eyes shut. When I open them again, I'll be lounging on our living room sofa, watching *The Chase* with a cup of tea. I won't be alone in an unfamiliar place, won't have to confront the terrifying ordeal of meeting my fellow campers.

God, snap out of it. This is your dream. You've wanted it for as long as you can remember. Sarel didn't become a star by hiding away, did she? At this rate, your family'll be the only ones who ever hear your music.

I get up to explore this space that'll be mine for the next four weeks. Wardrobe and built-in desk along one wall, single bed against the other with a cabinet beside it. The air smells like our house after the cleaner's been, of furniture polish and vacuumed carpet.

Star's having no trouble adjusting. The instant Jake put her bed in the corner, she curled up like a furry snail shell. I crouch beside her, stroking my guide dog's silky head. Soundbites of laughter and conversation waft through the open window. Fifty-nine teenagers breaking into cliques, forming bonds.

It's not fair, how making friends comes so easily to everyone else. You only have to walk down the school corridor to see it, huddles of students whispering secrets and planning their weekends. I'm left on the outside, an observer. No one's mean. Not on purpose, anyway. They'll say hi to me, ask for my input when we work on group projects. It just never occurs to them I might want to be included.

Don't think about school. My hand fists in Star's fur. Things will be different this summer; they have to be. If I can't find my people among musicians, what hope do I have?

2. MINA

I ADORE MY PARENTS, truly I do. I love cosy afternoons in the
kitchen with Dad, soft rain pattering against the window,
the air fragrant with spices as he prepares my favourite Arabic
dishes. I love going for meandering walks through Highnam
Court Gardens with Mum, the two of us arm in arm like sisters.
I love them even while there's this part of myself—a secret, vital
part—they'll never understand. Right now, though, as I see
them off from the front steps of Dukes Academy, I can't wait for
them to leave.

"You're quite sure this is what you want, galbi?" Dad asks,
using the Arabic word for 'my heart'. "You can still change your
mind, come home with us."

"Dad." I resist the temptation to roll my eyes. As if I could
simply throw it away, this opportunity I've dreamt of since
I was a little girl. Then again, my parents don't have a clue how
important this summer is, the hopes tied up in it.

"Samir," Mum reproves him and pulls me into a hug. "You'll
have a wonderful time, sweetheart."

Thank you, Lord, for giving me Mum on my side. I squeeze her
tight, resting my head on her shoulder. Dad wasn't against me
attending the summer camp—not exactly—but he's cautious
by nature. Unlike Mum, whose family has lived here for three
generations, Dad emigrated from Iraq to accept his place at
Cambridge. He's mellowed in the years since he and Mum fell in

love at medical school, but he still adheres to his strict Catholic upbringing.

When Mum releases me, my fingers slip into the pocket of my dress to fiddle with my phone. I've been itching to text Gareth since we arrived, but my parents insisted on helping me unpack and haven't left me alone for a moment.

Dad lays a hand on my back. "Before we head off, I think you and I should have a talk."

Did he read my mind? *Please, God, let the ground open up and swallow me like the blood of Abel.* Dad already had a lengthy conversation with the college to ensure I ended up in a single-sex flat. Poor Dad. He has no idea his efforts are wasted on me. If he did, he'd never look at me with that same unconditional love again.

Mum nudges me. "It isn't that your dad doesn't trust you. He never tires of telling people how sensible you are."

Oh, yes, Little Miss Sensible, that's me. I work hard at school, never flout my curfew, and attend church with him and Mum every Sunday. I'm the epitome of the good Catholic daughter—on the surface, anyway.

"So," Dad says, adopting his *I'm about to launch into a lecture* voice, "on the subject of boys…"

THE INSTANT MY parents' car is out of sight, I spin into a graceless pirouette right there in the deserted car park. Arms outflung, hair and skirt flying, I let the anticipation fill me up like warm caramel. At last, this magical summer can begin.

Once I've slowed to a stop, I extract my phone to check the time. Sugar. Unless I get a move on, I'll be late for the welcome meeting. I hurry into the foyer of the Dukes Building, ballet pumps slapping the polished wooden floor. A few stragglers are trickling in from the campus, thank goodness, and I duck around an elegant pillar to hide among them, texting Gareth as I walk.

They've just left. Coming to find you.

I've barely tapped 'send' when my phone lights up with a string of emojis—confetti balls, popping champagne corks, a person with their arms raised in celebration. My smile stretches so wide my cheeks ache. An entire month to devote to music and my best friend in the world. What could be more perfect?

Double doors lead off to one side of the foyer, and beyond them—my heart accelerates into a wild arpeggio—the famous Dukes concert hall. I follow the other latecomers inside, pausing to take it all in.

French windows line the walls, thrown open to let in a breeze and the golden evening haze. To my left, banks of seats upholstered in burgundy velvet rise towards the rear of the hall, and to my right, the focal point of the large space, is the stage. It's empty now, apart from a drum kit and the most gorgeous grand piano I've ever seen. I long to run my fingers over its keys, to send crystalline notes bouncing off the vaulted ceiling. So many artists have kickstarted their careers from this platform, and I, Mina Farhan, have the chance to perform from those hallowed boards.

I scan the assembled crowd for my friend. Most people are already sitting in huddles, but the more confident wander from group to group. A stocky white girl in a Manic Street Preachers T-shirt is slumped in the third row, her unruly bob the same colour as the golden retriever at her feet.

She has an interesting face. It captures my attention, not because of the strong jaw and deep-set grey eyes, but because of how expressive it is. Wariness, discomfort, hope…emotions play across her features like sunlight and shadow on the surface of a lake.

"Hun, over here."

I'd know it anywhere, that deep voice with the lilting Welsh accent. I tear my gaze from the girl and there he is, a couple of rows further back, his size and mop of red curls making him easy to spot.

Gareth Thomas—my Gaz—listed in my contacts as Gabby, a fictitious girl in my biology class. He's another of the countless deceits that make up my life and the only person who knows the real me. It kills me, lying to my parents on a daily basis, but what choice do I have? if I told Mum and Dad about our friendship, I'd have to explain how we met, and that would lead to questions I'm nowhere near ready to answer.

He waves, shoulders hunched as if praying no one else will notice, and I hurry towards him. Self-consciousness is a curious trait for a musician, especially one who sings and plays piano as beautifully as he does, but I've spent more than a few nights with him on WhatsApp, soothing his nerves before a school concert.

"You made it." Gareth leaps up as I reach him, pulling me into his arms, and it's like being enveloped by a teddy bear. His eyes, which have only ever met mine through a screen, are a brilliant emerald.

"No, *we* made it." I rest my cheek against the worn cotton of his shirt. He's here. After all the planning and dreaming and whispered conversations into the early hours, he's really here.

Gareth opens his mouth as a torrent of words prepares to spill out of me, but before either of us can say anything, the strum of an acoustic guitar issues from hidden speakers. He sits back down, tugging me into the seat beside him, and those who'd been milling around scramble to take their places. My attention, along with everyone else's, is drawn to the front of the hall.

A video plays, projected onto the backdrop, which I realise now is a giant movie screen. A single spotlight relieves the darkness, shining onto a stage from another place, another time. Perched on the edge, all soulfulness and molten-chocolate eyes, is a young black man. He sits with his long legs dangling, leaning towards the unseen audience as though sharing the secrets of the universe. He cradles a night-dark guitar to his body with such tenderness it could be his newborn child, and the melody he coaxes from it is sweet and full of love.

Then he starts to sing. He sings of happiness discovered and of the simple joy that comes from spending time with the people most precious to you. The espresso richness of his voice tingles in the hush, and I'm not the only one who's spellbound. My heart aches with the beauty of it, and with the knowledge of what came next, because I know this video. We all do. It's iconic, the performance that closed the last concert Marlon Dukes ever gave. The last concert before he set off to fly home to his wife and two-year-old daughter, only for his private plane to crash into the Atlantic.

When the final notes have faded, I turn to Gareth through my tears, and he gives me a watery smile. A striking woman with ebony skin and wrists adorned with a rainbow of bangles walks onto the stage. She wipes her eyes, then gazes out at us with a rueful chuckle.

"Sorry, that gets me every time. My name's Leticia Dukes, and it's my pleasure to welcome each and every one of you to our summer camp." Marlon's mother spreads her arms as if to enfold us in a giant group hug. "I set up the academy after my son's death, as a tribute to him, and for the past twenty years, it's helped many talented young people gain a foothold in the music industry. The programme is funded in part through the charity I established for that specific purpose, with student fees making up the rest. We'd love to be able to provide the course completely free, but sadly the running costs are too high. However…"

Leticia Dukes pauses and the tension in the hall intensifies. I grip my hands together in my lap. This is it, the reason we're all here.

"However," she continues, "we do offer one scholarship place to the student the panel deems would most benefit. Every one of you sitting in this room was selected for showing particular promise, and at the end of this four weeks, we'll be awarding someone a fully funded spot on our course beginning next September."

As she talks, explaining more about the scholarship, my imagination roams. I'm no longer simply here for the summer; I'm a Dukes student about to start my first term. It's a fantasy, a beautiful impossibility. My steady, practical parents— Dad a local GP, Mum an ENT surgeon—would never agree to it. They've always stressed the importance of a reliable career, one which will save me from the money worries that turned my grandparents' hair prematurely grey. How can I tell them all I want to do is write country songs?

But I've struck a deal with myself. If I win the scholarship, I'll pluck up the courage to reveal the truth—that my heart lies outside the medical profession. The chances of winning are slim, I know that, and I'll be up against fifty-nine unbelievably talented musicians. If, though, by some miracle I do manage it, maybe—just maybe—it will be enough to convince my parents my dream is worth a shot.

3. GEORGIE

T HE SCHOLARSHIP.
My fists clench in my lap. I need that full ride. Without it, my chances of convincing Mum to let me come here next year are smaller than Dad's last royalty cheque. She's already had to watch someone she loves pine for a failed music career. No way she's risking that for me.

I have to win.

"Our summer camp has become a real family affair," Leticia's saying. "In a moment, I'll hand you over to my granddaughter, Calypso, but first, let me introduce you to Dutch, my wonderful grandson-in-law who's working the projector."

"Hey, guys." A sleepy drawl floats from somewhere to my left.

Several of the people around me sigh. I can practically hear them melting into puddles of mush. Chris Holland—AKA Dutch—is the lead singer of indie rock band The Desired. Half the teenagers in the country are mad for him.

"Now here's my gorgeous Calypso," Leticia continues. "She'll tell you a little more about the camp schedule."

The hall explodes with clapping and wolf whistles. I straighten in my seat. Any second now, Marlon Dukes' daughter will walk out in front of us. Since releasing her debut at eighteen, her folksy pop sound has earned her a cult following. She's a total legend. And I'll actually get to meet her.

Calypso hurries onto the stage. Even her footsteps vibrate with energy, the same energy she brings to her music.

"Hey, everyone," she says, the smile clear in her tone. "I'm so looking forward to getting to know you all over the next month. I'll be taking the Music Through the Decades session every weekday at nine. We'll look at how different genres have changed through the years and see how you can gain inspiration for your own work. Then, after morning break, you'll have Performance Technique. These workshops will be divided according to preferred instrument, but you can find out more about the tutors and venues in your welcome pack. If anyone hasn't got their welcome pack, see me after this and I'll sort you out."

Calypso pauses for breath, her foot tapping a rhythm against the boards. It's like she just can't keep still.

"Of course," she goes on, "the most important aspect of your time here is that it gives you the space to explore your own creativity. That's why every afternoon is yours to spend on your music. You'll be separating into groups of between three and six, and this will be the band you perform with for the duration of the programme. However, we're doing things a little differently this year." She pauses again to gulp another lungful of air. "Normally, the camp staff have a discussion and decide who we think would work well together. This year, though, we thought it would be fun to let you choose your own bandmates."

Oh, no. My heart crash-lands in my stomach. It's school all over again. The class being told to split up for team projects. Me, always left out until the teacher takes pity on me and assigns me a partner. Humiliation after gut-shrivelling humiliation.

Calypso's voice seeps through my dread. "You have the rest of the weekend to get to know each other and decide who you'd like to work with. Come and see me after our session on Monday and I'll make a note of your bands."

A buzz travels along the rows, campers sounding each other out. I swallow my panic. This won't be like school. I can't let that happen, can't go to Calypso and admit I'm the only one without a band.

Calypso hands back to her gran, who talks us through the camp rules—no smoking indoors, no alcohol full stop, no using the pool unsupervised. She then invites us to head over to the welcome barbecue, and everyone stampedes towards the exits. I unhook Star's harness from the back of my chair.

"Up stand," I coax.

Star hauls herself to her feet so I can slip the harness over her head. Seriously, you'd think she was an old lady who'd been rudely woken from a nap.

Together, we retrace the route we took with Jake, across the foyer and out through the back entrance. When I explained to my guide dog trainer I'd be spending the summer holidays at Dukes, she arranged for us to visit in advance. Amy walked me over every inch of the campus till I had it down. Thank Christ she did. At least I don't have to rely on anyone to find my way around.

It's time for Star's dinner, so I direct her towards Osborne House. Our path winds through stripes of warmth and shade. A breeze carries the smell of charcoal and the chatter of my fellow campers as they head to the barby.

I'm not hungry; Me and Jake stopped for burgers at a service station. Still, I should probably go down once I've fed Star.

No use getting all snarled up about it. I need to put myself out there, meet people, make friends. After all, other than the scholarship, isn't that why I'm here?

Once Star's gobbled down her food, I take her into the back garden of Osborne House to do her business. I'm feeling around on the grass, poo bag on my hand like a glove puppet, when…

Voices.

Damn it. Everyone was supposed to be at the barby. Balanced on my haunches, I quickly scoop up the mess, listening. Probably they've stopped by their rooms to get changed. No reason for them to come out here.

Please, go away.

The sliding glass door rumbles open. What sounds like four or five girls spill onto the patio, trailing giggles and perfume. And here I am, crouched on the lawn with a bag of dog crap.

"Don't know why you're bothering. Seemed kind of moody to me," says a girl with a broad Scottish brogue.

"Blair," a second girl gasps. "He'll hear you."

Blair snorts. "So? Doubt he'd care."

The snick of a lighter cuts through the laughter. I push to my feet, inhaling the acrid tang of cigarettes. God, that smell. Reminds me so much of home. For an instant, I'm sitting under our apple tree with Dad, chatting to him while he has his post-dinner smoke.

Star tugs on her lead, eager to say hello. I thrust the memory away and draw her to me. What to do? To reach the bin, I'll have to walk right past the group on the patio. Talk about embarrassing.

"You have to admit he's hot." This girl has a voice like sandpaper dipped in dark chocolate. "I'm totally asking him to dance later."

"Good luck with that, Chan," Blair says. "He didn't seem the sociable type."

"Trust me, I can be very persuasive. Zephan won't be able to resist."

Come on, George, you can't stand here like a prat all night. Sod the poo bag. This is your chance. It's just…whenever I imagined meeting my campmates, I was always doing something cool. My favourite version had me seated on one of the benches around campus, picking out a tune on my guitar. Seriously, though, I'd have settled for a casual 'hi' as we passed each other in the hallway. But this… Even in my worst nightmares, I hadn't conjured up such a cringe fest.

I'm still rummaging inside myself for my courage when the girl with the husky voice squeals. "Oh my God, look."

She rushes over, bending to stroke Star. "Aren't you just gorgeous? Yes, you are. Boy or girl?" she asks me.

"Girl." I shift, attempting to hide the poo bag behind my leg. "Her name's Star."

"Aw, so adorable," the girl coos. I may as well not be there for all the notice she takes of me. I'm used to it. A lot of people feel more comfortable talking to my dog than to me. Well, it's my job to change that.

I twist Star's lead around my finger. *For Christ's sake, say something. The girl will get bored soon and I'll lose my chance.*

"So, uh, are you going to the welcome party?" The words catch in my throat. Hell, I sound like I've swallowed a wad of chewing gum.

"Thought we'd check it out, yeah." The girl pauses before adding, "Want to come with us?"

My face warms. Did she think I was fishing for an invitation? I wasn't. Not really. It's what I'd wanted, though, isn't it? To be included? No way I can turn it down. "Um, sure."

"Cool." The girl straightens. "We're meeting at Himari's. She's in flat one opposite. Room five. See you there around half eight?"

"OK." She's already walking away when it hits me. "Sorry, I don't know your name."

"Chanelle Clarke. I'll introduce you to everyone else later." Her footsteps click across the patio as she re-joins her friends. "Come on, guys, I'm dying of hunger here."

"And not just for barbecue, eh, Chan?" Blair says to peals of laughter.

Heels grind dog ends into the concrete and then the girls head indoors. Once everywhere's quiet, I rid myself of the stupid poo bag and follow. Might've been nice if they'd asked me to go to the barby with them, or even if Chanelle had asked my name. Still, you can't have everything, right?

Excitement fizzes in my gut. My first proper party, and maybe the start of some new friendships. I should text Jake, let him know. A grin tugs at my mouth. Yes, this summer will be different; I can feel it.

4. MINA

D URING THE WALK to the recreation building, Gareth and
I can't stop grinning at each other.

Early evening sunshine gilds the imposing buildings that edge
the campus, lending the red brick an ethereal magic. We wind
along one of the many paths that criss-cross the velvety lawn,
our route shaded by beech trees. And here I am, in the midst of
it all, as though the glossy pages of the college prospectus have
sprung to life around me.

When we reach the patio outside the dining room, we join
the line for the barbecue.

"Can't believe we're here," Gareth says for the umpteenth
time. "I keep thinking Mam gave me dodgy mushrooms for
breakfast."

I collect two plates from the trestle table and hand one to
him. "Then I must be part of your hallucination. Shouldn't
there be more leprechauns or flying sheep?"

"Flying sheep? What're you like?"

"Well, I don't know, do I? I couldn't tell a magic mushroom
from a morel."

We're still laughing when we reach the front of the queue,
where the guy manning the coals introduces himself as Rick.
I would've pegged him as a retired wrestler rather than a chef,
but he has a cheerful smile.

Once we've been served sausages and burgers and spiced
chicken on skewers, Gareth and I enter the dining room through

the French windows. It's done up more like a trendy restaurant than a school cafeteria with rich chestnut flooring and chairs upholstered in sage-green leather congregated around oblong tables. At the buffet, we help ourselves to salad and new potatoes, burger buns and ketchup, before carrying our loaded plates back outdoors.

Most of the picnic tables on the patio are occupied, everyone talking over each other and competing to be heard. Calypso's seated with a group of goth kids, her violet pixie cut and sequinned top a splash of colour amidst the black. Dutch, all sandy ponytail and lounging grace, has his arm around her. I pass so close I could've reached out and touched them. Thank goodness I have my hands full, otherwise I might've made a fool of myself.

Still more campers are sprawled on the lawn. We choose a spot beneath a beech tree, far enough from the crowd to give the illusion of privacy, and sit facing each other on the grass. From here, I can just make out the corner of the pool house, the sun glinting off sliding glass doors.

Gareth bites into his burger. "You had me worried back there. When you were late to the welcome, I reckoned your dad had changed his mind, like, and taken you home."

"I'm sure he thought about it. Not that Mum would've let him. Poor Dad. He doesn't stand a chance when we gang up on him." I begin sliding the pieces of chicken and red onion off their skewer. "I did get the lecture, though."

My stomach squirms, an echo of the embarrassment that always accompanies Dad's warnings about boys. After everything that happened with my sister, I can't entirely blame him for being protective. It's just that, where I'm concerned, it's utterly pointless.

Gareth rests a hand on my knee. "I hear you."

And he does. His dad's forever demanding to know when he'll finally get himself a girlfriend. He might be teasing, or so Gaz claims, but it's still reduced my friend to tears more than once. I meet Gareth's eyes and understanding flows between us—the understanding that bonded us almost two years ago.

I'd been to a sleepover for Allie's fifteenth birthday. The five of us that make up our friendship group had stuffed our faces with pizza and popcorn and binge-watched *The Summer I Turned Pretty*. Afterwards, when we were all snuggled in our sleeping bags, the girls started giggling over their crushes.

"You're very quiet." Allie, who had the sleeping bag next to mine, prodded me with her foot. "There must be someone you fancy."

"Really, there isn't." I was grateful for the darkness that hid my blush. Of course I had crushes, but it wasn't as if I could admit to them. Having a thing for Emilia Clarke isn't the sort of secret you can entrust to the daughters of devout Catholics.

My friends wouldn't let it go, and in the end I invented a crush on Harry Styles simply so they'd stop badgering me. I lay awake long after the others fell asleep, feeling more alone than I ever had, wishing I could be like my friends.

My parents had a work do the following evening. As soon as they left, I curled up in bed with my laptop and turned to the internet for help. It's inevitable, I suppose, that I wound up on a forum for LGBTQ+ teens. I must've read hundreds of stories, all of them written by people like me, people who were struggling with their sexuality. I never intended to post anything myself; it was enough to know there were others out there going through the same thing.

Something about Gareth's words called to me, though. He wrote about growing up in a former mining village in South Wales where the residents cling to so-called traditional values and your whole family lives within a ten-minute walk. When he described his claustrophobia, his inability to be himself for fear that everyone he knew would reject him, my pulse beat in recognition. I might live in Gloucester, a far cry from the Welsh Valleys, but the Catholic community is a close-knit one. If I were to come out, several of my parents' friends—maybe even most of them—would shun me.

So, I wrote back. Over the course of that night and the following weeks, we poured out our hearts to each other in a way neither of us had felt able to before. When we discovered our mutual love of music, our friendship was cemented. Without the other to spur us on, I doubt either of us would have had the courage to apply for the Dukes summer camp.

I pop a piece of chicken into my mouth, chilli and coriander tingling on my tongue. "At least you didn't have any trouble convincing your parents to let you come."

"Yeah, although I'm lucky we got here before midnight. Practically the whole bloody village turned out to see me off. So embarrassing." Gareth cringes.

I laugh. "It's sweet they're so proud of you. My family treats my music as if it's a lovely little hobby."

"I s'pose. Feels like a big responsibility sometimes, that's all. Everyone expects me to do well, to win." He takes an enormous bite of his burger, shutting himself up.

In all the hours we've spent planning for our time at camp, frothing over with what an amazing summer we'll have, we've avoided talking directly about the ultimate prize. We've tiptoed around it, envisioned what it might be like to be a fully-fledged student, but we never mention the possibility that one of us could actually win.

All the same, I know how much Gareth wants it. His parents don't earn much, barely enough to scrape a living. The scholarship is his only hope of getting into Dukes... and he deserves it. He truly does. It's just, if Gareth were to win, it would spell the death of all my dreams.

5. GEORGIE

IMAGINE IF EVERYONE at Brookminster Comp could see me now. Here I am, all done up in my best jeans and new Nirvana T-shirt, on my way to an actual party. They wouldn't recognise me. Blimey, I hardly recognise myself. Jake was psyched for me when I told him.

I finish off with a squirt of White Musk and clip on Star's lead. Maybe I'd be better leaving her in our room, but this is all kinds of nerve-racking. I need my furry friend with me for moral support. Also, she's the perfect icebreaker.

"Right, let's do this," I say to Star, slinging the guide dog harness over my shoulder. I'll put it on her once we're outside.

We head out of the flat and across the lobby. My heart bounces around my chest like a bloody pinball. I'm not totally sure where I'm going. Chanelle said flat one was opposite ours, and…there. My hand, stretched out in front of me, finds the door. First challenge completed. Now for my second challenge— getting to Himari's room.

I grip the handle. Next moment, it's jerked from my grasp and I stumble as the door flies inward.

"Oh my gosh," comes a girl's startled voice. "I'm so sorry. I wasn't expecting anyone to be there. Are you OK?"

"Yeah. Yeah, fine." I steady myself against the doorframe. *Fantastic start, George, almost nosediving into the carpet.*

Star trots forward, tail whipping my legs. Attention seeker. She'll sweet-bark anyone into making a fuss of her.

"Hey, sweetheart." The girl obliges, crouching to Star's level. "Is it all right if I say hello?"

"Be my guest. Her name's Star." *Don't mind me.* I lean against the wall and try to pretend I'm not here.

"Sorry, that was really rude," the girl says. *Damned face.* It must've given me away again. Still, she sounds like she means it.

"Really," she adds, tone earnest, "I didn't mean to imply I only wanted to talk to Star. I'm Mina."

"Georgie." I smile. Can't help it. Ridiculous how amazing it feels, introducing myself, like this is the start of something.

"Star's gorgeous," Mina tells me from the floor. "How long have you had her?"

"A couple of months. Wouldn't be without her now, though."

"I bet. You're so lucky. I've always wanted a dog—Dad, too—but Mum's allergic."

My grin widens. Talk about goofy. I'm so used to being pitied, never occurred to me anyone might envy me. It's sort of nice. Talking to Mina is nice, too. There's a warmth about her that puts me at ease.

"I am lucky to have her," I agree. "Star's changed my life. Gutting you can't have a dog."

"It really is. We do have a cat called Misty, and she lets me cuddle her when she's in a good mood." Mina laughs and gets to her feet. "Are you going to the party?"

I nod. "Walking over with some of the others. I'm supposed to meet them at Himari's."

"Oh, OK. If you follow the corridor along and to the right, hers is the door straight ahead. Can you find your way?"

"Should be able to. Thanks."

"You're welcome." Mina gives Star a last pat. "I might see you later then."

"See you." I step aside, drawing Star with me to let Mina through. As she slips past, I breathe in her scent. It's sweet and citrussy, like lemon meringue. Her light footsteps hurry across the lobby and she pulls open the door, letting in a waft of evening air.

"Bye," she calls. Then she's gone and the door closes with a muted thud.

I stay where I am, disappointment gnawing at me. Would've been fun to walk over to the party with Mina. Still, I can't stand Chanelle up, and hopefully, I'll catch Mina later. On the plus side, I've spoken to two of my campmates in as many hours. Definitely counts as a win in my world.

"Come on then," I say to Star.

Fingers trailing the wall to guide me, I lead her along the hallway. Even without Mina's directions, I would've found Himari's room no problem. Their chatter may as well be a GPS. The door must be ajar because, as I round the corner, Chanelle's husky voice carries loud and clear.

"But I promised. What if she turns up and we're not here?"

Wait. Are they talking about me? I bring Star up short, listening.

"Don't know why you had to invite her, anyway." That's the girl with the Scottish accent. Blair. "It's not like you wanted to babysit her all night."

"Well, obviously, but what could I say? She put me on the spot, asking if we were going to the party. Don't worry. I'm sure we can palm her off on someone else once we get there."

This isn't happening. Nausea rises in my throat. *Shit, don't let me throw up. Not right outside Himari's room.* Mind you, it isn't like I could feel any more humiliated.

How could I have been so gullible? Of course Chanelle only asked me out of obligation. That should've been obvious. I mean, she didn't even bother to ask my name. If I hadn't been so desperate to feel included, I would've seen straight through her. Mina, too. She'd seemed friendly enough, but it was all an excuse to pet Star.

My sinuses burn. I clench my fist until Star's lead bites into my skin. *Don't you dare cry, Georgie Wilde. You want these girls to see how much they've upset you?*

I retreat, tugging Star with me. *Please stay quiet, just till we're out of earshot.* Once we're safely around the bend, I turn and feel my way into the lobby fast as I can.

So much for things being different here. Why did I ever think they would be? A tear sneaks past my defences and down my cheek. I bat it away. Stupid, stupid, stupid. I was never going to any party, would never have fitted in with Chanelle Clarke and her friends. The *It* crowd. God, it would be funny if it weren't so fucking tragic. Nothing to do now except shut myself in my room and forget tonight ever happened.

6. MINA

"**G**az, you've been holding out on me." I pause mid-twist to poke him in the chest. "How come you never told me you could dance?"

Gareth grins, seizing my hand and raising it so I can duck under his arm. "Never knew I could. Skulking in a corner near the buffet table's more my style."

I laugh and allow myself to be twirled. My skirt fans out around me, turquoise with a design of seahorses. I have this thing for dresses in bright patterns—cherries, butterflies, cats—something my friends love to tease me about.

Actually, I think the girls would rather I skulked in a corner sometimes. My efforts have always owed more to enthusiasm than skill, but I've never let that stop me.

Gareth, on the other hand…you'd think he'd been dancing for as long as he could walk. For a big guy, he's incredibly light on his feet and he moves with a grace I can only marvel at. He seems to know instinctively what to do with his shoulders, how to roll his hips.

All around us, teenagers sway and writhe to the music with varying degrees of prowess, some in large groups, others in twos and threes. A few campers cluster on the fringes, preferring to talk than dance, but most are on the floor.

When a Missy Elliott song comes on, several people cheer and the atmosphere cranks up another notch. I throw back my head, revelling in the pulsating energy, the beat thrumming against the soles of my sandals and up my legs. The heat sticks my dress to my skin, and the air vibrates in time with the thumping bass.

The reception room is located in the Dukes Building, across the foyer from the concert hall. It's where students and their families can mingle after performances, sip champagne and hobnob with those influential figures in the music industry who have come to watch. Now, the space is awash with streamers and silver stars. A giant disco ball bathes everything in strobes of blue and violet, and with the French windows open to the purple dusk, the whole place has the feel of a magical twilight world.

Gareth leans in to shout in my ear. "I really don't look like a prat?"

"Really, you're a natural. See? You have an admirer."

"You're winding me up."

"I'm not. Behind you to the right. In the lime-green vest."

Gareth swivels his body in that direction, careful to make it appear part of the dance. The slender white boy is at the centre of the most boisterous group, but with his fluorescent top and the lights catching the blue tips of his spiked-up hair, he's easy to pick out from the crowd. There's a vibrancy to his movements, a sensuality that makes me blush. When I first sensed the boy's gaze several songs earlier, I thought he was watching me. It wouldn't be anything new, someone staring in fascination at my poor coordination. His interest, though, is all for my friend.

"Oh, God." Gareth turns back to me, cheeks glowing pink through the dimness. "He's hot, like."

I nod, smile mischievous. "And he obviously thinks you are, too."

"Oh, God." His steps falter and he almost trips over his own feet. "Shit, I can't dance now. Want to get some air?"

We weave our way between the gyrating bodies towards the French windows. I glimpse my flatmates and their friends but can't see Georgie among them. Pity. I'd been hoping to chat to her some more. She was nice to talk to, much less intimidating than the other girls I've met.

After the crushing heat inside, the breeze cools my flushed skin. Gareth takes my hand and we start along a tree-lined path, splashing through puddles of moonlight. The noise from the party grows fainter behind us, giving way to the distant strum of a guitar.

"He can't really have been interested in me, can he?" Gareth asks. "He was probably just wondering what a country bumpkin like me was doing on the dance floor."

"Are you serious? Bet he thought you'd come straight off the West End stage." I give him a playful shove.

Gareth's mouth twitches but he glances down at himself. "Could be he was just impressed with my moves, like. He might not be into big guys."

I squeeze his hand. Gareth's insecure about many things, but generally his weight isn't one of them. Why would it be? With his height and broad shoulders, the extra pounds suit him.

"You're gorgeous," I tell him, "and that boy obviously thought so. He was definitely checking you out."

"You think so?" The longing in Gareth's voice breaks a piece off my heart. It's lonely enough for me, hiding my sexuality from those I'm closest to. When you live in a village in the depths of the Welsh hills, it's even more isolating and dating opportunities are non-existent. All Gaz wants is a boyfriend, someone he can love and who will love him for who he is.

"I know so." I loop my arm through his. "This is going to be your lucky summer. I can feel it."

He turns to me, his smile brighter than the moon. "How about you? Should we find you a cute girl to fall in love with?"

I laugh, shaking my head. The prospect of telling my parents I want to pursue a career in music is daunting enough, but introducing them to my new girlfriend? Gosh, they'd be so shocked, so disappointed in me. Of course, I'll have to do it one day, maybe after I've left home and met the right person. Maybe then I'll feel better equipped to cope with their disapproval, but not yet, not so soon after everything with my sister. No, for the foreseeable future, romance is off the table.

7. GEORGIE

THE SILENCE OF the dead hangs over the flat next morning. I'd set my alarm for seven, sure everyone would sleep in after the party. Waking up so early on a Sunday isn't my idea of fun, but anything to avoid bumping into Chanelle or Blair. I can't face them. Can't face anyone ever again.

In the kitchen at one end of the living area, I measure Star's breakfast into her bowl. Dried pellets ping off the plastic loud as artillery fire. I wince. *Don't let anyone wake up. Not until I'm safely back in my room.*

As always, Star hoovers her food like she's half starved. Despite everything, I laugh. "You didn't even taste that, did you?"

Star wags her appreciation. I fill her bowl with fresh water and fix the lead to her collar, then let us out through the sliding glass door. Cool air blows against my face, earthy and sweet with dew. It soothes the grit from my eyes.

On the lawn, I lengthen Star's lead to give her more freedom to explore. My head throbs. I lay awake for hours last night, the conversation I'd overheard playing on repeat. Still, I refused to cry; Chanelle and co didn't deserve my tears. As I finally sank into a coma, the lyrics to a new song swirled around my brain.

> *Why can you not understand,*
> *I'm just a girl like you?*

Star does her business and I bend to tidy up after her. At least we don't have an audience today. I walk Star to the patio and drop the poo bag in the bin, thoughts churning.

So, what next? I could call Jake. He'd come pick me up if I asked, but he'd also want to know why. God, someone slit my throat now. Then there's the fact that it would mean giving up, admitting I'd failed at the first hurdle. Dukes has been my dream for so long. Am I really going to abandon it without a fight?

As I reach for the door handle, someone calls out to me. "Hey. Georgie, isn't it?"

Blinkin' hell. Star's lead slips in my grasp. Even if I hadn't heard it yesterday, I would've recognised that voice from her interviews. And she knows who I am. Calypso Dukes, absolute bloody legend, knows my name.

"Sorry." She joins me on the patio. "Didn't mean to ambush you. I came out for a puff and saw you, thought I'd come say hi."

"Uh, hi." My reply wobbles. You'd think I'd never had a conversation before, but God, Calypso isn't just anyone. I knew, obviously, she'd be taking some of the workshops, but for her to single me out like this… It's surreal. Surreal and properly kind.

Calypso lights up with an audible flick of her lighter. "Didn't think any of you guys would be up yet. Not after partying into the early hours."

I shrug, forcing a smile. I'd rather eat dog food for a month than tell this cool young woman the truth—that I'd spent the evening barricaded in my room like the loser I am.

"Still." Calypso nudges her hip against mine. "I'm guessing that beautiful dog of yours doesn't let you sleep in too long."

My grin's real this time. "Nope. Star's very particular about her breakfast."

Calypso laughs, and warmth spreads through my chest. Forget last night's humiliation. It would've been worth coming here for these few minutes with Calypso.

"Will I see you and Star at the picnic this afternoon?" she asks.

And just like that, her question snuffs out my happiness. I could go. I could sit on the grass with Calypso and Star, chatting over sausage rolls and egg mayo sandwiches. But that would risk bumping into Chanelle and the others. What would they do? Blank me? Put on a fake show of concern, ask why I never showed? Either way, the whole thing would have me vomiting into my plate.

"Maybe," I say, hedging. "Have a bit of a headache, though."

"Oh, that sucks." Calypso sounds genuinely concerned. "Rest this morning and hopefully you'll feel better by lunchtime. Rick's made his famous chocolate fudge cake. It's worth coming just for that."

I smile, but my heart's not in it. Damn those girls. It would've been awesome, getting to spend more time with Calypso, but I'm nowhere near ready. Oh, I know I can't hide in my room forever. Sooner or later, I'll have to stick up my chin and face my campmates. Just…not yet.

8. MINA

THE NOISE FROM the picnic reaches us long before we round the corner of the recreation building. Red-and-white-checked blankets have been draped over the lawn outside the dining room, several wicker hampers clustered to one side. Some campers sit in groups while others mingle, showing off dresses and band T-shirts, piercings and hair dyed every shade of the rainbow.

Gareth and I fill paper plates and find a spot on the edge of the gathering, near a boy with a ponytail strumming an acoustic.

"We should probably start sounding out potential bandmates," Gareth says, popping a Scotch egg in his mouth.

I nod, although my mind's elsewhere, still on our exploration of the campus. The study block had been locked, but we skirted the exterior, peering through the windows at the classrooms with their comfortable chairs huddled around octagonal tables. After that, we climbed to the upper floors of the rec building to check out the practice rooms. At our first sight of a piano, we tumbled onto the bench and launched into an elaborate rendition of 'Chopsticks', all twiddly bits and unexpected key changes.

And some lucky so-and-sos get to study here full time. Yearning squeezes my chest. No quadratic equations or diagrams of the human nervous system for them. Just music all day, every day. It must be paradise.

"Anyone in your flat who might want to team up with us, like?" Gareth asks.

I swallow a bite of chicken sandwich. "Think they already have their band sorted. How about yours?"

"God, no. I've somehow ended up with a load of thrash metal fans."

"Would certainly be original. Pop with influences of country and metal."

"Yeah, doubt there's anyone on the planet who'd want to hear that." Gareth nudges his knee against mine. "You know her? The one in black?"

I glance beyond the guitar player to the girl sitting beside him. She catches me looking, her eyes blackberry dark against her pale skin, and the intensity in them has me averting my gaze.

Gareth whoops. "Hun, you're blushing. You should go talk to her."

"Shush." I open a bag of Doritos and bury my scalding face in it. "You know I'm not interested in dating."

"Who said anything about dating?" Gareth appropriates one of my crisps. "Think of it as a summer fling, like."

I'm about to argue that the girl isn't my type when a shadow falls across us. "Mind if I sit here?"

The soft Manchester accent belongs to the boy from the party, the one who'd been watching my friend. All Gareth's casual talk of flings blows away on the breeze and he gawps at the newcomer, lips parted.

"Of course not," I say, since Gaz seems incapable of responding.

"Cheers." The boy settles on the blanket and crosses his legs in their skin-tight denim. "I'm Art Dabrowski."

38

He smiles between us—a lazy, beautiful smile. If cats could smile, I'm pretty sure this is how Misty would look as she curls into her favourite sunny spot on our patio. His sleeveless T-shirt is the exact same turquoise as his eyes and shows off supple, golden arms.

"I'm Mina Farhan." On the pretext of shifting position, I jab Gareth with my elbow. "And this is Gareth Thomas."

"Hi." Gareth's voice rasps as if he's recovering from laryngitis, but his answering smile puts the afternoon sun to shame.

"Hi back." Art toys with a sausage roll, although he's too busy staring at Gareth to eat. "Saw you dancing last night. Bloody amazing."

"Oh, God." Gareth laughs, throwing up an arm to shield his face.

"I'm serious. You go dancing much?"

"Me? Nah. For one thing, I live in this shitty little village in the middle of nowhere. For another, I spend most of my time in front of a piano."

"A pianist, huh?" Art studies Gareth's hands from beneath long lashes.

It's easy to guess what he's thinking. The blatant interest in his gaze has me flushing, and I'm not even the one he's looking at. My insides squirm. Gareth deserves the chance to flirt and have fun, but that doesn't mean I want to be a bystander.

"I love your hair," I tell Art.

He remembers my existence and turns his smile on me, running a hand over the blue-tipped spikes. "Thanks. I can do yours for you, if you like. You'd look awesome with a blue streak…or maybe purple. Yeah, definitely purple."

"Wow, I don't know. Maybe." Longing seeps into my tone. I've always dreamt of doing something more adventurous with my hair but have never been brave enough.

Art grins at me, and it's as though he knows what I'm thinking. "Don't worry, mate. It washes out after a couple of weeks. My dad wouldn't exactly approve."

I grin back at him. "All right. I might take you up on that."

"Cool." Art bumps Gareth's knee with his. "How about you, mister?"

Gareth shakes his head. "Not sure I'm a streaked hair kind of guy."

Art's gaze travels over my friend, lingering on his mop of red curls and the broad shoulders only partially disguised beneath the baggy shirt. His eyes lock onto Gareth's. "Nah, you're fine as you are."

Colour floods Gareth's cheeks, but his expression contains more light than I've ever seen. I finish my sandwiches and try not to feel shut out. Yet, as the two of them drink one another in, I may as well be invisible.

9. GEORGIE

ONCE MY FLATMATES have gone down to the picnic, my growling stomach tugs me from my room in search of food. Man, I'm ravenous. Haven't eaten since yesterday's pub lunch with Jake.

While Star laps from her water bowl, I raid the kitchen cupboards. Pretty good haul. Crisps, dried pasta, cereal, biscuits. I find the bread and drop two slices in the toaster.

"Sorry about this, Star." I open the fridge and delve around for the butter. "This isn't much fun for you, is it? You'd much rather be at the picnic, eyeing up the sandwiches."

To prove my point, Star heads away from me to explore the living area. Her nails *click-click* on the wooden floor.

"Not sure what to do." I work my way through the drawers and cabinets, rooting out plates and cutlery. "We can't shut ourselves away all summer, but how the hell am I meant to face them?"

The toast pops up. I fish it out, burning my fingertips, and begin slathering it with butter. What would Jake tell me, if I weren't too embarrassed to confide in him? Well, that's a no-brainer. He'd tell me to ignore them. He'd say I can't let a few spiteful girls ruin this for me, and he'd be right. They have ruined it, though. So much for finding my people. With a few cruel words, Chanelle and co have smashed my hopes to bits.

"Hey there."

The knife slips from my grasp and clatters to the worktop. The voice came from the far end of the living area. I remember there's a couple of sofas grouped around a TV. Oh, God. Heat prickles my whole body. I hadn't heard the door open. Whoever it is must've been here the entire time, while Miss Clueless here chatted away to her dog like a total plank.

Before I can make a bigger prat of myself, my brain clocks his tone. Soft, coaxing. He was obviously talking to Star. Cringing, I feel for the knife and grip it. Who cares if this boy thinks I'm a nutcase? There are worse things…probably.

"Cool dog."

This time, I manage not to jump. The boy has a blunt way of speaking. It's like words cost the Earth and he's determined to grab a bargain.

"Thanks." I focus on cutting my toast in half. Is it worth starting a conversation? After yesterday's fiasco, it's tempting to find a cave in the Himalayas and never speak to anyone again, but…

Oh, what the hell? No one can accuse me of not making an effort. "Her name's Star. I'm Georgie."

The boy's silent. So, he's going to blank me. Better than fake friendliness, I suppose, and at least I tried.

I've picked up my plate, about to slink back to my room, when he says, "Zephan."

The name strums a chord in my memory. This is the boy Chanelle had been talking about, the one she thought was hot.

"Hi." I lean against the worktop with my plate. See? Not running away. Jake would be proud. "You, uh, didn't want to go to the picnic?"

"Nope." Paper rustles. He must be reading. Damn. If he'd turned a page earlier, I would've known someone was there.

"Chanelle'll be gutted." It escapes before I can think it through. My face burns, and I shove a piece of toast into my mouth.

"Who?" He sounds only mildly curious. Clearly, whoever Chanelle is, she can't be as fascinating as his book.

I like this boy.

"One of the girls in our flat. Think she fancies you." It's petty, spilling Chanelle's crush. Still, I feel a mean satisfaction.

"Oh." Zephan pauses. Then he says, "The loud one. With the braids."

A laugh snorts out of me. God, Chanelle would be miffed, hearing herself described like that. "She was banking on chatting to you at the party."

"Good job I didn't go then."

I grin through a mouthful of toast. Zephan's the most genuine person I've met at Dukes so far. I think about the two of us last night, holed up in our separate rooms while everyone else was at the party. Makes me feel a smidge less alone.

10. MINA

"Sure you're all right with this?" Gareth angles to face me, expression anxious. We're seated at one end of a corner sofa in the packed student centre, the buzz of music and voices mingling to mask our words.

No, actually, since you ask, I'm not all right with it. Jealousy pricks my heart, the same jealousy that's been lodged there ever since Art held Gareth back after the picnic to see if he wanted to hang out later, just the two of them.

Still, I paste on my biggest smile. "Of course. I'll be fine."

"It's just… I don't want to be that guy who abandons his best mate for a boy, like. Why don't you come with me? I'm sure Art wouldn't mind."

"I'm sure he would. Me tagging along would totally cramp his style."

I nudge him, and he grins, a blush stealing up his neck. Gareth's wanted this for as long as I've known him—wanted a boyfriend, to be loved. Am I really petty enough to begrudge my closest friend in the world the chance at a romance simply because I feel excluded? The thing is…this was supposed to be our summer, Gaz's and mine, our first taste of friendship in real life. Now, I can feel our precious time together slipping like a fiendish guitar solo through my fingers.

I swallow my resentment with an effort. It leaves the bitter tang of burnt toast on my tongue, but I hug him, hiding my guilt against his broad shoulder. "Go on. Go get your boy."

I stay where I am after he's gone, feeling conspicuous, the only person sitting on her own. Not that I have anywhere else to go. My gaze wanders around the student centre, a cross between cosy café and sports bar. At one end of the large room, comfy sofas and armchairs cluster around low coffee tables, while at the other, a small crowd is cheering on a game of pool. Along one wall are machines dispensing snacks, as well as hot and cold drinks. The rattle of coins and the *thud…thud…thud* of cans being disgorged carries over the conversation, all of it competing with Rita Ora blasting from the jukebox.

The door from the lobby bursts inwards, admitting my flatmates and their friends. They pour themselves onto my sofa in a vibrant tangle of chatter, flowing hair and elegant limbs, Chanelle Clarke at their centre. The way she presides over the group—legs tucked beneath her, scarlet halterneck brilliant against her dark-brown skin—is reminiscent of a princess with her ladies-in-waiting.

"We should share the vocals," Himari's saying. "You know, like The Spice Girls."

Blair snorts, tossing her mane of red curls. "The Spice Girls? How old are you, Grandma?"

The girls collapse into one another, helpless with giggles. Gosh, I need to escape from here. It isn't that I have anywhere else to be, but their laughter and clear sense of togetherness makes me feel all the more alone.

Before I can stand, Himari touches my arm. "Mina, sorry, we didn't mean to ignore you."

"Yeah, we were saying earlier." Patrice tucks a spiral strand of her gorgeous afro behind one ear. "There's space in our band if you'd like to join."

I smile at her, pathetically grateful, and get to my feet. "That's really kind of you, but I'm already forming a band with my friend."

"Your loss." Chanelle shrugs. "With what we've got going on, one of us is bound to win."

She says this with a smirk, but I'm not entirely convinced she's joking. In the midst of these girls with their beauty and self-assurance, why wouldn't she be confident? I can't possibly compete. Inadequacy weighs on my belly, keeping company with the loneliness.

I'm about to flee the suffocating din, maybe go for a walk, when it hits me. All at once, I know where I want to be, the only other person besides Gaz I'd like to talk to, and I turn back to the group. "Do any of you know where Georgie's room is?"

11. GEORGIE

TOAST FOR LUNCH. Toast for dinner. I'm getting sick of the stuff. Still, it beats the alternative—braving the dining room and hovering like an arse till someone helps me at the buffet table. Plus, Chanelle's bound to be there.

Unlike mine, Star's lust for toast holds firm. She's seated near as she can get to my cross-legged perch on the bed, patiently waiting for a crust. Not that I ever feed her anything other than her food and the odd dog biscuit. The folks at Guide Dogs are strict about things like that; don't want their charges breaking off mid-walk to snuffle at discarded takeaway cartons. Star lives in hope, though.

Dodgy's 'Staying Out for the Summer' blasts from my phone. I'd set it as my ringtone the day before I came to Dukes, back when the weeks ahead were still bright with promise. What a joke. Cringing, I lick the butter from my fingers and reach for my mobile.

"Watcha, George Porge." Dad sounds so close he might be in the room with me.

Blinkin' tears. I force them back and try for upbeat. "Watcha, Dad. You OK?"

"Yeah, all good. Just missing my girls. It's kind of quiet without you."

"Right, because me and Star are so loud."

He chuckles. "You missed a treat earlier. I made my famous summer pudding."

"You did not!" God, I can practically taste it, the sharp berries and sugary sponge. My stomach grumbles. "So unfair."

"Well, we needed something to cheer us up. Anyway, how's it going? I almost didn't call, thought you might be busy."

Ha-bloody-ha. "Nope, not busy. Just in my room." That's the truth, at least. Dad doesn't need to know I've more or less been shut up in here for the past twenty-four hours."

"Ah, having a bit of a rest after your late night?" He teases. "Jake said you were headed to the party with some friends."

My heart drops. What to say? No way I can tell Dad what actually happened, the things I overheard. It would crush him.

"You know," I say, "I don't think those girls are friend material. We don't really have much in common."

"Shame." Dad sounds disappointed, but I'll take that as a win. "Still, never mind, eh? It's early days. You have the whole summer to make friends."

"Yeah, the whole summer," I say, and wish I believed it.

Even after I've hung up and cleaned my plate of crumbs, I don't move. Isn't like I have anywhere to be. Star's retreated to a corner with her bone, a poor substitute for toast. Homesickness cramps my gut. I want to go home.

The lyrics that formed on the verge of sleep last night come back to me. This time, a snatch of melody follows on their heels. Galvanised, I set my plate aside and dig out my guitar. Fender hugged to my body, I sit on the edge of the bed and lose myself. I play around with chord sequences, the tune slowly taking shape. Words unspool like pages from a printer.

I'm the one whose eyes are blind,
But it's you who cannot see,
It's you who'll never glimpse beyond,
Beyond my disability,
Why must you always treat me like,
I'm something strange and new?
Why can you not understand,
I'm just a girl like you?

12. MINA

MUSIC TRICKLES FROM beneath Georgie's door, a haunting ballad played on the guitar. The melody's full of so much yearning it makes my chest ache. It tugs at me, compelling me to stay and listen…but I can't. It would be wrong to eavesdrop without her knowledge, or to disturb her when she's obviously engrossed. Ah, well, there will be other opportunities. Disappointed, I tear myself away and wander back outside.

The evening is heavy and close, pasting itself to my skin. I can't face returning to my lonely room, so I meander along a path until I reach the circular lily pond that marks the heart of campus. At its centre, as if he has just emerged from the water, stands a fountain in the form of a brown-skinned boy. He's playing a guitar, his lips curved in a faraway smile.

I've always loved the sound of water—waves, tumbling streams, the patter of rain on my bedroom window. When I was little, I spent hours in our paddling pool, filling my plastic teapot and emptying it again, simply for the fun of it.

A bench crouches in the denser shadow of a beech tree, facing the pond. I slump onto it and watch the water glitter and sparkle as it catches the moonlight. The fountain sings its tinkling song, trying to soothe me.

Hopefully, Gareth's having a better night. That treacherous jealousy rears up again, coiling around my heart, but I bat it aside. I want this to work out for him. Truly, I do. It's just that, whenever I pictured my first evenings at Dukes, I was never sitting alone.

The moonlight sparks off something violet at the periphery of my vision, and then Calypso drops onto the seat beside me. "You all right out here?"

"Yes, thank you." My smile trembles at the corners, but it's a commendable effort. I should be in awe—a star of the music world, the daughter of a modern-day legend, sitting less than a foot away. Somehow, though, I can't summon any excitement.

She lights a cigarette, the flame darting like a firefly in the darkness. "Saw you sitting on your own, wanted to check in. Sorry, I don't know your name."

"It's Mina."

"That's pretty. Nice to meet you, Mina. You settling in OK?"

"Yes, absolutely." I rouse myself to glance around at the sprawling campus. Lights glimmer in the windows of the houses, rectangles of amber warmth in the blackness. "This place is amazing."

Calypso's teeth flash in a grin. "Glad you think so. Got your band sorted yet?"

"Not exactly. There's the friend I came with, but we haven't decided on the rest. Well." I hesitate, pleating my skirt between my fingers. "Gareth may have found us another member. It depends how things go tonight. That's where he is now, with this guy we met at the picnic."

I only just prevent myself from blurting the part about it being a sort of date. What's wrong with me, almost outing my best friend to a total stranger? There's something about Calypso, an open friendliness that invites confidences.

"Ah." Calypso's quiet for a while, drawing on her cigarette. Then she asks, "Have you come across Georgie?"

"Briefly. Just in passing."

"Great. Thing is, I get the feeling she's having a hard time settling in, that she's a bit isolated."

Really? This hadn't been my impression when she was on her way to meet Himari and the others. Then again, I hadn't spotted her in the chaos of the party, and she definitely wasn't at the picnic this afternoon.

"Look." Calypso glances sideways at me. "It's entirely your decision. The last thing I want to do is interfere, but how would you feel about asking Georgie to be part of your band?"

13. GEORGIE

How long have I been lying here? Feels like a bloody millennium since I took Star out for a last wee. I'd crawled into bed and willed myself to fall asleep. Just let this disaster of a weekend be over. Now, I reach for my phone to check the time. *Eleven twenty-eight*, voiceover informs me. God, is that it? I must be stuck in some weird time warp.

The window's open, for all the good it's doing. My baggy T-shirt and shorts stick to me in the stuffiness. I toss my phone onto the bedside cabinet and kick off the covers. A breeze creeps around the curtains, stroking my face. It carries the thrum of music and laughter from the student centre.

My heart twists. They're all over there, my campmates— joking around, having fun. It's like those grown-up parties when I was little, being sent to bed while my parents and their friends stayed up. I'd listen to the clink of glasses, the hum of adult conversation, sure I was missing out on something special.

Star lets out a snuffling snore from the corner. At least I'm not on my own. And probably Zephan's down the hall, nose in his book. Should be comforting, having a partner in loneliness. It's not the same, though. If he wanted, Zephan could be over at the student centre, flirting with Chanelle. He isn't too humiliated to show his face.

I roll onto my side, knees hugged to my chest. Tomorrow'll be a nightmare. Bad enough that I'll have to leave my sanctuary and brave the world. Somehow, I'll have to tell Calypso I don't have any bandmates. The poor little blind girl. She'll feel sorry for me, have to ask the others if any of them would 'very kindly' let me join their band. Christ, I could be the first person in history to die from embarrassment.

This is stupid. I reach for my phone again to open Audible. Listening to an audiobook always calms me when my brain's on overdrive. I get lost in the lives of ordinary teens leading ordinary lives, hanging out with friends, falling in love. Sometimes I can even kid myself I'm one of them.

I pop in my headphones and tap play on the latest Kasie West. As the narrator's voice fills my ears, I bury myself in the unfolding romance. Anything to block out the horror to come.

WEEK ONE

Wake up, live your life
and sing the melody of your soul.

– Amit Ray

14. MINA

"BE HONEST," GARETH says the moment I open my bedroom door on Monday morning. "I look like a Brussels sprout, don't I?"

A surprised laugh bubbles out of me. I thought it might be difficult, hiding my bruised feelings from my best friend, but I needn't have worried. Confronted with that self-deprecating half-smile, my resentment melts and I pull him into a hug. "You wally. You look hot."

He truly does. The shirt accentuates his biceps and broad chest, and the olive green lends fire to his curls.

While I return to brushing my hair in front of the wardrobe mirror, Gareth throws himself on my bed. "What did you do last night? Am I forgiven for abandoning you?"

"Don't be silly. I was fine, sat with the girls from my flat for a bit." I cross my fingers at the white lie and rush to change the subject. "But how did it go?"

Gareth's grin illuminates his entire face. "It was… Well, it was bloody amazing."

"Really? Come on, I need details. What did you get up to?"

"Nothing much. Hung out in Art's room and listened to music, mostly. And we talked, like…a lot. Turns out he's half Polish and his family's Catholic like yours. His dad's a builder, runs his own firm, and his brothers are all tough, macho types."

"Wow." I replace my hairbrush on the desk, remembering the graceful boy with the dyed hair and skin-tight jeans. Art, too, must understand what it's like to feel an outsider. "So I'm guessing they don't know about him being gay."

Gareth shakes his head. "Definitely got the impression they wouldn't be too thrilled, like."

Before I met Gaz, I genuinely believed there wasn't another soul going through the same conflict as me. Now, I'm discovering this whole subculture of people who are too afraid to come out to their families.

I open my jewellery box, everything arranged according to colour, and take out the bangle I want. It's heavy and silver, decorated with bees that match the ones on my dress. I slip it onto my wrist and peep over at Gareth. "So, I assume you'll want Art to be in the band. What's his instrument?"

"Drums, and yeah. Only if you're all right with it, though. We talked about it, obviously, but I said I'd have to check with you."

Gosh, how could I have been so petty? I beam at him, warmth igniting in my chest. "Of course he can join, and there's someone else I'd like to ask."

Gareth listens while I fill him in on my conversation with Calypso, her suggestion that I include Georgie. He shrugs. "Fine with me. Four's a good number for a band, and her dog's adorable."

"She really is." Actually, I think the girl's pretty adorable, too, but I keep this to myself. Can't have my best friend believing he can play matchmaker.

Gareth's phone chimes and he reaches into his pocket. As he glances at the screen, it's as if his mouth is too small to contain his smile. "You ready? Art's waiting for us outside."

We leave my room, making our way into the morning freshness where the pastel sky and buttery sunshine hint at another perfect day. I breathe the air into my lungs and let it fill me up with its promise.

Art's leaning against the wall by the entrance to Osborne House, but he isn't alone. A lanky boy with shaggy hair and dark-brown skin stands a short distance away, shoulders hunched, thumbs hooked into his belt loops.

"Hey." The instant he spies us, Art comes over and takes Gareth's hand. The gesture is so sweet and natural, it causes a pang in my heart.

"Hey." Gareth entwines their fingers. His expression reveals the same awe as if the boy in front of him were a beautiful sunrise.

Art extends his smile to encompass me and indicates his companion. "This is Zephan Oduro from my flat. If he had his way, he'd stay cooped up in his room all summer."

"Yup," Zephan mutters.

"Zeph, has anyone ever told you you're a grouch?"

"Art, has anyone ever told you you're irritating as fuck?"

Art laughs. The infectious sound sets Gareth off, and then the three of us are cracking up. Zephan rolls his eyes heavenward as if to say *who are these idiots?*

"Zeph isn't as much of a grump as he'd like everyone to think," Art says, grinning. "That's my theory, anyway, and I'm on a mission to prove it. You don't mind if he joins the band, do you? I've heard him on bass. Fucking unbelievable."

He directs the question at me. I have no idea why he thinks I'm in charge, or maybe he already knows Gaz will go along with anything he asks.

I study Zephan, staring off into the distance and scuffing the ground with the toe of his battered trainer. He looks as though he wants to die, like he'd rather be anywhere but here. Probably shy.

"Of course not," I say. "Five's every bit as good as four."

We merge with the current of campers flowing towards the Dukes Building. Gareth and Art walk ahead, hands interlocked, Zephan and me trailing behind. He seems content with his silence, so I leave him to it, instead scanning the grounds for Georgie.

15. GEORGIE

Look at me, the great Georgie Wilde, expert in hiding and avoidance. Pity Dukes doesn't offer a scholarship for that; I'd win hands down. It means dragging myself out of bed at the arse crack, but it's worth it.

Once I've fed Star and wolfed down my own breakfast, I slink back to my room with a cup of tea. Curled on the bed, fingers clenched around my mug, I listen to the flat waking up. Doors bang. Showers run. Chanelle lets out a throaty laugh. At twenty to nine, I shift my bum into gear. If I head over to the workshop now, I can get settled before everyone else arrives.

The July air smells of earth and dew-soaked grass. I breathe it in, swallowing my nerves. A few people mill around, but no one takes any notice of us. I strap Star into her harness, grasp the handle in my left hand, and turn us in the direction I want to go.

"Forward," I tell her, sliding my right foot out in front, and Star leads me along the winding path to the Dukes Building.

When the door swings shut behind us, the thud echoes in the quiet of the foyer. I fling my arm to the side.

"Find the door," I urge Star, and she steers me towards the reception room.

"Hey, Georgie. Hey, Star," Calypso says, tone bright. You'd think there was no one in the world she'd rather see. "Here, take my arm. I've put out some cushions for you guys to sit on and I don't want you tripping over them."

I drop the handle, keeping hold of Star's lead, and Calypso guides me to the front of the room. Damn. If it'd been up to me, I would've picked a spot at the back. The price I pay for being early, I s'pose. No skulking in a corner for me. I slump onto my cushion, Star sprawling beside me.

Calypso flops down nearby. "Missed seeing you both at the picnic. You feeling better?"

Takes me a second to twig what she's talking about. Oh, right, the fictitious headache. "Yeah, thanks."

"I'm glad," Calypso says.

God, I suck, lying to her when she's been nothing but friendly. Still, no way I could've faced the picnic.

"Don't suppose you managed to find yourself any bandmates," she adds. "Being sociable's the last thing you feel like when you're under the weather."

I shake my head, cheeks hot.

"Ah, no worries. We'll wander over to the dining room after the workshop and see what we can sort out."

I drop my gaze. Calypso's being so nice, practically dealing me a get-out-of-jail-free card. See? I'm not a social outcast, after all. I was just too ill to leave my room. What a fraud. If I could, I'd crawl inside my cushion and die.

Campers start to drift in. Calypso greets most of them by name; must've gone out of her way to get to know us over the weekend.

"Hey, Mina," she calls. "Come grab a seat."

My shoulders stiffen. Thank God the cushions closest to me are already taken. All the same, I hug my knees to my chest like this will make me invisible.

Last time we ran into each other, I was on my way to Himari's room. Feels like a past life—one where I was actually hyped for the summer. I thought we'd shared a moment, Mina and me. Whatever. I'd been kidding myself, just as I had with Chanelle and all the others over the years.

"Right, let's get started." Calypso claps and the chatter peters out. The direction of her voice shifts as she paces. "Welcome to sixties week."

Several people groan.

Calypso laughs. "I see we have some sceptics among us. Trust me, by the end of our workshop on Friday, you'll be a hippy wannabee."

"Bet you fifty quid I won't," says a guy with a Liverpudlian accent.

Calypso laughs again. "Kai, I'm pretty sure my gran would have something to say about me winning money from a student, and I would win, you can bank on that. I mean, what's not to love? The sixties was the decade when this country finally shook off the shackles of the Second World War and learnt to have fun again. It was a time of revolution, of increased freedom for women and of experimenting with psychedelic drugs. Most of all, and this is what we'll be looking at in today's session, it saw the explosion of rock 'n' roll onto the music scene."

A chorus of cheers, and another boy pipes up in an exaggerated Texas drawl, "Sex, drugs, and rock 'n' roll, baby."

"You got it, Andre." Calypso comes to a halt in front of me. "There's this famous saying that if you can remember the sixties, you weren't there. Of course, rock 'n' roll was born in the fifties, but it was during the following decade that it really caught fire. The Beatles, Jimi Hendrix, The Who, The Stones…these artists all helped shape the genre and continue to influence music in the twenty-first century. What I'm going to do now is play you some of the most iconic tracks from that era. Then we can talk about what makes them stand out and if there's anything we as musicians can learn from them."

The grate of electric guitars blares from a surround sound system. *Revolution*. Grandad must've played it to Jake and me a zillion times. A doomed effort to induct us into his Beatles' fan club.

I try to concentrate on the music, but dread has my insides in a fist. All I can do is count down the minutes till break and steel myself for certain humiliation.

16. MINA

"You go on," I tell Gareth and Art as we exit the Dukes Building after Calypso's workshop. Zephan must've slipped out already because he's nowhere to be seen.

"Good luck." Gareth punches me on the arm. "She looked kind of fierce, like."

I roll my eyes. "You have a sister. You're not allowed to be scared of girls."

Gareth laughs and turns to Art. "Shall we go grab a table then?"

Art nods, taking Gareth's hand, and they amble away across campus. Watching them—fingers entwined, heads close together—you'd never guess they only met the day before.

A wooden bench is set against the wall to one side of the main entrance. I sit on it to wait while campers wander past in clusters and head towards the dining room. I find myself humming the last track Calypso played us, 'I'm into Something Good' by Herman's Hermits. They might be cheesy, some of these sixties songs, but they do get stuck in your brain.

Actually, Gareth's right. Georgie did look sort of fierce huddled on her cushion at the front of the room, jaw set, arms strangling her knees. Has someone upset her? Because, if they have, I'd dearly love to give them a piece of my mind. Not that Georgie seemed in need of my protection. She appeared ready to battle the entire world.

The door to the foyer opens. Georgie emerges first, fingers curled around the handle of Star's harness, attention on giving instructions to her dog. Calypso follows, falling into step beside her as the two of them start along the path.

I leap to my feet and hurry to join them. "Georgie! Wait."

They pause to let me draw level. Other than a slight tautening of her shoulders, Georgie doesn't react to my presence.

"Hey, Mina, how did you like the session?" Calypso asks.

"It was really great," I say. "I'm definitely going to check out some more sixties stuff."

"Then my job here is done." Calypso winks. "Look, do you girls mind if I run on ahead? I need to sort out who's in what band. Come see me in a bit."

She waves and lopes away across the ground, her legs in their aquamarine shorts eating up the distance in long, easy strides. Silence blows in to fill the space she leaves behind. Georgie scuffs her Converse against the concrete, making no move to break the awkwardness.

"I looked for you over the weekend," I say. "Where were you hiding?"

She shrugs. "Had a headache."

"Oh, poor you." Perhaps that explains her aloofness this morning. My sister's suffered with debilitating migraines since she was a child, and she's always a bit out of it the day after.

Silence descends between us once more, and I chew on my lower lip. This isn't proving as easy as I thought it would. What happened to our effortless connection of the other day?

"So," I venture, "my best friend and I are putting a band together with a couple of others. I'm sure you have your own band by now, but if you don't…would you like to join ours?"

"Oh." Georgie's tone gives nothing away.

I shift my position to get a better view of her face, but there's no play of sunlight and shadow today. It's like staring at a flat stretch of water under an overcast sky.

I hurry on. "As I said, though, you probably already have a band—"

"No." Georgie's hand tightens on Star's harness, the single word seeming to cost her an enormous effort. "No, I'd like to. If…if you're sure."

Still no smile from her, merely a brief flicker of relief. Surely it would have taken more than a headache to bring about such a change. Something happened over the weekend, something that upset her. Well then, it's up to me to try and cheer her up.

"Great," I say with all the brightness I can muster. "Let's find the others and tell them the good news."

AFTER BREAK, THE five of us wander next-door to the study block where we separate for Performance Technique. At the end of the ground-floor corridor, I step into a bright room with chairs arranged in a semicircle around a gorgeous upright. Chanelle—surprise, surprise—has taken the central seat, her girls ranged on either side.

"Hey, Mina." She offers me a wave as I take the empty chair beside Himari. "Looking forward to the session?"

I beam. "Give me an excuse to sing and I'm there."

"She's good, too," Himari says. "Heard her singing in the shower this morning."

I smile at her, touched.

Patrice lolls in her chair, gaze dreamy. "Who cares about the singing? We get to spend an entire ninety minutes with Dutch. Man, he has the sexiest arse."

"Yeah." Blair pokes her in the arm. "And the sexiest wife."

"Hey, stop raining on my parade." Patrice sticks her tongue out at her, and the five of them crack up.

As campers trickle into the room around us, I pleat the material of my skirt between my fingers. I've never felt comfortable in cliques like this, the ones characterised by faux bitchiness and boy talk. My mind goes to Georgie, how quiet she'd been during break, her definite coolness towards me. Had I mistaken the spark of friendship we'd shared the other evening? I'd been looking forward to getting to know her, but perhaps she doesn't feel the same. Perhaps she only agreed to be part of the band because she had no other option, or perhaps there's something else going on I don't understand.

"So, Mina." Chanelle reclaims my attention. "Saw you with the blind girl earlier."

The blind girl? I wince. It isn't as if Georgie's lack of vision defines her. Was Chanelle being deliberately offensive? When I search her expression, though, it reveals only innocent curiosity. Maybe she's simply thoughtless.

"Georgie, yes," I say. "We're in the same band."

"Aw, that's so sweet of you." Chanelle reaches across to pat my knee. "Taking her under your wing. Well done, you."

I frown. Her patronising tone makes me want to slap her, or it would if I were the kind of person who waltzed around hitting girls in the face. Does she really believe I asked Georgie to join our band out of pity, that she's some charity case? If anything, she's doing me a favour. With Gareth wrapped up in Art, it'll be nice to have someone to chat to.

Before I can explain any of this, the door opens and Dutch saunters in. He moves to the piano, all toned limbs and sinuous grace, and perches on the stool facing us. When his lazy grin travels around the circle, Patrice almost slides off her chair in a swoon.

"Hey, guys, and welcome to the vocals section of PT."

The buzz of chatter dies and everyone focuses on Dutch, expressions showing varying degrees of awe. The Desired might not be my cup of tea, but seeing him up close—close enough to feel the force of his charisma, to inhale his woody aftershave— it's impossible not to get a thrill.

"Really," Dutch continues, "we're just going to have a bit of fun together. Each week, I'll choose a couple of tracks from the decade you're exploring with Calypso, and we'll play around with it, experiment with harmonies and whatever."

Some of my fellow vocalists exchange intimidated glances, maybe nervous about singing for this celebrity, but I'm not among them. Singing has never held any terror for me. If anything, it's when I feel the most confident, the most myself.

"So, let's get this show on the road." Dutch retrieves a stack of printouts from the top of the piano and tosses one to each of us. "We're kicking off with 'California Dreamin'' by The Mamas and the Papas. The harmony's super fun. Here are the lyrics for anyone who doesn't know them. I'll play you the original first, just so everyone's on the same page."

Dutch fishes his phone from his baggy jeans and taps the screen, the lilting guitar intro pouring out of the speaker. It's like magic, the way music can make me forget everything else. As the overlapping vocals eddy around me, my annoyance with Chanelle and my worry over Georgie fades into the background.

17. GEORGIE

TIME FOR OUR first rehearsal.

I clip Star into her harness, sling my guitar case over my shoulder, and tramp across campus. The toast I forced down for lunch roils in my stomach. A scene flashes into my mind, a premonition. Me, unpacking my Fender in front of my bandmates and puking all over it. What an impressive start that would be.

For Christ's sake, get it together. This is what you wanted, isn't it? You found a band without Calypso's help. And Zephan'll be there. Not exactly a friendly voice, but one I can trust. I met the other guys at break, too, and they seemed cool with me. Still, doesn't mean they really want me around. More likely, Mina felt bad for me and convinced them to go along with it.

As I steer Star towards the rec building, Mina calls my name. She must've been on the lookout.

"Hey," she puffs, running to meet us. "You OK? We saved a seat for you at lunch."

I tilt my face away, hiding my guilt. Hadn't occurred to me they'd do that. "Yeah, sorry. Star kept yawning, so I grabbed something while she had a nap."

True, but not the whole of it. Fact is, I chickened out. I imagined my bandmates chatting over plates of pasta or chilli con carne and figured they'd have more fun without me.

"Aw, poor Star." Mina matches our pace. "How was PT?"

"Good. The tutor's great." Nate Rogers, a potty-mouthed Geordie with a big laugh, plays lead guitar for The Desired. Zephan and I snagged a corner where we could strum along to 'House of the Rising Sun' without drawing attention. "Um, how was Vocals?"

"Loved it. Well, I got to sing for ninety minutes, so I'm a happy girl."

In the rec building, we lug our instruments up two flights of stairs to our assigned practice room. Mina pushes open the door to quiet voices and the twang of a bass.

She stops on the threshold so that I almost barge into her. "Ugh. Enough with the canoodling. There're other people present, you know."

"Hasn't bothered them so far," Zephan mutters.

Art laughs, the sound drifting as he moves to the far side of the room. "Sorry, Zeph, didn't realise we were embarrassing you."

Zephan scoffs and goes back to tuning his bass. Mina leads me to the chair next to him, then takes the one on his other side. Across from us, Gareth starts running scales at the piano. I set Star free and she lies down next to me.

"So, I have the perfect name for our band." Art taps out a complex rhythm on the drum kit. He adopts the dramatic tone of someone making an announcement. "Artisan." Then, switching back to his normal voice, he adds, "Zeph's on board. Right, Zeph?"

"Sure." Zephan's reply is flat. "As in, Art is an enormous pain in my arse."

Art gasps in mock horror, while Gareth and Mina crease up. Even through the nerves, a smile tweaks my mouth. These guys are funny.

"I'm curious," Mina says, unzipping her instrument case. "Does anyone here come from a musical family?"

"You know I don't." Gareth snorts. "Unless you count Dad murdering The Stereophonics in the shower. Their songs, like, not the band."

I hide a grin as I lift out my guitar. Gareth's such a goof. You can't not warm to him.

"My parents can hold a tune," Mina says. "They're both in our church choir, but they're not going to win any awards."

Art pulls off a swift drumroll. "It's just me in my family. Everyone else is completely tone deaf. Reckon I'm adopted."

"How about you, Zeph?" Gareth asks. "You're pretty quiet over there."

Zephan huffs. "So would you be if your family was the Ghanaian equivalent of the fucking Von Trapps."

"Ooh, *The Sound of Music* is my sister's favourite film," Mina says. "That must be so cool, growing up in a house of musicians."

"Musicians, dancers, bloody exhibitionists… It's a nightmare. Can't hear yourself think for all the arias and violin concertos and oversized egos."

He sounds so narked, it's impossible not to laugh. Poor Zephan. Would be easy to get lost among so much talent, such big personalities. He probably came to Dukes for the peace.

"What about you, Georgie?" Mina tugs me from my thoughts.

I twist the tuning peg, adjusting my D string. Not my favourite topic. Oh, I don't mind people knowing I have a sort-of-famous dad. It's just the only thing my classmates ever ask me about. Well, when they aren't pelting me with dumb questions.

"How many fingers am I holding up?"

"Do you need help tying your shoelaces?"

Still, this was bound to come up sooner or later.

"My dad was in a band," I tell them. With any luck, they'll assume it was some college thing that never went further than playing the local pub.

Fat chance.

Everyone except Zephan jumps on the news.

"What were they called?"

"Did they ever hit the charts?"

"Were they famous?"

Eventually, I crack. "They were called The Wilde Landers."

"Rings a bell." Art sounds pensive.

"Yeah, you know," Gareth says. "They did that song, the one that goes *'it's a high without a comedown, dessert with extra cream'.*"

Gareth launches into the chorus, Mina and Art joining in. "*'A band that always turns up trumps, when you achieve your dream'.*"

I cringe into my Fender. Why does their biggest hit have to be the most toe clenching?

"Classic," Art says. "What happened to them? They kinda disappeared."

I test a few chords, fingers forming the shapes automatically. "My Uncle Sean was killed in a car crash, skidded off the road in the rain."

"Wow, I'm sorry." It's what you're supposed to say, but Mina sounds like she means it.

I shrug. Me and Jake never knew Dad's youngest brother, since he died before we were born. "Dad and Uncle Rob might've carried on, but Uncle Sean was their front man. Without him, their label wasn't interested."

That's been the hardest part, living with Dad's regret. All my life, he's pined for a music career that ended too soon. It's why Mum's so wary of me going down this path; doesn't want me to get hurt.

"We still need a band name," Art says, "since you so rudely scoffed at my idea. We should pick one that pays tribute to Georgie's dad. The Wilde Cards, or…no, I've got it. Wilde Oats."

Gareth splutters. "Trust you to come up with that. How about Wilde Summer?"

"Or Wildest Dreams," Mina suggests, "because that's what we're all following, isn't it? Georgie, what do you think?"

If I smile any harder, my face'll split in half. Could be my bandmates are trying to suck up to me, but I don't think so. The gesture feels genuine. Also, the name has a good vibe. Dad would be touched.

18. MINA

"CHRIST, WHAT'VE I done to deserve this?" Zephan's grumbling trails in his wake as he's marched along the alley that cuts between the study block and the rec building.

"No idea." Art walks behind him, hands on the taller boy's shoulders, steering him towards the pool house. "It must've been something bloody good, though, to be landed with me."

Zephan snorts. I nudge Gareth, grinning, and he tears his shining eyes from Art to grin back.

He takes my arm, drawing me to a stop, and drops his voice. "So? What do you think?"

"Of Art?" My gaze drifts to the boy ahead of us, all swaying hips and supple grace. His laughter burbles towards us on the breeze, vibrant and infectious, and I smile at Gareth. "I think he's lovely."

"God, he totally is. Can't believe my luck, to be honest."

I hug him. "Luck has nothing to do with it. You're gorgeous and funny and the sweetest guy I know. Art's obviously smitten. The way he looks at you, it makes me blush."

Gareth exhales a shaky breath, cheeks flushing, and squeezes me tight.

"Oi, Mina!" Art calls. "Get your hands off my man."

He and Zephan have reached the entrance to the glass-fronted pool house and are waiting for us. We break apart, laughing, and go to join them.

"You see?" I murmur in Gareth's ear. "Crazy about you."

He shakes his head, though whether in denial or incredulity I'm not sure. Either way, he can't hold back his smile.

"Come on, mister, let's check out this famous swimming pool." Art extends a hand to Gareth, who takes it, the two of them heading through the sliding doors in the direction of the changing rooms.

Zephan raises his eyebrows as if to say *looks like it's just you and me.* Then he slouches through the door after them and crosses to the far corner. There, he settles onto one of the cushions strewn like giant Starbursts around the edge of the water and buries himself in his book.

I follow more slowly, pausing to remove my ballet pumps. The instant I step inside, that familiar chlorine-scented humidity wafts into my face. The oval pool is crowded with campers, some fooling about, others bobbing on inflatable doughnuts, their splashing and laughter bouncing around the cavernous space.

Wow, my sister would love this. Unlike me, who would rather float on a Lilo with my headphones in, May has always been the swimmer of the family. His little water baby, Dad used to call her. She cried whenever it was time to get out of the pool and go home, and this isn't your average pool.

The one thing Marlon Dukes was known for, besides being an incredible musician, was his love of the sea. His interviews were full of his latest trip to swim with dolphins in Miami or dive with stingrays in the Cayman Islands. When Leticia Dukes created her vision for an academy to nurture the talent of budding stars, she also designed this pool as a memorial to her son's lifelong passion.

I weave my way between the small groups sprawled on their cushions. With its front of tinted glass and the mist-blue lights set into the rocky ceiling, I have the sense that I've entered a subterranean cave. Beneath my feet, tiles the dark gold of wet sand slope to meet turquoise waves. The bottom of the pool is lit up, illuminating the intricate mosaic—shimmering seahorses and shoals of tropical fish entwined with the fronds of marine plants. It's mesmerising. The water calls to me, begs me to submerge myself, but instead I flop onto the orange cushion beside Zephan's pink one.

He glances at me from behind his book, an Agatha Christie Poirot mystery. "Not going in?"

"Waiting for Georgie." I adjust my swimsuit beneath the sleeve of my dress. "How about you?"

He shrugs and turns a page. "Gotta draw the line somewhere."

"Fair enough." I stretch out on my back and stare up at the ceiling, tracing the pits and crags in its surface.

Where can Georgie have got to? I'd asked her to come to the pool with us, but she said Star needed a wee and a drink first. Thinking back, her tone strikes me as evasive. There's no denying the wariness that's hung about her since I sought her out at break.

A splash, followed by a chorus of shrieks, yank my attention to the pool where Blair and Patrice are hastening to avoid a deluge. Gareth emerges, spluttering and pushing sopping curls out of his face. His eyes go straight to Art, who's smirking at him from the safety of the tiles.

"No pushing, guys." Dutch, acting as lifeguard, gestures to the sign over Art's shoulder. "It's all there in the rules."

"Sorry, mate," Art says, not sounding it in the least.

"You're gonna pay for that," Gareth tells him.

The moment Art slides into the pool, Gareth ducks him under the water. Art surfaces, laughing and dripping, and the two of them wrestle like a pair of otters. It's lovely to see Gareth so happy, and yet I can't help but feel excluded.

Though Gareth's stripped down to his swimming shorts, Art's still wearing his purple vest top. Art Dabrowski hasn't struck me as the coy type. If anything, I would've expected him to seize the first opportunity to flaunt some skin.

"Hey." Cold droplets shower my bare legs. I squeak and glance over to find Gareth waving at me. "You coming in, or what?"

"Yeah, in a bit. Just waiting for Georgie."

Not that I really believe she's coming. For whatever reason, Georgie's cooled towards me since Saturday and is going out of her way to avoid the group. If only I knew why. Then I might be able to fix it.

19. GEORGIE

NOTHING WAKES YOU up faster than a cold nose to the face.

I kick off the damp tangle of sheets, free myself from my headphones and pause the book. My phone says dinner started ten minutes ago. Explains why Star's so hungry. Explains, too, why the house is silent as the grave. Reckon it should be safe to leave my room. I run a hand through my wild hair and snag Star's lead.

Outside in the hallway, I stop. Sounds from the kitchen. Crockery rattles, cupboard doors bang. Shit. What if it's Chanelle? My muscles urge me to back up before whoever it is notices me. But Star needs feeding. It wouldn't be fair to make her wait just because I'm a spineless melt.

"Hey," Zephan says.

"Hey." Star trots ahead, tail whirling, and I follow in relief. "Thought everyone was at dinner."

Zephan crouches to pat Star, shoes squeaking. "Had enough socialising for one day. Sandwich?"

The offer catches me off guard, coming from him. Will make a nice change from toast, though. "Cheers."

While Zephan cobbles our meal together, I feed Star and take her for a sniff around the garden. When I get back, Zephan waits for me to wash my hands before passing me a plate.

"Thanks." I lean against the worktop and bite into my sandwich. Thick and buttery and delicious. My stomach purrs.

"You're welcome." Zephan retreats to the worktop opposite. "Not that you deserve it."

"Huh? What did I do?"

"Abandoned me, that's what. If I have to sit by the pool being sociable, least you can do is show up."

"Oh." I chew my lip. It was kind of Mina to invite me along, but she's a kind person. I could tell that much the first time we met. It would be easy to latch on to her kindness, to kid myself it means more than it does, but I can't. Not again.

We fall quiet. Star crouches in front of me, breath warming my thigh, alert for crumbs as ever.

After a while, Zephan says, "Mina kept looking for you."

"Did she?" I lick butter from my fingers. Really hadn't thought she'd miss me. "I was worried… I didn't want to butt in."

Zephan considers. Then he says, "Pretty sure she wouldn't see it like that."

His words niggle at me for the rest of that day and into the next morning.

I hunch on a cushion before Calypso's workshop, my exhausted brain on a loop. I've got Mina all wrong. She'd waited for me at the pool, Zephan said, kept looking out for me, was gutted when I didn't show. I'd say Zephan was just being nice, but…well, pretty sure lying to make someone feel better isn't his style.

"Hello."

And here she is, like my confusion has conjured her up. Mina takes the cushion behind mine, breath tickling my neck.

I jump. "Uh, hi."

Where was my head? I'd barely noticed my campmates come in. I tune into the chatter competing with Marvin Gay's 'Heard It Through the Grapevine'. Why's Mina even talking to me? I've treated her like crap, pushed her away. Would serve me right if she wanted nothing more to do with me.

"Where did you disappear to yesterday?" Mina asks. "I looked for you in your room, but there was no answer."

"God, sorry. Didn't hear you. Fell asleep with my headphones in."

"That's OK. I was worried I might've upset you, that you were avoiding me."

I duck my head, hiding behind my curls.

"Gosh, I did." Mina sounds near to tears. "I knew there had to be something. Georgie, I'm so sorry. Whatever it was—"

"No. You... You didn't do anything."

"Really? So, why...?"

I fiddle with the knee of my jeans, nail poking a hole through the denim. How to explain? Mina's been nothing but welcoming to me, and what have I done? Let past disappointments blind me to a genuine offer of friendship. I'll have to tell her everything. What choice do I have? I only hope she'll understand.

Marvin Gay finishes and Calypso claps for quiet. "OK, let's get started. As you've probably gathered, we're moving on to sixties soul."

"Now that's what I call real music," the boy with the Liverpudlian accent calls.

"Glad it meets with your approval, Kai. There's no doubt soul's had a massive impact on the music industry, although in fact, the rise of the genre here in Britain owes a lot to the birth of rock 'n' roll in the fifties. The original R & B was immensely popular within the mod subculture. The Beatles were huge fans, as were bands like The Who and The Kinks."

"Shame it didn't help them write better music," Kai says, and several people snigger.

"OK, so you're not a convert," Calypso says. "Let's see if I can find you something more up your street. So many soul artists who began their careers in the sixties are still revered today. Stevie Wonder, Aretha Franklin, The Supremes, James Brown…these are all household names and continue to influence musicians in the twenty-first century. The first track I'm going to play you is by Sam Cooke. It's called 'Bring It on Home to Me.'"

Piano gushes from the speakers. I scarcely hear it. My hands clench into fists. *Just ask her. But what if she doesn't want to know? Why would she after you've done your best impression of Oscar the Grouch?*

Mina's voice grazes my ear. "You OK?"

Why's she being so nice? I sure as hell don't deserve it. At least she still seems willing to talk. Maybe I can save this, or maybe it's too late. Either way, I have to try.

Feels like one of the tuning pegs from my Fender has lodged in my throat. I swallow and twist to face her. "Uh, can we… Would you come for a walk with me at break?"

20. MINA

WE WANDER THROUGH campus, the sun a reassuring hand on our backs. I study Georgie, who's focused on directing Star, shoulders rigid, a tautness to the set of her mouth.

"You don't have to do this," she says. "I'm sure you have better things to do with your break."

I laugh. "What? Like providing the captive audience for Gareth and Art's romance of the millennium?"

One side of Georgie's mouth shivers. It isn't quite a smile, but it's the promise of one, and I call that progress.

The splash of water carries towards us a few moments before the path opens onto the paved area encircling the fountain. I take Georgie's arm. "Come on. Let's sit down."

We settle on the low brick surround of the lily pond, Star lounging on the concrete at our feet.

"So…" I trail my fingers in the cool water, watching the lily pads bob and sway in the ripples. My unspoken question dances in the air between us.

Georgie angles her body away from mine, concealing her expression. "Sorry."

"What for?"

"For avoiding you."

"Oh." I'd suspected as much, that Georgie's been keeping her distance, but my heart still sinks. What could I have done to make her so wary?

"It wasn't anything you did." She twists her hands together, tone urgent. "But when someone invites me to do something, it's usually out of pity, or…or because they've been told to."

Haltingly, as if she has to drag each word from the depths of her soul, Georgie pours out her story.

It was Year Eight, a typical Monday. Georgie had been forced to endure lesson after lesson of her classmates enthusing about some party they'd been to over the weekend, a party she, as usual, hadn't been invited to. By last period—an art lesson—she was miserable enough to confide in her teaching assistant. Georgie vented to Kate about her isolation, how much she longed to be treated like a human being. A couple of weeks later, a girl in her English class, who always made a point of saying hi, mentioned she was having a few friends round for pizza on Friday night and asked if she'd like to come.

"I should've put it together." Georgie kicks her heel into the wall behind, her voice more self-deprecating than bitter. "I mean, it wasn't like Emma ever wanted to hang out before, but I was so chuffed to be included, I didn't make the connection."

Poor Georgie. My heart hurts for her, that hopeful twelve-year-old who'd been so desperate to find her place. "What happened? I'm guessing it didn't go well."

"Hardly." She snorts.

At Emma's house on Friday evening, Georgie was returning to the lounge after a visit to the downstairs bathroom when she caught the other girls' conversation. According to Emma, Kate had been sounding out their classmates to see if any of them would be willing to absorb Georgie into their friendship group.

Georgie adopts a singsong voice, imitating Emma. "I couldn't exactly say no, could I? I do feel bad for Georgie. She must get lonely."

"Gosh." I wince. "I can't imagine... That must've been so—"

"Humiliating? Just a bit." Georgie shrugs like it's nothing, simply to be expected.

She'd gone home after that, pretended she felt sick and called her dad to pick her up. The girls were all kind enough, she says, fetching her a glass of water and sitting with her on the sofa, but Georgie could tell they were relieved to be rid of her. Emma did ask her over a few more times, but Georgie always made some excuse, and the invitations dried up.

There have been more incidents over the years, more uncomfortable visits to classmates' houses, reluctant acceptances onto lunch tables and into project groups. Then, shoulders hunching in on themselves, she tells me about our first night here. When I hear how my flatmates and their friends treated her, the cruel things they'd said, I want to cry... or hit someone... or both. Yes, definitely both.

"I'm so sorry." I touch her arm. "Those girls are cows. You're better off without them."

Georgie puffs out a long breath and some of the stiffness leaves her body. "I know that now. It's just..."

"Just what?"

"It's stupid, but, well, I kind of hoped things would be different here. Not sure why, really. No reason why anyone at Dukes should want to hang out with me any more than the kids at school."

"I want to hang out with you."

Georgie swivels to face me, a glimmer of hope in her eyes. I can tell she wants to believe me, even as experience warns her to be cautious.

"I do." Since she can't see my expression, I pour all my sincerity into my voice. "I've wanted to get to know you since the other night."

This time, Georgie's smile breaks free. It's the first smile I've seen from her since our meeting at the weekend. "Really?"

"Really."

It's true, every word, and yet… I remember Calypso seeking me out on the bench directly across from where we're sitting now, her suggestion to ask Georgie to join our band. I would have done so anyway, if I'd known she wasn't already part of one, but how might it look to Georgie if she found out?

I swallow my unease. "Want to grab a drink before PT?"

As we walk to the dining room, guilt coils around my heart. Should I come clean? Calypso might've planted the idea in my head, but I'd felt drawn to Georgie before that. Given past events, though, I'm not sure she'd believe me. More likely, the knowledge would hurt her, and hurting Georgie is the last thing I want to do.

21. GEORGIE

THE DAYS SLOT into a pattern. Music Through the Decades with Calypso first thing, Performance Technique after break, jamming sessions in the afternoon. Amazing how well we play together, given our different styles. With each practice, we gel more as a band.

There's no more sitting alone in my room, living off tea and toast. Instead, the five of us take over a table in the dining room with its smell of coffee and spices. Over plates of carbonara or chicken bhuna, we volley ideas and take the piss out of one another. And I could've missed out on all this—the awesome food, the in-jokes, being part of something for the first time in my life.

"Can't believe you're having seconds," Mina tells me on Wednesday evening. Her tone lands somewhere between amusement and incredulity. "You already had two helpings of pasta."

I pop another spoonful of cherry pie into my mouth. It melts on my tongue, a blend of tart fruit, buttery pastry and Jersey cream. "Would be rude not to when Rick's gone to so much trouble."

"I'm with Georgie," Art says. He's polished off his own pie and returned with a slice of lemon cheesecake. "Why waste your energy deciding what to go for when you can have a bit of everything? That's my philosophy and I'm sticking to it. Nice fruit salad, Mina?"

"Oh, shush. Can I help it if my parents are both fitness freaks?"

"No, but you can ditch their poisonous ideology and follow the true path."

Gareth scoffs. "It's pudding, hun, not Buddhism."

"Pudding is a religion," Art says. "Right, Georgie, mate?"

"Right," I agree through another mouthful of pie. "All disciples kneel before the holy trinity of crumble, ice cream and butterscotch sauce."

Zephan snorts from behind his book, while the others burst out laughing. At me. I can't stop grinning. I've waited my whole life for this moment, this sense of belonging. My bandmates' laughter. It fills me up, sweet and addictive as Rick's cherry pie.

AFTER BAND PRACTICE on Thursday, Mina and I sit on the edge of the pool. I dip my feet in the water, the chill zinging up my calves.

Mina squeals and withdraws her legs in a cold spray. "It's freezing."

I nudge her. "You'll soon get used to it."

"All right, I can do this." Mina shifts beside me, lowering her toes towards the surface. She retreats with another squeak. "Or maybe not."

I crack up. "Wimp. It's not that bad. Just go for it."

"Actually, I've changed my mind. Let's go back to my room and listen to music."

"We could." I hum, pretending to consider. "Or..."

Before Mina can guess what I'm about to do, I twist and shove her off the side. She shrieks, grabbing for me as she falls, and the two of us tumble into the pool. The smack knocks the air from my lungs. I surface, gasping and blinking. Mina emerges beside me, half coughing, half laughing.

"No pushing, girls," Dutch calls.

"Sorry," we say together. Then we collapse into one another, convulsing with laughter.

"I can't believe you did that," Mina says, still giggling.

I grin and scrape the wet hair away from my face. "Guessing you don't have a brother."

"No, just an older sister, and she's way too serious about swimming to mess around. It would be like burping in church."

"How about you?"

"Hmmm, I wouldn't say that, exactly." Mina launches herself at me and dunks me under the surface.

I emerge, spluttering, and tackle her. We roll in the water, wrestling and tickling each other. Our limbs get tangled up, her slender frame against my stockier one. Mina's skin is silky smooth beneath my hands. I flush all over. Suddenly, my heart's beating way too hard.

When Dutch tells us to calm it, Mina snags us a giant rubber ring. We float, holding on to opposite sides. Slowly, my pulse steadies. The waves lap at my shoulders, cool and gentle. It's like drifting in an underground lagoon. Doesn't matter that we're surrounded by campers; we may as well be in our own private bubble.

"Let's play a game," Mina says. "Pretend you're a famous musician and I'm a radio DJ doing one of those quickfire interviews. You know. McDonald's or Burger King."

"OK, but we'll take it in turns." I fold my arms on the rubber ring and rest my chin on them.

"That's fair. I'll start." Mina thinks for a moment, then asks, "Soaps or quiz shows?"

"Quiz shows. Geeky or what?"

"Totally. Is that your question?"

"No." I splash her. "Rom coms or action flicks?"

Mina laughs. "Neither. Horror films."

"Hey, you can't just make up your own options."

"Can, too. My game, my rules."

"Cheat." I kick her under the water. "Thought you'd be all Disney princesses and happy endings."

"I'm full of surprises." Mina hooks her ankle around mine, trapping it.

A current tingles up my leg. "Your turn."

"Hmmm. Favourite takeaway. Indian or Chinese?"

"Indian," I say. "The hotter the better."

"You sound like my dad. I'm more of a korma girl."

"Yeah, thought so."

"Hey, are you calling me a wuss?"

"Yup." I duck Mina's return splash, laughing. "OK, how about this one? Believer or atheist?"

"Ooh, you've gone all philosophical on me." Mina pauses, considering. "I've been brought up Catholic, and I do believe in God, but I don't agree with all the little rules."

"Like what?"

"Like euthanasia being forbidden, or that even married couples should only have sex when they're trying to have a baby. I mean, my parents are really devout, and even they don't follow that one."

"Mina!" I snort.

"What? You've never heard your parents having sex?"

"If I have, my subconscious blocked it out. God, something like that could scar you for life."

We crease up. Once we start, we can't stop. I laugh until my stomach hurts and tears sting my eyes. So this is how it feels to have a friend. The high of it buoys me up until I could bob on the water like the rubber ring.

22. MINA

FRIDAY AFTERNOON BRINGS our first test of the camp. I hug my banjo, fingers slippery with perspiration. *For heaven's sake, Mina, pull it together.* I never get this nervous before a performance, and this isn't even a real one, merely a demonstration of our progress. Still, it feels important, and the others sense it, too.

My gaze travels the practice room, taking in my bandmates— Georgie clutching the neck of her guitar hard enough to splinter wood; Gareth, a quivering mass of apprehension at the piano; Zephan, rigid-backed and deadpan. Only Art appears unaffected, lounging in the corner by the drum kit, sticks dangling at his sides.

Calypso throws herself into the seat by the door and smiles at us. "No need to look so worried. I'm not judging you."

I take a deep breath, but it does little to calm my racing pulse. Calypso might not be judging me now, but she will be. When I come to give the performance I hope will land me the scholarship, she'll be there, assessing me, and how I do over the next few weeks is bound to influence her decision, even if she doesn't mean it to.

"OK, guys." Calypso leans back, legs crossed. "Let's hear what you've been working on."

Art gets into position, adjusting his grip on his sticks. "Ready? On the count of four. One…two…three…"

Gareth comes in a beat too soon. Immediately, he realises his mistake and his fingers slip on the keys, producing a cacophony of discordant notes. In the silence that follows, Gareth turns to look at us, expression stricken. Then Art doubles up over his drum kit, helpless with laughter. Calypso joins in, and soon the whole lot of us are in hysterics. Even Zephan's shaking his head, mouth quirked.

"Fancy giving that another go?" Calypso grins. "And don't beat yourself up about it, Gareth. Happens to the best of us."

"Yeah, babes, you can do it." Art's gaze locks onto Gareth's, his eyes alight with confidence.

Gareth's spine straightens. This time, when Art counts us in, we launch into the song in perfect unison. My fingers fly over the strings, seemingly of their own accord. Why was I so anxious? This is what I love, the thing I was born to do. All the same, I'm glad we decided to do the entire piece in four-part harmony, Zephan refusing to sing. With my voice blending with those of my bandmates, I feel less exposed, one segment of a unified whole.

When the final chord fades, Calypso leaps to her feet in a standing ovation. "That was awesome, guys, really awesome."

The air leaves my lungs in a hurricane of relief. At the piano, Gareth closes the lid and slumps onto it as though he's just completed Sorabji's four-hour *Opus Clavicembalisticum*. Zephan rolls his eyes, swatting at Art, who's performing a victory drumroll on Zeph's shoulders.

I turn to Georgie, wanting to share this moment of triumph. Her grip on her guitar has loosened and she's propped her cheek on the chestnut wood, holding it as though it's a newborn puppy. I reach out to take her hand. A smile flows across her face and she interlaces our fingers, palm brushing mine. Warmth floods my belly. It's nothing. Just the thrill of our performance and of this budding friendship. My friends and I hold hands all the time, offering comfort, buoying each other up before an exam. It's no big deal.

Calypso's moving towards the door, and I force my brain to tune in to what she's saying. "You've obviously gelled really well as a band, but you've each kept your own individuality. It's lovely to see." She pauses with her hand on the knob to smile at us. "I have a few more bands to catch up with but hope to see you all at the sixties night later."

As soon as she's gone, Art slides onto the piano bench beside Gareth and slips his arms around him, murmuring something into his neck that makes him blush. Really, those two are so all over each other.

I nudge my knee against Georgie's. "What do you think? Should we check out the sixties night?"

"I dunno." Her features scrunch in a grimace. "Can't dance to save my life."

"Trust me, however bad your dancing is, it can't be as bad as mine."

"True fact." Gareth smirks at me over Art's shoulder.

"Hey, I don't remember asking for your opinion." I stick my tongue out at him before returning my attention to Georgie. "Seriously, though, we don't have to dance if you'd rather not. We can just sit and listen to the music."

Georgie's expression relaxes and she grins. "I'm up for that."

"Yay!" My heart floats to the roof of my ribcage. I honestly don't mind what we do, so long as we do it together. I turn to Zephan, who's plucking a melancholy tune on his bass. "And you'll come, won't you, Zeph? Bet you're hiding some killer moves."

"I'd rather swim naked through a sea of stag beetles," he says, and Georgie and I double up.

23. GEORGIE

C HANELLE CLARKE MIGHT be a bitch, but you have to hand it to her. She has a badass voice—Whitney with a shovel-load of Amy Winehouse grit.

Saturday's open-mic night in the concert hall, and anyone who wants to can strut their stuff. The members of Wildest Dreams are sprawled on the grass outside the Dukes Building. I stroke Star, the performances wafting towards us on the mild air. They've all been incredible, but Chanelle's on another level. She's putting her own spin on Aretha Franklyn's 'Respect', acoustic and contemporary.

God, what am I doing here? No way I can compete with that.

"She's good," Art says.

Is that envy? Like Art Dabrowski has anything to worry about. He went up a few performances back, Gareth accompanying him on the piano as he belted out Queen's 'Somebody to Love'. The power behind it would've put Adam Lambert to shame.

"So're you," Gareth tells Art. "No one should be allowed to play the drums like that. I could jump you right now."

"Please don't," Zephan mutters from his prone position beside me.

Star rolls over, plonking her head in my lap. I rub her ears while Chanelle goes for it. Her licks would've done Mariah proud. It's like she's been performing all her life. Well, she probably has. Wish I had a tenth of her punch. I can only hope the judges see something else in me.

Ugh. There's the wet slurp of kissing, full-on snogging with plenty of tongue action. I cover my ears.

Zephan groans. "Make it stop. My retinas are melting."

"Sorry, mate." Art disengages with a pop. He couldn't have sounded less sorry if he tried.

Chanelle ends her song to noisy cheers, and Mina's leg bumps mine. "Fancy going up?"

My stomach lurches. The idea of stepping onto the stage, performing in front of my campmates, is bloody terrifying. "I've, well, I've never done it before."

"What? You've never sung in front of people?"

"Yeah. Well, my family, but I'm not sure that counts."

"It totally counts. We can duet. It'll be fun. I'm itching to try out that grand."

I want to. I do. More than that, I need to. How will I ever make music a career if I don't put myself out there? It's just... everyone's so talented.

I take the coward's way out. "Maybe later. You go first."

"All right, but I'm not letting you off that easily." Mina slaps my knee and scrambles to her feet. "Back in a bit."

She leaves, taking the sun with her. The space beside me feels cold and empty. A guy's singing now, crooning a James Blake track with a ton of soul.

"Hi, boys."

That voice, sandpaper and dark chocolate. Shit. I've somehow managed to avoid her so far, but it seems my luck's run out.

"Hey, Chan," Art says. "Nice job back there."

"Cheers, babes." Her shadow falls across me, then moves on. "How about you, Mr. Elusive?"

"What?" Zephan sounds irritated. You'd think he'd been interrupted just as he was about to solve the mystery of life. I duck my head, grinning.

Chanelle continues, unfazed. "Gonna get up on that stage and show us what you can do?"

"Nope."

"Aw, come on. Not gonna hold out on us, are you?"

"Yup."

"Spoilsport." Chanelle sighs. "If you're shy, we could always sing together. I promise to hold your hand." She drops her voice to a seductive purr.

"Uh…" Embarrassment comes off Zephan like heat from a radiator.

Poor Zeph. I'd tell Chanelle to back off if I thought she'd take any notice.

Chanelle laughs, voice retreating as she walks away. "The offer's there when you're ready. See you around, boys."

"Ooooh!" Art bursts out the moment she's out of earshot. "Someone's got an admirer."

"Shut the fuck up," Zephan snaps.

The three of us crack up. Funny. Chanelle hadn't acknowledged me, not even to pet Star. A few days ago, her snub would've stung. Now, sitting on the grass with the bandmates who're fast becoming my friends, I couldn't give a toss.

The opening bars of a piano piece spill from the concert hall. I fall quiet, waiting. Not a song I know, but it has an upbeat country vibe. It's about finding a love you never knew you needed, about not realising there was this hole inside you until someone fills it.

I've heard Mina sing before. Hell, when is that girl not singing? If she isn't working out harmonies in rehearsals, she's accompanying one of her playlists. When she doesn't know the lyrics, like at the sixties night, she hums.

This, though… Mina's putting her heart and soul into it. Her voice is pure and sweet and totally stunning. She's obviously having a ball up there. The joy of it is catching. It lodges in my chest like a secret, nestles beside the ache I can't put a name to.

24. MINA

I EXIT THE CONCERT hall, still humming the Carrie Underwood song I'd chosen. The original was written for the guitar, so I had to adapt it, but there was no way I would've passed up my first chance to play on that spectacular piano. The thrill of performing on Dukes' famous stage still thrums through my veins. My fingers flex, itching to be reunited with those satin-smooth keys, to let the gorgeous sound wash over me and know I was responsible.

My friends are on the grass where I'd left them—Zephan lying behind the shield of his arms; Gareth and Art leaning into one another, talking softly; Georgie stroking Star, who has her head in her lap. When I reclaim my spot, Art gives me the thumbs up.

Gareth ruffles my hair. "Incredible, hun."

"It really was." Georgie smiles at me with a softness that fills my chest with hot toffee sauce.

"Not bad, Farhan," Zephan says, which is high praise coming from him.

"Thanks, guys." A grin engulfs my entire face. I touch Georgie's leg, her skin warm through the denim. "Want to duet, then?"

She bites her lip, emotions flitting across her features—apprehension, uncertainty, longing. "I dunno. Not sure I'm ready to sing on my own. Maybe I could do the harmony?"

"Of course. Whatever you're comfortable with." I trawl my mental music library. "How about 'When You're Gone', Bryan Adams and Mel C? You know it?"

"You kidding? My dad's a massive Bryan Adams fan. Always plays his albums in the car."

"Mine, too. Do you need the lyrics? I can pull them up on my phone."

"That's OK. They're burnt into my brain."

"Same." I scramble back to my feet. "Come on. Let's go and wait our turn."

"Right. Zeph, would you hold on to Star for me?" Georgie extends the lead towards him.

He lowers a hand to take it. "Sure. Star and me are best buds. Right, Star?"

Georgie laughs and eases herself out from under Star's head. Star huffs, disgruntled, and shuffles closer to Zephan, laying her chin on his stomach. Georgie stands and I give her my arm. Her skin slides against mine, warm and dusted with fine hairs the colour of spun gold.

With Gareth and Art cheering us on, we head into the concert hall where Leticia Dukes is overseeing the proceedings from her perch on the edge of the stage. She has her tablet in hand, noting down those campers wanting to perform and calling them up. When she catches sight of me, her teeth flash. "Couldn't stay away, eh?"

"Trust me. I'd glue myself to that piano if I could."

Leticia chuckles, and once she's added our names to the list, we take seats a few rows from the front. Twenty or so campers sit in clusters, either waiting to perform or supporting their friends.

"Who's that?" Georgie murmurs in my ear, nodding towards the stage.

Her breath sends a shiver up my neck and I clear my throat against a sudden dryness. "Blair McIntosh. Good, isn't she?"

"Yeah, sadly," Georgie says, and I laugh.

After Blair, Kai takes his place at the piano and holds us enthralled with a gorgeous version of John Legend's 'All of Me'. He's followed by a group of girls singing an acapella rendition of Little Mix and a boy with a green mohawk growling his way through a heavy metal track. Georgie's still wincing when it's our turn.

"Kind of wish I had my guitar," she says as we navigate the aisle between the seats.

"Here." A girl from my vocals workshop hops up from the front row. She's wearing a hijab and an Iron Maiden T-shirt and holds out a midnight-blue acoustic. "You can borrow mine. I'm Nazneen, by the way."

Georgie allows the girl to thrust the instrument into her arms, looking stunned. "I'm Georgie. Wow, you sure?"

"Totally. Just do something awesome with it, yeah?"

"I'll try. Thanks."

Since Georgie has her hands full, I slip my arm through hers, and the two of us climb the steps to the stage. There's a smattering of applause and a few whistles as we take our places, me at the piano, Georgie leaning against it with the guitar's leather strap over her shoulder.

"Ready when you are," I say.

Georgie sucks in a deep breath. Her eyes are wide, panicked, and for a moment, I'm sure she's about to change her mind. I actually open my mouth to assure her we don't have to do this, but then she straightens her spine, positions her fingers on the frets, and strums the first chord. I join in, improvising the piano part as I go, and we're off.

Georgie begins tentatively, and I hush my voice so I don't drown her. As the song progresses, however, she grows more at ease, inhibitions dissolving right there in front of me. Her playing becomes assured, her vocals rising to match mine. Why was she so self-conscious? She has a great voice, quirky and distinctive, like a gruffer Lola Young. I could listen to it all day.

My fingers fly over the keys, spurred on by Georgie's confidence. Our vocal styles are so different, they shouldn't work together, and yet they do. I study Georgie, relaxed and into it now, her face alive with that joy musicians only experience when they perform.

As I watch her, something happens inside me. My chest feels strange, light and full at the same time, a meringue bursting with whipped cream. It's like when I first met Gaz, the thrill of finding a kindred spirit—the relief, the words that tumbled over one another in their hurry to be shared. At the same time, it isn't like that at all. In a way I can't define, my friendship with Georgie feels utterly different.

WEEK TWO

*The most exciting rhythms seem unexpected
and complex, the most beautiful melodies
simple and inevitable.*

– W.H. Auden

25. GEORGIE

WHEN I EXIT the house on Monday morning, I'm met with the last voice on Earth I want to hear. She calls a greeting and I wince. *Christ, not her.* She must be speaking to someone else, though. Chanelle has no reason to seek me out.

The air hangs heavy and damp. It pastes itself to my skin like clingfilm. As I direct Star onto the path that winds across campus, a spot of rain splatters against my cheek. The weather app on my phone forecasts thundery downpours, so I decided to walk Star early. My dog hates getting wet, won't even step through puddles. Of course, she thinks nothing of leading me through every puddle on our route. Just so long as her paws stay dry.

"Hey, wait!"

Footsteps pursue me along the path. Damn it, she *is* speaking to me. I tell Star to stop, heart plunging.

"Hi." Chanelle joins me, breathless. "Can I talk to you?"

Talk to me? She hasn't so much as acknowledged my existence since orientation weekend. I shrug. "Need to walk Star before the workshop."

"No worries. I'll walk with you."

Why can't I be one of those kickass heroines from the books I read? I'd tell Chanelle Clarke just what I think of her. Since I'm stuck being me, though, I bite my tongue and urge Star forward.

"How's it going?" Chanelle asks. "You enjoying the camp so far?"

"Uh, yeah?" My confusion turns it into a question. *"No thanks to you,"* the kickass heroine would've added.

What's she after? Not a friendly chat, I'd stake my guitar on that.

"Awesome." Chanelle drops her voice. "Look, you're in the same band as Zephan Oduro, right?"

"Right." So that's it. I should've known.

"Could you talk to him, find out what he thinks of me?"

Man, hilarious. I angle away from her, pointing Star onto the left-hand path. Given his indifference when I brought up Chanelle's crush, I doubt Zeph's spared her a thought. Should I tell her as much, stop her wasting her time on him? It would be the kindest thing to do, maybe. I scoff. Since when did I owe Chanelle a crumb of kindness?

"You mustn't make it obvious I put you up to it," Chanelle goes on. "Just bring it up casually in rehearsals, OK?"

God, could she be any more patronising if she tried? "Why don't you ask him yourself?"

"I would, but we always seem to miss each other. He's never in his room when I knock."

Strange. I hide my snort behind a cough. He's always there when one of us calls for him. I mean, I doubt he'd leave his room at all if we didn't coax him out.

"Choke up." Chanelle pats me on the back, a careless gesture with no concern beneath it. "Just see what you can find out, yeah? I'm meeting up with the girls now. See you around…"

Her heels *click-clack* away. I slow our pace, frowning. Something about her last words sounded off, like she'd left the sentence hanging.

Oh, wow. I bring us to a halt. Is that girl for real? I shake my head, not sure whether to be amused or annoyed. Chanelle went to all the trouble of enlisting my help with her love life, and she hadn't even bothered to remember my name.

26. MINA

I WAIT OUTSIDE THE Dukes Building, scanning the stream of campers. The clouds loom heavy and ominous, and what began as the odd raindrop has increased to an intermittent drizzle. I press myself into the doorway, but a fine mist still glues my skirt to my legs.

There she is. My heart twirls and I forget all about my damp clothes. Georgie has hold of Star's harness, the two of them a seamless unit, weaving their way between the groups of musicians. The rain has turned her hair the dark gold of wet sand and tendrils curl against her cheeks. It's ridiculous how happy I am to see her, considering we were up chatting till two in the morning.

"Hi." I grin as she reaches me. "Let's get inside. Looks like it's going to bucket down."

In the foyer, a familiar melody drifts out to greet us—the iconic guitar solo that closes 'Hotel California'. Georgie draws Star off to one side and crouches to unclip the harness. As if summoned by my words, the clouds burst, hurling a downpour against the windows.

"Wow." Georgie slips the harness over Star's head, pausing to scratch her under the chin. "Glad we didn't get caught in that. Wouldn't have liked it one bit, would you, girl?"

"Aw, no. You were lucky." I stare out at the torrent, now coming down so hard the glass appears opaque.

Georgie stands with a laugh, swinging the harness over her shoulder. "Kind of, although we did run into Chanelle."

"Really? Don't tell me she deigned to speak to you."

"I know. Turns out I'm an actual person with a brain and everything. She wants me to talk to Zeph, find out if he fancies her."

"She what?" How dare Chanelle Clarke ask favours of Georgie after the way she behaved, the things she and her friends said. I might be a gentle soul, but my palms itch to slap Chanelle across her gorgeous face.

Georgie shrugs. "It's kind of funny. I mean, Zeph's clearly not interested."

"True. Are you going to tell him?"

"Later. Don't want to ruin his week so early on a Monday."

I giggle, offering Georgie my arm, and we head into the reception room. Calypso's already here, dressed in a tie-dye T-shirt, talking to Kai and a few others. I don't recognise the song playing now, something with a lot of heavy bass.

"Black Sabbath," Georgie tells me when I complain about the racket. "And don't say that when you meet my brother. Jake loves them."

It warms me right through, the way Georgie talks about me meeting her brother, as though it's a certainty. It does feel certain, the fact that our friendship will extend beyond this summer.

I spy the boys in the far corner. Gareth and Art have squeezed themselves onto the same cushion, their heads almost touching. Zephan's seated nearby, arms folded, looking as if he wishes the wall would swallow him.

We skirt the room towards them, passing Chanelle and her posse. At the sight of her, seated like a queen at the centre of the group, my fingers curl into a fist. Please, God, I think I could bear not winning the scholarship so long as Chanelle Clarke doesn't get it.

"Hey." Gareth beams as we settle onto the cushions they've saved for us.

Art leans past him to study Georgie's T-shirt. "Blind Melon? Like, as opposed to the melons that stare reproachfully at you as you're about to eat them?"

She shakes her head. "I can't wait till the fourth week. About time you got a proper education in nineties music."

Art laughs and nestles his cheek into Gareth's shoulder.

"OK, let's get started," Calypso calls, then waits for quiet. "Bell-bottoms, the Vietnam War, Pacman, and the first ever gay pride parade…this week we're journeying back to the seventies."

"Nice top, Calypso," Kai says to a chorus of wolf-whistles.

She gives him the thumbs up. "The popularity of rock exploded during this decade. It saw the creation of so many iconic songs—'Bohemian Rhapsody', 'American Pie', 'Stairway to Heaven'—songs we all still know and love today. From heavy metal bands like Led Zeppelin and Black Sabbath, to the softer sounds created by Fleetwood Mac and Chicago, through Southern, progressive, acid, new wave, and all the incarnations of rock in between. Honestly, I could've spent the whole four weeks exploring the subgenres and how they developed. Since we only have a single session, however, I'll give you a taste of as many styles as I can." She pulls out her phone. "This first track, very appropriate given the weather, is 'Who'll Stop the Rain' by Creedence Clearwater Revival."

The room fills with an upbeat guitar intro, which immediately has me jiggling my knee.

Under cover of the music, Gareth leans in close. "So…we did it."

"You what?" It takes a second for his meaning to sink in, but then my eyes go wide. "Oh. You mean…you and Art?"

Gareth nods, his smile radiant.

My own smile stretches to mirror his. "What was it like?"

Gareth's lips part but no sound emerges. All the same, the joy in his expression when he looks at Art reveals more than words ever could.

27. GEORGIE

AFTER PRACTICE THAT afternoon, Mina and I shelter in the student centre. Rain drumrolls against the windows, almost drowning the conversation and clink of pool balls. Mina guides me to a sofa, then goes to investigate the hot drinks machine. Star curls up on the carpet, while I toe off my trainers and sink into the cushions, legs tucked beneath me.

"Wow," Mina calls. "I've never seen so many herbal teas. Camomile, peppermint, ginger, honey...would you like one?"

My nose wrinkles. "You trying to poison me?"

Mina laughs. Man, I love her laugh, sparkling and full of warmth. The sound sets my insides fizzing like I've eaten a bag of Tangfastic.

"Fine," she says, "but I'm determined to convert you by the end of the summer."

"Not if I lure you over to the dark side first."

"I accept the challenge. For now, they've got plenty of your heathen teas. PG Tips, Earl Gray, Twinings, Yorkshire..."

I consider. It's cosy in the student centre, the air spicy with dinner prep from the kitchen. "Actually, I think it's a hot chocolate day."

"Ooh, yes." Mina sets the machine in motion with a whirr. "Two hot chocolates coming up."

A few moments later, she joins me on the sofa and hands me a plastic cup. When her knee touches mine, tingles zip up my thigh. I tilt my face away and sip my drink. It's rich and creamy, tons better than the watery stuff you usually get out of a machine.

"Whose turn is it?" Mina asks.

I grin. The game that began in the pool carried on through the weekend. Our questions have ranged from the silly to the deep. With each answer, I learn more about this girl who's become the focal point of my life.

"Yours, I think." I cradle my drink. Chocolaty goodness slides into my stomach, feeding the butterflies.

"OK." Mina hums to herself. "Ooh, how about this? What's the one thing you can't do but wish you could?"

I don't need to think. "Drive."

"Really?"

"Well, yeah. To be able to just jump in the car and go wherever I wanted…how amazing would that be?"

Mina sighs. "Dad thinks I'm too young to drive, no matter what the law says. He claims there's no need, since he or Mum are always happy to taxi me wherever I want to go, and they are, but it isn't about that, is it?"

I shake my head. It's about freedom, not having to rely on anyone else. I get that more than most, since independence is something I've had to work twice as hard for.

"Anyway," Mina adds, "Mum must've talked Dad round because they bought me some driving lessons for my birthday last month."

"Yay for your mum. So, what do you wish you could do that you can't?"

"Buy a motorbike."

The horror film revelation should've prepared me. Still, Mina with her bangles and floaty dresses riding a motorbike? Surprise snorts out of my nose. "You're winding me up."

"Am not." Mina laughs. "There's a Harley Davison I have my eye on. Probably best to keep that from my dad, though, or he'll cancel my driving lessons."

I bump her shoulder. "Your secret's safe with me, so long as I get to be the first one to ride on the back."

"Deal." Mina lets her arm rest against mine.

The gentle heat of her. It seeps through our clothes and into my chest. I stop breathing.

Mina's phone pings.

She straightens and air fills the space between us. I slump against the cushions. A WhatsApp message, probably from the group chat she has with her friends at home. Seems like it never shuts up.

God, stop being a jealous arse. Mina's allowed other friends, you know. Still, each chime taunts me with the truth. Unlike me, Mina has a crowd beyond Dukes, a crowd she'll go back to when camp's over. A crowd that doesn't include me. Will she want to keep in touch, or will the memory of this fade like a summer fling?

"Hold this for me?" Mina passes me her cup. She digs out her phone, then creases up.

"Who's it from?" I try to keep the heaviness from my voice.

"Gaz. He's sent a pic of him and Art. They look like they swam back to the house. Glad we didn't venture out in that." Mina taps out a reply, keypad clicking, then puts her phone away. "All right, your turn."

She relieves me of her drink, shoulder settling once more against mine. It feels natural, as if it belongs there. Electricity spreads from the contact, down my arm and into my fingertips. I hide a grin in my cup.

God, I like this girl. I really, really like her.

28. MINA

PERHAPS ART FEELS guilty about monopolising my best friend—not that he has any reason to. I miss spending time with Gaz, obviously, but in the thrill of my burgeoning friendship with Georgie, his absence cuts nowhere near as deeply as it would've done. All the same, Art's waiting to ambush me when I emerge from Performance Technique on Wednesday.

"Still want me to dye your hair?" he asks as we head along the corridor to the lobby.

I glance at him, surprised. Honestly, I'd assumed the offer had been a throwaway comment, made on the spur of the moment and forgotten about. "I'd love it, if you're sure you don't mind."

"'Course not. Come to my room after dinner and I'll fix you up. Georgie, too, if she wants." Art flashes his infectious grin, then spies Gareth ambling towards us and bounds to meet him.

THAT EVENING, I'M installed in Art's desk chair, my dress protected beneath a dye-spattered T-shirt of Art's, an old towel spread over the carpet to catch any splashes. Georgie's taken Star for a walk, and both Gareth and Zephan declined the invitation to watch my transformation. Since it's just the two of us, this will be the perfect opportunity to get to know Gareth's boyfriend better.

"What're we listening to?" I raise my voice above the music spilling from the Bluetooth speakers on Art's desk. It's an EDM track that wouldn't normally be my thing, but there's an energy to it that has me tapping my foot.

He looks over from where he's squeezing purple dye into an empty Tupperware container and his entire face lights up. "Adam Lambert. He's my idol."

"He's the one who tours with Queen, right? His vocals are incredible."

"They really are. I love how he merges genre—pop, rock, dance… It's what I want to bring to my own music."

Art's eyes sparkle. Until now, for all his prowess as a drummer, I've assumed Art's primary purpose in being here is to have fun, but I've misjudged him. It's clear how passionate he is, how much he wants this.

I smile at him. "You definitely have the talent."

"Thanks." He averts his gaze, blushing, and stirs the dye with a tint brush. "Adam Lambert's such an inspiration. I mean, he's this international superstar, but when he was at school, he was a bit of a loner, always afraid of being bullied."

"I love stories like that. So inspirational. Still, I doubt that's a problem for you. You're the coolest person I've ever met."

Art chuckles, a humourless sound at odds with his usual contagious laugh. He moves to stand behind me, setting the Tupperware and brush on the bedside cabinet. "What're we doing then? I can do a strand, or if you think your parents will mind, I'll just dye the tips. That way, I can cut them for you when camp ends and they'll never know."

I shrug. "Mum won't care. My dad's pretty conservative, but it's not like he's going to beat me just for dying my hair."

"That's good." I'd meant it as a joke, but Art takes my reply at face value, as though he wouldn't have been at all shocked to learn that my parents regularly dole out physical punishment. "So, shall we go with a strand?"

"Yay! Let's do it," I tell him, although I'm still processing that strange response. Did he really think I was being serious?

Art dips his brush in the tub of dye and sets to work. "Your family's Catholic, too, right? Gaz mentioned it."

"Yeah. My parents go to church every Sunday, more during Easter and Christmas, and Dad's president of our local Catenian circle."

"Snap. And I bet they make you go to church with them."

"Gosh, no." I'm about to shake my head, but this probably isn't the best move. It's just…the idea of my parents forcing May or me to do anything we don't want to is ridiculous. "I mean, it's always made them happy when my sister and I attend church, especially Dad, and I generally don't mind going, but if we ever have other plans, they don't mind."

Art's quiet, his focus on painting the dye along the length of my hair. At last, he says, "You're lucky."

"Are…" I hesitate. Might this be a sensitive subject? Then again, he's the one who brought it up. "Are your parents very strict?"

"You could say that. Well, my mam died when I was little, but my dad…he takes his religion very seriously." His tone is flippant, but it can't disguise the hardness underneath.

I chew my lip. "Gaz said… He said he doesn't know…"

"I'm gay? Fuck, no. If he did… Let's just say my dad has strong views about what makes a real man." He emphasises the last words with bitter sarcasm. "I have three older brothers, every one a carbon copy of our dad. Big, powerful men's men who all work for the building firm and spend their Saturday afternoons watching the footie at the pub. The perfect sons."

Whereas Art... He doesn't spell out his dad's opinion of him, but the truth hangs between us. I peer at him from the corner of my eye, this slender boy with the delicate features and blue-tipped hair. Since we met at the picnic, I'd had him down as a carefree party animal, outgoing and full of fun—someone who didn't give a monkey's what anyone thought of him and whose confidence carried him through school with indecent ease. Whatever I'd hoped to learn about Art, it wasn't this, and my heart breaks for him.

29. GEORGIE

"Hey, Mum," I say, digging my phone out of my pocket. The chuckle of water tells me we're near the fountain. I extend my foot, feeling for the wall of the lily pond, and plonk my bum down. Star flops onto the path, clearly glad for a break from our walk.

"Hi, babes," Mum says, voice breezy. An engine rumbles in the background.

I smile. Maybe it's because she had Jake and me when she was barely out of her teens, or maybe because she's way more career woman than domestic goddess. Either way, Louise Wilde has always felt closer to a big sister. "You on your way home?"

"I wish. No, en route to a conference. It's at a hotel in Birmingham so we're all staying over and driving back in the morning."

A spot of drizzle lands on my cheek. I pull my hoodie tighter against the chill and roll my eyes. Whatever she says, Mum would far rather talk shop over glasses of champers than tuck into Dad's Bolognese. Mum went back to work a couple of months after me and Jake were born, so it was mostly Dad who took care of us. Once we started school and he set up Wilde Land Records, Nana and Grandad looked after us until our parents got home.

"Dish the goss then." Mum's eagerness crackles across the distance between us.

So, I do. I tell her about camp life, the workshops and getting to meet Calypso and Dutch. I tell her about my friends, our jamming sessions and mucking around in the pool. Most of all, I tell her about Mina, our late-night chats, sharing secrets and our favourite songs. The only thing I leave out is what happened with Chanelle and co. Mum would go all lioness on me, roaring down to Dukes to protect her cub. No point getting her riled up. Not when none of it matters anymore.

"Wow," she says once I've finished. "Don't think I've ever heard you talk so much. Sounds like you're having an amazing time."

"I really am." My grin's so broad it's actually painful. I pause. Should I risk spoiling the mood? Oh, what the hell. "Being here… It's made me even more sure this is where I want to be. Music's what I want to do."

Mum's sigh gusts through the speaker. "Georgie, we've been through this."

We have. Mum's arguments are branded into my brain, we've rehashed the subject so often. And I get where she's coming from. I do. The past twenty years must've been tough, watching Dad pine for his lost music career. She's seen firsthand how disappointment can gnaw at someone, wants to shield me from that pain. I understand, but it doesn't make me any less determined.

Still, I don't want to get into a row. Time for a topic change. The best thing about having a mum who's like a sister? I can talk to her about pretty much anything.

"There's someone I like. A girl." My face heats up.

"There is? Who?" Mum's annoyance vanishes, the way I knew it would. "No, let me guess. It's your friend Mina, isn't it? I could tell."

My heart swells. "Yeah. She's... She's one of the sweetest people I've ever met. I'm not sure she thinks of me like that, though."

"Then find out," Mum says, all confidence. "Sounds to me like she feels the same, but if she doesn't, it's her loss. Plenty more fish in the sea."

After we hang up, me and Star wind our way back to Osborne House. Is Mum right? Easy to be pragmatic when you're Lou Wilde. From Mum's stories of her teenage years, she was never short of boys vying for her attention. Out of all the screaming fans packed into the pub that night, she was the one who snagged Dad's eye. If she'd ever suffered unrequited love, she would've picked herself up and moved on.

"Find the door," I tell Star, and she veers right.

Sighing, I let myself into the lobby. Mum could never understand what it's like to be me. Mina's the best friend I've ever had. I won't—can't—risk that by pushing for something she might not want. What we have is too precious to lose.

30. MINA

WE STRUM THE final chords—Georgie, Zephan and me in perfect sync—a well-oiled, music-making machine. With a last flurry of notes from Gareth, Art taps out the closing beat and the song comes to an end.

Fingers stilling on the strings of my banjo, I glance around at my bandmates. "Everyone happy?"

Wildest Dreams has gone for something a little different this week. We've taken a classic seventies disco track, 'Knock on Wood' by Amii Stewart, and turned it into a rock ballad. It probably shouldn't work, but it does. At least, I hope it does—hope Calypso will like it when we perform it for her tomorrow.

"Hmm." Art rubs his drumsticks together, expression deadpan. "I think it's missing something. Maybe what it needs is—"

"Don't say it." Zephan thrusts a palm in his direction, as if anything short of a freak earthquake could stop Art from finishing that sentence.

Georgie and Gareth are already shaking with silent giggles, and I cast my eyes heavenwards, preparing myself for what we all know is coming.

"A drum solo!" Art tosses his sticks in the air, catches them deftly, and launches into a furious routine that would give Steve Sinatra a run for his money.

"Oh my God." Zephan drops his chin onto his guitar with a groan and shuts his eyes.

The rest of us clap, egging Art on. To look at him now, his vibrant energy filling the room, it's impossible to believe this is the same boy from the night before—the boy who spoke of failing to live up to his dad's ideals of manliness.

Art rounds off with a flourish and Gareth shakes his head, gazing at Art with a mix of amusement and tenderness. "Exhibitionist."

"Guilty as charged." Art grins at him, eyes softening. "Speaking of which… Is everyone up for the seventies disco tomorrow? Georgie? Mina?"

"We'll be there. Have to show off my new look." I toss my hair like someone in a shampoo advert, displaying the vivid purple streak that now adorns it from root to tip. It makes me feel quirky, exotic, like the star I hope to be someday, and I love it.

"Plus," Georgie adds, "we can't let you and Gaz steal all the spotlight. The floor needs our dancing prowess."

"Like a rock band needs a kazoo," Art says with a wicked smirk. "How about you, Zeph, mate? You know I'll get you onto the dance floor sooner or later."

"Over my mutilated corpse," Zephan mutters.

"What?" Gareth twists on the piano bench, raising a mischievous eyebrow. "You're not going to ask your admirer to the disco?"

Zephan flings Gareth a filthy look, clearly deeming this unworthy of a response.

"Right. How can you resist the tenacious Chanelle Clarke?" Art says. "And you get to witness a master in action."

He throws himself into a hilarious parody of his usual dance moves, all thrusting hips and exaggerated footwork. His drumsticks leave his hands again, but this time when he attempts to catch them, they spin away from him and thud to the carpet. One rolls into the far corner, the other disappearing under a chair.

"Bugger it." Art shakes his head at himself and goes to retrieve them.

Gareth's slumped over the piano, howling with laughter, while Zephan has his face hidden in his arms. That's why neither of them sees, but I do. As Art kneels in front of the chair, delving beneath it for his stick, the hem of his vest rides up to reveal a slice of pale skin. There, faded but still standing out starkly above the waistband of his jeans, is an angry, purplish wheel— a perfectly preserved imprint of what looks horribly like a belt buckle.

31. GEORGIE

Before the seventies disco on Friday, I knock for Zephan. Silence.

I roll my eyes. "Zeph, only me."

Still nothing.

Then there's the rustle of movement and the lock rattles. "Where's my best girl?"

"Nice to see you, too. Star's chewing on her new bone. It'll keep her busy while we show Gaz and Art up on the dance floor."

Zephan grunts and steps aside to let me past. As soon as I'm inside, he shuts the door and re-locks it.

I feel my way over to his bed and perch on the end. "You can't hide in here forever. If you just talked to Chanelle—"

"Already tried." He flops onto the mattress, stretching out his long legs behind me.

"Really? When?"

"Cornered me when I came back from dinner. Wanted to know if I was coming to the disco."

"And what did you say?"

"What do you think? I said 'no' and legged it in here."

I snort. "You're such a charmer. Still, fingers crossed she's got the message and won't be pestering either of us again."

"I wouldn't bet on it," Zephan says. "She definitely said something about getting me on the dance floor before the end of the summer."

I grin. "Fighting talk."

"It's not funny. She's fucking terrifying."

"Yeah, she kind of is. Chanelle's right about one thing, though. You should come tonight."

"Oh, no." Zephan wriggles away from me until he's pressed against the wall. "No, no, no."

Knew he'd say that. Still, Chanelle Clarke isn't the only one who can be persistent. I slip a wheedling note into my voice. "Come on, Zeph. Come with us. It'll be fun."

"What? Playing the fifth wheel to two couples? Yeah, so much fun."

I splutter, cheeks catching fire. "Me and Mina...we're just friends."

Zephan scoffs.

"What?" I say. "We are."

"But you like each other." Zephan prods me with his foot. "A mole in a blindfold could see that."

I fiddle with the hem of my Def Leppard T-shirt, biting back a smile. *Don't get your hopes up, George.* "What makes you think that? That Mina likes me."

Zephan's quiet for about a decade. It's his way. Ask him a serious question and you can be sure he'll give it proper consideration. Honesty, that's what you get from Zephan Oduro. No bullshit. Still, I fidget like there's a whole colony of ants in my pants.

"So." When he finally speaks, he sounds as though he's being force-fed kangaroo nuts. "Whenever she sees you, it's like... Christ, I dunno. Like she's woken up on Christmas morning to find she's got everything she fucking asked for."

The flames spread from my face, engulfing my entire body. Mina isn't the only one who's full of surprises. Who would've thought Zeph could be so poetic? Is it true? Does Mina really look at me like that? Wish I could see for myself, to be sure. Since I only have his word for it, though, I clutch it to me like a talisman.

32. MINA

ELTON JOHN LAUNCHES into the chorus of 'Crocodile Rock' and the entire room joins in. I seize Georgie's hands, her fingers curling warm and firm around mine. We leap about to the music with no rhythm or skill whatsoever and sing along at the tops of our voices.

The seventies disco in the Dukes Building is packed. A few people are gathered around the giant punch bowl, while still others occupy the clusters of chairs in the corners, chatting and sipping from plastic cups. The majority, though, are showing off their moves on the dance floor. It's chaotic and loud, the air sticky with heat and the fruity sweetness of punch.

I pull Georgie into a spin until we're dizzy, both of us laughing so hard we can barely manage the tune. Disco balls transform the high ceiling into a mini galaxy, the dozen smaller ones glittering and revolving like planets around the largest body at its centre. A shower of coloured stars flicker in the darkness—pink, blue, green, gold, crimson—splashing Georgie's skin in a rainbow constellation.

"You OK?" I shout over the deafening piano.

Georgie appears wild and mysterious in the shifting light, and her grin encompasses a universe of joy. Her hair flies in all directions, stray curls sticking to her cheeks, and I have the overwhelming urge to smooth it back.

She leans in closer to be heard above the noise. "Shall we get a drink? I'm dying of thirst."

"Sure." I swallow. Her breath caresses my ear, sending goosebumps up my spine. "I'll let the boys know."

I release her hands and turn to Gareth and Art. They're not touching, and yet their dance moves appear synchronised, their bodies conducting a secret conversation only they can understand. It puts our inelegant stomping to shame.

I tap Gareth on the shoulder as 'Crocodile Rock' leads into 'The Jean Genie' by David Bowie. "We're going to get a drink."

He tears his gaze from Art, pushing his sweaty fringe off his forehead, and raises a hand in acknowledgement.

"Good thing, too. You girls are seriously cramping our style." Art smirks.

Georgie pokes her tongue out at him, linking her arm through mine, and I lead a meandering path between the dancers towards the glimmering silver of the punch bowl.

"Want to get some air?" I ask, ladling punch into Georgie's cup.

She nods, so we head for the nearest set of French windows. A curtain of iridescent beads hangs across the opening. I hold them aside for Georgie, and they clink and shimmer behind us as we step onto the patio. The drizzle that's been on and off all day has stopped and the night air's deliciously fresh after the crush of bodies. A cool breeze traces my exposed skin, bringing with it the scent of damp earth and cigarette smoke.

We settle on the bench near the main entrance, mostly dry thanks to the overhang. Music and laughter drifts to us from the disco, though it feels oddly distant. Apart from a few smokers grouped at the far end of the patio, we're alone out here.

"That's better." Georgie leans against the wooden slats and takes a gulp of punch.

I sip my own drink. It's tropical and sparkling and wonderfully cold, soothing my parched throat. I shift position so I'm angled towards Georgie. We're mostly in shadow, but a soft glow spills from the foyer window, illuminating her features. "OK, here's one for you. Who was your first crush?"

"Oh." She huffs out an embarrassed laugh. "Like, proper crush? My brother had this mate when we started secondary. Will Parker. He was the only one of Jake's friends back then who really spoke to me."

The punch turns sour on my tongue. All at once, the dazzling promise of the night has faded, as though God has turned down a celestial dimmer switch.

"What happened?" Even to my own ears, my voice sounds forced.

"Nothing, other than that I spent hours fantasising about him asking me out. His family moved away in Year Eight and he and Jake lost touch."

"Were you devastated?"

"Totally gutted, at least for a couple of weeks. Then my history teacher paired me with Nafeesa Akhtar for a project on the Romans and I forgot all about Will. Fickle, right?" She grins at me over her drink.

Happiness bubbles up inside me. It fills me to the brim, spreading to the very tips of my fingers and toes, bright and effervescent as the punch.

33. GEORGIE

*J*UST ASK HER.

My heart's thumping so hard Mina has to hear it, which is stupid. It's not like I've held back from asking stuff before. Trouble is, there isn't normally so much riding on her answer. The longer I don't know for sure, the longer I can cling to the hope. It's just…Zeph seemed so certain.

I swallow another mouthful of punch. No idea what it's got in it, but it's bloody amazing. "What about you? Who was your first?"

No reply. 'Sweet Home Alabama' floats through the French windows, filling the quiet between us. The trees shake off the earlier rain with a soft *drip…drip…drip.*

The silence stretches, a guitar string wound too tight. My nails dig into the knees of my jeans. God, have I stuck my foot in it, stepped across some invisible line? If only I could see her expression; might help me figure out what she's thinking.

Eventually, I crack. "You don't have to tell me. Not if you don't want to."

Maybe it's better this way. Means I can hang on to the hope a while longer. All the same, it hurts. I've shared everything with Mina these past ten days. It doesn't matter that we haven't known each other long; I'd trust her with my life, thought she felt the same. Have I been kidding myself?

Perhaps my face gives me away yet again, because she says, "It isn't that I don't want to tell you. I do. It's just, well, I find it hard to talk about."

The hope slides from my grasp, slippery as seaweed. Is she in love with someone else? Never mind whether she's straight or not. Would be just my bloody luck, falling for a girl who has feelings for someone back home.

"I get it." I force the words through the crushing disappointment. If it's true, I'd rather not know. "Really. Forget I asked."

Mina puffs out a breath. "It's fine, I promise. The thing is… Gosh, I thought it would be easier the second time, after telling Gaz." She takes my free hand, holding so tight it's painful. "OK, so, I had this crush on my friend Allie."

Oh. Jealousy knees me in the gut. Jealousy towards a girl I've never met. Mina talks about Allie sometimes, but I hadn't thought anything of it. Why would I? They're friends. At least, that's what I assumed. "Does she… Did anything ever happen?"

"Not even a little bit. Honestly, the crush only lasted a few weeks. It was when I first knew her, at the start of Year Seven, before we actually became friends."

I let out my breath. The jealousy gushes out of me like poison from a wound, leaving me giddy with relief.

"I think," Mina says, then hesitates. I hear her take a sip of her punch. "I think that's when I began to accept what it meant to be a lesbian. I'd fancied female celebrities, of course, but I sort of presumed that was normal. When I was crushing on Allie, and all the other girls could talk about was the boys they liked, I realised I was different."

She keeps her hand in mine. I'm way too aware of the feel of it, her fingers silky smooth apart from the callused tips. My thumb twitches. I want to stroke her palm, trace every bump and groove, like a psychic divining the future.

I settle for a gentle squeeze. "That wasn't so scary, was it? Telling me, I mean."

"Truthfully?" Mina snorts. "It was absolutely terrifying. Will it ever get any easier, do you think?"

"Not sure. Maybe it's different for everyone. Until now, I've never had anyone to come out to besides my family."

"And they were cool with it?"

"More than cool."

Long before I had a name for it, I knew I fancied both boys and girls. I never thought twice about it, thought everyone was like that. Didn't occur to me to keep it from my parents. For their part, Mum and Dad took it in stride. They never once acted like me being bi was anything out of the ordinary. It was only at school, eavesdropping on my classmates, when I twigged I might be different.

"You're so lucky," Mina says.

"I know it. You said I'm only the second person you've told. You're not out to your parents?"

"Goodness, no. I'll need an entire orchestra's worth of courage before I can face that one."

"Why? You think they'll have a problem with it?"

"They're devout Catholics. How can they not? Oh, I know they love me. They're not going to disown me or anything, but it has to be tough for them."

I rest my head against the wall behind me, face tilted to the night air. A raindrop splashes onto my cheek. Must be shitty, having to hide a vital part of yourself from the people you love. Lonely, too.

I press her hand. "Glad you told me."

"Me, too." She returns the pressure, palm flush against mine.

The opening drumbeat to 'We Will Rock You' drifts from the reception room.

Mina gets to her feet, tugging me up with her. "Come on. Let's get back to showing the boys how it's done."

34. MINA

I'M STILL HUMMING 'We Will Rock You' as I carry my nighttime camomile tea back to my room. Other than the audience laughter from a comedy show seeping from under Patrice's door, the flat is quiet.

Snuggled up in bed, I sip my tea and listen to the rain pattering against the window. Snapshots of the evening scroll across my mind—Georgie's face enigmatic in the star-strewn darkness; the brush of her fingers against my palm; both of us leaping around to the music, neither caring if we were making fools of ourselves. Then there'd been that sensation, the strange fluttering in my belly when Georgie talked about her crushes...

There's a soft tap at the door, and I shuffle into a more upright position against the pillows. "Who is it?"

"Only me," comes Gareth's hushed reply. "All right if I come in?"

"Of course. Quickly, though, before anyone sees."

He slips inside, closing the door behind him. I shift over and pat the space beside me. This, it occurs to me as Gareth perches on the edge of my bed, is precisely the sort of thing Dad was aiming to prevent when he insisted on a single-sex flat. It was a sound strategy, given the rule about not having a member of the opposite sex in your room after curfew and my own tendency to follow rules to the letter. Still, Gareth wouldn't be here if it weren't important.

"What is it?" I ask. "You and Art haven't had a fight, have you?"

"No. No, nothing like that. Art's…well, he's incredible, like. It's just…" Gareth shakes his head, clearly struggling to find the words. He glances at me. "Thought Georgie might be here."

Absolutely no reason at all for me to be blushing. It's an innocent enough comment, given how much time we spend together. My cheeks obviously haven't got the memo, though, because they flood with heat.

"We just said goodnight," I tell him, burying my face in my mug.

Gareth touches my knee through the duvet. "I've been a shitty friend, I know that. Never thought I'd be the kind of guy who abandoned his mates the moment he got a boyfriend."

"I understand." I reach for his hand, entwining our fingers. "Really. This is all new and exciting, and maybe…maybe if you hadn't met Art, I wouldn't have got to know Georgie so well."

"I'm glad you have her. She makes you happy, like." He smiles at me.

"She's a good friend. The best." Gosh, if my face grows any hotter, it'll spontaneously combust. I nudge Gareth with my knee to distract him. "So, what's going on?"

He groans and flops backwards across my legs, arms flung up to hide his face. "I'm probably being an idiot."

"Probably, but tell me anyway."

"Cheers, hun. The thing is… God, this is embarrassing. Do you reckon… Is it normal for someone to only want to have sex in the dark?"

I choke on a mouthful of tea. "Excuse me?"

"No, really, serious question."

"Right, sorry, you just… I honestly don't know. It's not like I'm a sex guru, but if that's how you feel most comfortable—"

Gareth shakes his head from beneath his forearms, cutting me off. "Not me. Art."

OK, this is unexpected. I wouldn't have believed Art Dabrowski capable of coyness when it came to sex—not unless…

Gareth lowers his arms to look at me, eyes troubled. "He has a real thing about it. Even when we did it in the shower—"

"Wait. You had sex in the shower?"

It's his turn to flush, although he waves my words away. "That's not the point. The point is, even then, he insisted we keep the light off. I dunno. Maybe that's normal. Maybe that's what people do. I just can't help wondering…"

My brain's still snagged on the discovery that my best friend's had sex in the shower, and I disentangle it with an effort. "Wondering what?"

"Wondering, well, what if he's hiding something?"

"Something really embarrassing, you mean? Like… Like a tattoo of Pikachu?"

Once he's stopped convulsing with giggles, Gareth flashes me a sheepish grin. "Yeah, I'm being an idiot, aren't I? Probably it's completely normal, or else it's just some weird fetish, like."

I return his smile, feeling like the most terrible liar on the planet, because it's obvious to me why Art would prefer Gareth didn't see him naked. The memory of yesterday's rehearsal flashes across my vision—the moment when Art's vest rode up to reveal the angry wheel on his back.

I can't say any of this to Gaz, though. It isn't my truth to share, and Art doesn't even know I saw. Whatever's going on with him, and it doesn't take a genius to determine what, Art will tell Gareth when he's ready. Until then, his secret's safe with me.

35. GEORGIE

"Hey," Art calls through my closed bedroom door on Saturday evening. He performs a rapid drumroll on the wood. "This is your knight in skintight armour, here to rescue you from a night of boredom."

Mina and I are sprawled on my bed, sharing songs from our Spotify playlists. I free my legs from hers and scramble to sit up. "Bloody hell. You gave me a heart attack. What's going on?"

"It's party time! Snacks, alcohol, drinking games…you don't want to miss it. See you in Zeph's room."

"Um, does he know?"

"Good point," Art says. "Come on, babes, let's go and deliver the happy news. Meet you girls there."

"Not sure that's wise," I say, but his and Gareth's feet are already scuffing away along the hall.

Mina sits up next to me, drawing her knees to her chest. "Uh, did he just mention alcohol?"

"Yup." My grin threatens to split my face in half. I swing my bare feet to the carpet and stand, waiting for Mina to follow. When there's no rustle of movement, I turn back to her. "What's up?"

"I don't know." Anxiety bleeds into her tone. "I'm not sure this is a good idea."

"Why not?" Art's laugh floats along the hall. I bounce on my toes, impatient.

Mina huffs. "We're not even supposed to have alcohol. It says so in the handbook. Leticia Dukes mentioned it in her welcome speech. What if we get caught? If my dad found out, I'd be grounded for life."

"We won't get caught. The staff hardly ever check on us, and Art will have something figured out. You know what he's like."

"That's what worries me. Think about it. We're not only risking a telling-off here. We could get kicked out of the programme. It could affect our whole future. Is it really worth it?"

Silence drops between us. It's a physical thing, thick and cloying as day-old custard. I hug my chest, wrestling with myself.

"I just…" The words stick in my throat. I shouldn't. It would be manipulative. But I want this. "I've never had the chance to do anything like this before, never had anyone to do it with. I thought it might be fun."

I cringe. It's a low move, designed to appeal to Mina's soft heart. Not that it isn't true. I've spent countless Saturday nights wishing I had anything to do other than watch *Britain's Got Talent* with my parents. I'd imagine what my classmates might be up to, the wild parties and movie marathons. Now I get to experience it for myself. All the same, guilt leaves a chalky film on my tongue.

"It's fine." I backtrack, stomp on my disappointment. "You're right. It isn't worth it."

Mina puffs out a breath. "No, it's OK."

"Really?" A smile plucks at my lips.

"Come on." Mina slides from the bed, although she still sounds far from convinced. "I'll probably live to regret this, but let's go."

My smile breaks free. Excitement fizzes along my nerves. I call Star to heel, and the three of us head along the hall.

"Great," Zephan says when we appear in the open doorway to his room. His voice comes from the direction of the bed. "The invasion continues."

I laugh. I'm too used to Zeph's grouchiness by now to take any notice.

"At least you've brought the guest of honour. Hey, girl." His tone softens. Star trots over to him, panting happily.

"Come on in," Art says, "and shut the door. It's time to get this party started!"

So, THIS IS what it's all about. I'm seated on Zephan's floor, back resting against his wardrobe, Mina beside me, Gareth and Art opposite. It's like I've slipped into this whole other world. I'd known it existed, just not how to get there. It's a world where alcohol pumps through your veins, numbing and deliciously warm. In this world, inhibitions are peeled off like a pair of too-tight jeans and everything's so much funnier than usual.

Only one thing mars the magic. Mina shifts next to me, and I bet she's checking the door again. Tension blows off her like the hot air from a fan heater. I can feel it, even though we aren't touching. Was I wrong to talk Mina into this? She was obviously afraid of her parents finding out, had only agreed because I'd emotionally blackmailed her into it.

Not that Mina has any reason to worry. I was right about Art having everything figured out. He brought his own snacks with him, completely within the rules. These just happen to include half-litre bottles of Coke pre-spiked with vodka. There's a film playing on Zeph's laptop, bags of Doritos and popcorn on the carpet between us. If a staff member does poke their head in, they'll be greeted with a group of friends having a movie night. Nothing to see here, folks.

"Let's play a game," Art says. He raps the metal bedframe, which twangs like a tuning fork. "Oi, Zeph, you party pooper. Get your arse down here."

"Nuh-uh." The mattress creaks under Zephan's weight. Clearly, he's putting as much distance between himself and us as possible. "And just so you know, if we're busted, I'm throwing the lot of you under the bus."

"Cheers, you're a pal," Art tells him, and me and Gareth crack up.

No, I couldn't have passed this up. The illicit drinking and stupid jokes, anticipation frothing in the pit of my stomach. It's what I've dreamed of since my first day at secondary, to be invited into that secret club called friendship. Secret to me, anyway. Now I'm in, it's everything I hoped it would be. If I could only be sure Mina isn't mad at me.

Art kicks off a round of Musician Name Game. We go around the group, each of us coming up with a solo artist or band member whose first name begins with the same initial as the last musician's surname. Simple enough, right? Except that you have to keep drinking for as long as it takes to think of an answer. Then there's the fact that my brain feels like it's on a merry-go-round.

"Erm…" What had Mina said? Someone called Ashley Gearing? So I need an artist beginning with 'g'. "Ger…ger… ger…Gorillas!"

Art imitates the wrong answer buzzer from *Family Fortunes*. "Yellow card. No band names allowed. Next time, you'll be disqualified."

"Fine." I keep drinking, try to think through my giggles. "Ooh, George Ezra!"

Everyone cheers and play moves to Gareth.

"Elton John," he says at once, tone mushy. Bet he's remembering last night, being on the dance floor with Art.

"Uh." Art takes an audible gulp from his bottle. "Oh, John Legend."

"Leanne Womack." Mina jumps in lightning fast. No way she's going to drink more than she has to.

And now she's landed me with a 'w'. *Thanks for that.* I tilt my bottle to my lips. It's almost empty, proving how crap I am at this game.

"Wuh…wuh…wuh…" My thoughts spin. I scrabble about in the chaos until I seize on a single name. "Wayne Rooney!"

The others fall about in hysterics.

"Red card," Art announces.

Oh, God, what made me say that?

Mina subsides into me, convulsing with laughter. The alcohol heightens every sensation—her uneven breath on my neck, the coconut scent of her hair.

I twist until my mouth's against her ear. "Am I forgiven?"

"Silly girl. There's nothing to forgive." Mina slides her hand into mine. The satiny brush of her skin sends goosebumps up my arm. My insides fill with something molten. Something thrilling and dark that thrums in time with my racing pulse.

36. MINA

GRADUALLY, AS THE night passes in a hilarious rush of banter and drinking games, I stop expecting to be caught at any minute. I stop jumping at every footstep in the corridor outside, stop bracing to hear a rap on the door.

The fear of disappointing my parents is still there—it always is, especially since everything with May—but it's receded to a distant hum. I've only swallowed a few mouthfuls of my vodka-laced Coke, but the alcohol sings through my bloodstream and lends an extra sparkle to the evening, as though it's been sprinkled in fairy dust.

"Never have I ever…" Art trails off, brow creased.

"Aw, listen to him," Gareth says, "trying to come up with something scandalous he hasn't actually done."

"Hey, I resent that. I'm a good boy."

"Yeah, and I'm a porn star."

Art doubles up, which sets off the rest of us. Georgie leans into me, the warm silk of her arm whispering against mine. Happiness froths inside me, more intoxicating than Art's Coke.

I let my head fall against Georgie's shoulder. "I love this game. I haven't done anything, so I always stay sober while everyone else gets drunk. It's hilarious."

"I've never played before." She rests her cheek against my hair and speaks so only I can hear, her words melting around the edges. "But I've read enough books to get the gist."

Gosh, Georgie's missed out on so much, all the regular teenagery things the rest of us have taken for granted. This taste of normality must mean everything to her, and I made the right decision agreeing to come tonight.

"Sure you don't want to play, Zeph, mate?" Art calls.

Sprawled on his bed, Zephan glances at us with weary amusement and shakes his head.

"Right." Art focuses on me, eyes glittering in a way that means business. Uh-oh, he must have overheard my claim to Georgie. "You've asked for it. Never have I ever…made an excuse to get out of church."

Georgie and Gareth let out a collective "Ooh!" as though they're spectators at a football match and Art has brought down a rival player.

Indignation has me shooting upright. "I call foul. There's no way you've never done that."

"Like I'd dare. The only time Dad ever let me off church was when I had a temperature of a hundred and two." An edge of flint cuts through his nonchalance, and I wonder again about his home life.

"You, though…" Art jabs a finger at me, all teasing now. "Come on, mate, drink up. Can't believe you're still on your first bottle."

"Fine." I huff and unscrew the cap, releasing a hiss of carbon dioxide. "But what about the rest of you?"

"My family isn't religious, remember?" Georgie says.

"And mine only go to church at Christmas and Easter," Gareth adds. "Sorry, hun, you're on your own with this one."

Defeated, I roll my eyes and take the teensiest sip I can get away with, then fix Art with a deliberate gaze. It's time he discovered two can play at this game. "Never have I ever…had sex in the shower."

Gareth gasps in mock outrage. "She didn't."

"She did." Art's lips twitch. "Mina, you do know the idea is to try and find out stuff you didn't know about the players, not use stuff against them, right?"

"All's fair in love and drinking games. Are you going to report me to the *Never Have I Ever* Police?"

Georgie creases up, almost spilling her drink, and I can't contain my smile. I love this version of myself who's emerged over the past fortnight, my ability to make people laugh, the streak of wickedness beneath the good-girl exterior.

"Fine, you win. Not like we're ashamed of it, right, babes?" Art clinks his bottle against Gareth's. "Cheers."

While they drink, Georgie's thigh nudges mine. "You're badass, you know that?"

She may as well have told me I've outshone Reba McEntire in a sing-off. I lean into Georgie's side, our arms brushing from shoulder to elbow, and everywhere we touch tingles with tiny electric pulses.

"OK, my turn." Gareth's attention remains trained on Art, as though there's no one else in the room, and his voice trembles with sudden intensity. "Never have I ever…been in love."

The words have barely left his tongue when he raises his bottle to drink, but he's the only one who does. Georgie stifles a sound, something between a choke and a laugh. My heart has begun a rapid drumbeat in my chest, as if I'm a witness in the docks about to be interrogated.

Art fidgets under Gareth's gaze. "What's with all the rule breaking? You're not supposed to pick something you've done yourself."

"Fine. I'll drink twice as a penalty, like." Gareth takes another swig and continues to study Art, expression defiant. "There."

Art laughs, an embarrassed exhale that holds no amusement. He glances around the room, begging someone to come to his rescue, but none of us moves. The playful atmosphere of a moment ago has evaporated, fled out of the open window to dissolve into the misty dark.

Gareth's expression dims, becoming stricken. "You're not going to drink, are you?"

"Babes…" Art extends a hand as if to touch him before appearing to think better of it and pressing his palm to the floor. "It isn't that easy. You can't just drop something like that."

"Oh, I'm sorry. I thought we were on the same page. Clearly not."

Gareth slams his bottle onto the bedside cabinet, cheeks flushed, and lurches to his feet. Movements jerky, he stumbles over to the door.

"Gaz, wait." I call after him.

He ignores me, his knuckles bulging as he grips the doorhandle. I turn to Art, beseeching him to make this right. Art looks blindsided, like his hand on the carpet is the only thing holding him up.

"Mate, don't," he says, his plea little more than a whisper.

Gareth hears it, though, and rounds to glare at him through his tears. "Don't what, Art? Have feelings? Well, I'm sorry if it inconveniences you and all that, but some of us actually have that thing called a heart."

Before anyone can stop him, he's disappeared into the hallway and shut the door behind him with a slam.

37. GEORGIE

"I'M DYING." I clutch the toilet while my stomach turns itself inside out. My head has become the spinner in a game of Twister. It's like an annoying toddler keeps spinning it around and around until I want to yell at them to cut it out.

From the door to my en suite, Zephan has the nerve to chuckle. He's the sole witness to my humiliation and enjoying it way too much.

"Glad you find it so funny. Think how bad you'll feel when I keel over in front of you and the last thing you did was laugh."

"It'll make an entertaining story to tell at your funeral, though."

My groan swallows any hope of a snarky response. Nausea cramps my belly and I lean over the bowl. Through my misery, I hear Zephan retreating. The amusement value of watching me spew my guts up must've worn off.

Gradually, the wave subsides. Weak and shaky, I collapse against the wall and rest my head against it. The tiles are cool on my hot face. My insides feel like someone's scoured them with a wallpaper scraper.

Is this what all the fuss is about? Every Monday morning, my classmates boast about how legless they got over the weekend. Is this what they mean?

First…the high. You stop worrying whether what you're about to say is stupid, whether to take that person's hand. Might they read too much into it? Do you want them to? All that falls away in a rush of giddy confidence.

Then…the crash. A night ending with you in a shivering huddle on the bathroom floor, wondering if it was worth it. And is it? Would I go through this all over again just for the buzz?

Man, my head hurts.

"Here." Zephan crouches in front of me, pushes a glass into my fumbling fingers. "Water. Drink. You'll get dehydrated."

So, he didn't abandon me. Tears sting my eyes. *Stupid tears. Stupid, stupid.* I blink them away.

"Thanks." My voice cracks. I accept the water and gulp some down. It's ice-cold and soothes my raw throat.

"Steady," Zephan warns. "Don't want to bring it straight back up. Better?"

"Bit." I set the glass on the floor and close my eyes against the dull throb. "I'm never drinking again."

"Right. Never heard that one before."

"I'm serious. Why would I deliberately make myself ill?"

"Don't ask me. Ask one of the mugs who poison their body every weekend."

"Smug bastard."

"Drunk moron."

I start to retort, but my stomach roils and I have to bend over the toilet again.

Over my retching, I'm aware of a knock at the bedroom door. Zephan goes to answer it. Has someone else come to gawp at the spectacle? I don't have the will to care, not until she's there, all concern and lemony perfume.

"Hey, I'm here." Mina presses gentle fingers to the nape of my neck. "You're going to be OK."

How's Gareth? The question stumbles around in the fog of my brain but can't find my mouth. He must have calmed down if Mina felt able to leave him. A more urgent worry shoves thoughts of Gaz aside. God, I must look a state. Tears stream down my cheeks, mingling with the snot, and curls stick to my forehead in sweaty clumps.

"You shouldn't have to see this," I mumble between heaves. I need her to leave, and yet…I want her to stay. I want to melt into her touch and let her stroke it all away.

"Don't be silly," she says, rubbing slow circles on my back. "As if I'd leave you like this."

Turns out that regurgitating a day's worth of meals doesn't leave much energy for arguing. I can only submit as Mina holds my hair away from my face. *Christ, let it be over. Let me dissolve into a puddle on the bathroom floor and bring this humiliation to an end.*

38. MINA

"I'M SO SORRY." Gareth's words drift through the partially open door of Art's room next morning. "I can't even tell you."

Outside in the hallway, I pause, fingers tightening on the bulging carrier bag until the plastic gouges my palm.

"Don't worry about it, mate." Art sounds exhausted, as though he hasn't slept.

"How can I not? Christ, I don't know what got into me."

"A shitload of vodka, maybe?"

Gareth snorts out a shaky laugh, and I smile, even as guilt worms its way into my conscience. This is a private moment. I shouldn't be eavesdropping, but Gareth hasn't been answering his phone and when I went to his room, there was no response. I need to know he's OK—that he and Art are OK—because if they're not, it'll break my best friend's gentle heart.

"Babes, look," Art's saying. "I didn't mean to hurt you. That's the last thing I wanted to do. It's just—"

"Too soon, like. Yeah, I get that." Gareth's words tumble over one another, becoming entangled. "I behaved like a dick, putting you on the spot, throwing a tantrum when you didn't play along. You're not ready, and that's fine. I can wait. I'll wait for as long as you need. Just tell me I haven't ruined everything."

Art's quiet for a long time, and I hold my breath, teeth sinking into my lower lip. The rush of running water floats around the bend in the corridor, accompanying Chanelle's husky alto as she sings along to Emili Sanday.

"No," Art says at last. "No, 'course you haven't."

Gareth releases a noise somewhere between a whoop and a sob. There's the rustle of movement, and I shift to peer through the crack. Art has his arms around my friend, Gareth hugging him as though he'll never let go. The air leaves me in a whoosh; they're going to be all right.

With a new lightness in my step, I continue along the hallway to tap on the next door. At a muffled "Come in" from Georgie and a welcoming bark from Star, I push it open. "Hey, girls."

"Hey." Georgie scrambles into a sitting position on the bed, mouth curving in a sheepish smile.

I bend to stroke Star, although my gaze remains on Georgie. She's pale and slightly puffy around the eyes, but otherwise looks better. Her curls are damp from the shower and she's wearing joggers and a soft grey T-shirt.

"How're you feeling?" I ask.

"Oh, God." She buries her face in her arms. "I'm so embarrassed."

"What? Why?"

"Because I made a prat of myself."

I laugh. Star nudges my hand and I scratch her under the chin. "Don't be silly. It's not like you're the first. Allie stole a bottle of champagne at her parents' last New Year's Eve party and threw up in her mum's antique vase."

"Wow." Georgie raises her head, clearly entertained. "Were they furious?"

"They would've grounded her till uni, but luckily, we managed to convince them Allie had come down with a stomach bug."

"And they fell for it? No way I'd be able to pull that off."

"Yeah, her parents are pretty sheltered." I move past Star to dump my carrier bag on the desk. "Anyway, thanks to Allie, I've learned a few things about hangovers. I've brought snacks."

"Mina," Georgie says with the fervour of someone about to declare they've found religion, "I love you."

A startled laugh gurgles out of me. *Gosh, there's no need to blush.* It isn't as if she's being serious. All the same, heat blooms in my cheeks, mirroring the warmth that flared inside me at her words.

"No, really," Georgie says. "Zeph made me some toast earlier, but I haven't been able to face anything else."

"Aw. That was sweet of him." My mind returns to last night, Zephan sitting with Georgie while she vomited up a stomach full of vodka, not touching her or holding back her hair, but simply being there. "I think he has a crush on you."

She snorts. "Shut up. I'm dying of salt deprivation here...or is it sugar? No, definitely both."

"In that case, you're in luck." I begin unpacking the supplies, reeling off the options. "Coke, Dr Pepper, kettle crisps, Chipsticks, pretzels..."

Georgie plumps her pillows against the headboard and leans against them, shuffling over to make space for me. We're soon stretched out side by side on her bed, a bag of kettle chips resting across our thighs.

"Have you seen Gaz this morning?" Georgie reaches for a crisp and the bare skin of her arm grazes mine.

I swallow the dryness in my throat with a mouthful of Coke. "No, but I heard him in Art's room just now. Sounded like they were patching things up."

"You think they will?"

"Gosh, I hope so. I've never seen Gaz this happy."

"They're sweet together," Georgie says, "even if I do get the urge to stick my fingers in my ears and sing 'My Old Man's a Dustman' every time they start kissing."

"'My Old Man's a Dustman'? Seriously?"

"What? It's the least sexy song I could think of. My granddad sings it whenever Nana tells him to put the bins out."

We shake with giggles, smothering the sound behind our hands. Georgie collapses into me, her head on my shoulder, and suddenly I'm not laughing anymore. Air lodges in my windpipe, makes it difficult to breathe. Every one of my senses is attuned to Georgie's closeness—the solid warmth of her against me, the tickle of her hair on my neck, the apple scent of her shampoo…

39. GEORGIE

I WAKE WITH MY head resting on Mina's shoulder. My laptop's balanced across our legs, playing an episode of *Young Sheldon*. I feel better after a nap. My headache's buggered off and my stomach's no longer sloshing around like the water in a washing machine.

I'm also starving, so we wander over to the dining room for roast beef and Yorkshires. Since the boys are AWOL, the two of us have the table to ourselves. The remnants of our late night and drowsy afternoon wrap us in a contented languor. As we eat, we switch between idle chat and easy silence.

After I've wolfed down a second bowl of apricot crumble, we walk arm in arm back to the house. The evening air slides fresh and cool against my skin. Every now and then, a spot of rain pings off my cheek.

"Can I...?" Mina hesitates. "Is it all right if I ask about your sight?"

I squeeze her arm. "'Course."

"It's something I've been curious about. I just wasn't sure if it would be insensitive."

"Maybe, if it was the first thing you ever said to me, but not now. Anyway, it isn't like I'm touchy about it."

It's true. You can't miss something you've never had. I've been blind since birth, so why waste energy being bitter about it?

Of course, that doesn't mean I don't get sick of my classmates acting like my disability's the only important thing about me.

"Just wanted to make sure." Mina's shoulder brushes mine. "So, you can't see anything at all, right? Not even vague shapes?"

"Nope."

"But sometimes, when it's really bright, your eyes react to it, the way a sighted person's would. How come?"

I grin at her. "Not sure, really. For all I know, it's the same for all blind people, but I have a theory. I think it's because, technically, there's nothing wrong with my eyes. Problem is, I was born without any optic nerves to carry the signals to my brain. In every other respect, my eyes behave normally, like reacting to light."

Mina's quiet for a moment. She pushes open the door to Osborne House, waiting until it swings shut behind us. "Do the doctors have any idea why it happened?"

I shrug. "Mum almost miscarried when she was five months pregnant with me. They think that might've caused it, but no one knows for certain."

We head for Flat Two and along the hallway to my room. I unhook my arm from Mina's and fish out my key.

"So," Mina says as I slip it into the lock, "if scientists were able to grow an artificial optic nerve, you'd be able to see?"

The latch clicks. I step inside, earning a sleepy wag from Star's corner. "In theory? Yeah. In practice, though…maybe not." I flop onto my bed, automatically shifting to make room. "Because I don't have any visual memory, don't even know what colours are, it would be a total sensory overload. My brain would probably explode."

Mina throws herself down beside me, laughing. "On the subject of exploding brains, let's watch a horror film."

I groan. For someone as sweet and gentle as Mina Farhan, her love of all things gory is a mystery.

"Come on." She rolls over, entwining her fingers with mine. "I'll describe all the gruesome bits to you."

"Cheers." The air hitches in my throat. Her fingers are warm in mine and her breath ghosts against my lips.

"Please?" Mina nuzzles her nose into my neck, sensual as a cat. "Pretty please with chocolate drops and rainbow sprinkles?"

God, she's so close. My heart pounds, an out-of-control drumbeat. I can't breathe. Do I dare? It would be so simple. All I'd have to do is raise myself a few millimetres.

A bit more.

Almost there.

Still a chance for either of us to pull back, and then...

Our mouths brush. It's so soft, barely a touch, but...oh my God. My belly fills with molten heat. It spreads through my entire body, throbbing, electric. I want... I want...

Mina's lips are so smooth, like satin, and she tastes of apricots and cream. I don't move, holding my breath. When she doesn't pull away, I kiss her properly. I get lost in the softness of her mouth, the curved shape of it.

And Mina kisses me back.

I reach up to cup her neck. Need to be closer, to feel her against me...

A shrill ringing blares from across the room. At once, Mina flings herself away from me and off the bed. She scrabbles about on the desk, crisp packets rustling.

"Blast it." The jangling grows louder as she unearths her phone, then goes silent. "That was Dad. Sorry, I just remembered. I…I promised to phone home. I need to call him back."

"Oh, OK." I touch my mouth, still tingling from the kiss. "Will I see you after? We can watch that film."

"Actually, I think I'll have a shower and an early night." It spills out of her in a panicked avalanche. "Catch up tomorrow, OK?"

She's gone before I have a chance to answer, to persuade her to stay. The door clicks shut behind her and I'm left in a confused heap on the bed.

Christ, what have I done?

WEEK THREE

*Music was my refuge. I could crawl
into the space between the notes
and curl my back to loneliness.*

– Maya Angelou

40. MINA

TENDRILS OF MORNING mist shimmer beyond the kitchen window as I wait for the kettle to boil. I lean against the worktop and rub my eyes, scratchy and sore after a sleepless night. What have I done? Images chase each other through my brain—Georgie's hair a tangled lion's mane on the pillow; her eyes so close to mine I could see the flecks of silver in her irises; the hurt that creased her expression an instant before I fled.

Camomile tea made, I wander with it over to the glass doors. The sky is a pearly grey, but the blush on the horizon promises the first rain-free day for a week. In the dawn light, Gareth's hair glows like the embers of a dying fire. He's perched on the picnic table, his back to me, mug cradled in his hands.

At once, I'm sliding the door open and rushing onto the patio, concrete cold beneath my bare feet. My friend needs me. Finding him out here so early…and on his own…can't be a good sign. I wrap my dressing gown tighter against the freshness and hoist myself onto the table beside him.

Gareth glances sideways at me. "Christ, you look like shit."

"So do you." Shadows the colour of ripe plums stand out against his pale skin and his eyes are puffy and red. "What're you doing out here?"

"Couldn't sleep."

"But I thought… Did you and Art not make up?" Just in time, I stop myself blurting the fact that I'd overheard their conversation.

Gareth releases a long breath. "Yeah. At least, I think we have, but…"

"What?"

"Art seems kind of off. Really sweet, like, but…distant. What if I've pushed him away?"

"I'm sure you haven't." I sip my tea. "Maybe if you give him some space."

"Yeah, maybe. I need to be patient. That was a big thing I dropped on him." Gareth drapes an arm over my shoulders. "Me and my stupid mouth."

"Not stupid. I think it was really brave, putting it all out there." The exact opposite of my own cowardice. I snuggle into Gareth's side, but his solidity can't shield me from what I've done.

Gareth winds a strand of my hair around his finger. "So, what's keeping you awake? Did something happen?"

The question veers so wide of the truth, it's almost funny. I touch my lips, remembering the tentative brush of Georgie's mouth, how she'd tasted sweet, like crumble. "We kissed."

Gareth whoops, the sound unnaturally loud in the stillness, and I bury my face in his chest to hide my blush.

"Hey." He tugs on my hair. "This is a good thing, right? I've watched the way you are with her. Thought this was what you wanted, like."

I close my eyes, seeking refuge in the darkness behind my lids. For the hundredth time, I relive my reaction to the kiss, allow myself to feel every sensation. The mere memory has my entire body tingling, starts a throbbing in parts of me I'd barely known existed. Yes, I'd wanted it. I'd wanted it so much it terrified me.

Gareth lays a hand on my back. "You do like her, don't you? I haven't got that wrong?"

"You know you haven't."

"So…?"

"I ran, Gaz." I push myself upright, let him see the misery that must be gushing from every pore. "After it happened. I just ran."

"But why?" He blinks, clearly confused, and I can't blame him. If Art were to come out here right now, kiss him the way Georgie had kissed me last night, Gareth would hold on to him and never let go.

I avoid his gaze, mug clutched so tightly the heat of it scalds my palms. The sun has risen higher while we've been sitting here, gilding the top of the hedge in rose gold. "My dad called. He sort of interrupted us, and I…I panicked."

Leaving Georgie huddled on her bed, no doubt wondering what on Earth she'd done wrong. How bewildered she must have felt, how abandoned. But when the familiar number flashed on the display—that reminder of home, of my parents' expectations—it was all too much.

I returned Dad's call but was scarcely able to concentrate on his words, something about the hole-in-one he'd shot during his Sunday round of golf. All I kept thinking was *I kissed a girl. I've experienced the most magical moment of my life*, yet if I were ever to tell Mum and Dad, they'd suck the magic out of it, transform it into something shameful, a mistake. Accepting my own sexuality is one thing. I have accepted it, believe with all my heart that God loves me for the person he created. I've even made peace with the fact that, one day, I'll fall short of my parents' expectations…just not yet.

Gosh, but that kiss…

"What're you going to do?" There's no judgement in Gareth's tone, only empathy. It's more than I deserve.

The sigh comes from a place deep inside me. "I don't know, Gaz. I really don't."

41. GEORGIE

I'VE SCREWED UP.

The wall of the lily pond has soaked up the morning sun. Its warmth seeps through my jeans as I sit down and rest my chin in my hands. Picking up on my mood, Star lays her head in my lap.

How had I got it so wrong? Mina's body pressed to mine, her face nuzzling into my neck. She could've pulled back, stopped things going too far. God, I'd been so sure. In that instant before our mouths touched, I would've staked my life it was what she wanted.

The air snorts from my nose. Yeah, I'd misread that big time. Mina was clearly horrified, couldn't get away fast enough.

I squeeze my eyes shut and press my knuckles into the sockets. Shit. I'd trade my Fender for a time machine. If I could rewind to just before my lips brushed Mina's, I'd save myself from making that epic cock-up. Right now, I should be psyched for another day at camp. With Mina. Thanks to that stupid kiss, I'll never be able to face her again.

Campus wakes up around me. Voices drift on the breeze, campers reconnecting with friends from other flats. I dig out my phone. Still twenty minutes till the workshop. If I head over now, I'm more likely to miss Mina.

What? You really think she'll be waiting for you like nothing's happened? Yeah, right. If her disappearing act last night's anything to go by, it's a safe bet Mina's as keen to avoid you as you are her. All the same, better not take any chances.

"Hey." I've directed Star onto the main path when Zephan falls into step beside me. "Recovered from Saturday?"

"Ugh. Don't remind me." Already a snake pit of knots, my stomach roils at the memory.

Zephan moves ahead to hold the door open. Star guides me into the foyer where we're hit with the chorus of 'Should I Stay or Should I Go' by The Clash. Talk about fitting. Damn, the eighties definitely isn't my favourite decade for music.

"You waiting for Mina?" Zephan asks.

I shake my head. "Let's go in. We can save the others places."

Anyone else would've wanted to know why, cracked some joke about me and Mina being joined at the hip. Not Zeph. All he does is lay a light hand on my back and steer me into the reception room. Even when I snag his usual cushion in the corner, he doesn't comment.

"Sure you're OK?" Zephan sits beside me. "You don't look it."

"Cheers." I unclip Star's harness and she curls up on the sun-warmed floor.

The Clash fades into something by U2. 'Still Haven't Found What I'm Looking For'. Or is it 'Angel of Harlem'? Most of their stuff sounds the same. I lean against the wall and wrap my arms around my calves. Zephan's question hangs between us, unanswered. I could confide in him. He'd listen, give it to me straight, no crap. I bury my face in my knees. Man, kill me now.

"There you are."

Mina's voice yanks me from my thoughts. I hadn't realised before, hadn't realised I was clinging to a shred of hope. Maybe everything would be all right. Maybe, just maybe, I haven't blasted our friendship to shrapnel.

So much for that. Mina's tone gives her away. It's too high, too bright, like the top notes of a glockenspiel.

She settles on the cushion in front of mine. Star snoozes between us, her bulk a welcome barrier. "Gaz and I waited for you."

"Where's lover boy?" Zephan drawls. Dunno if the change of subject is for my benefit, but I could hug him.

"Outside," Gareth says, "Chatting to some of his other friends, like."

Another one who's rubbish at hiding their feelings. He sounds exhausted, like his sadness is a ten-ton weight. Was Mina wrong about Gaz and Art sorting things out?

Art joins us just as the song—definitely 'Angel of Harlem'—comes to an end. He's barely breathed a quick "Hi" when Calypso claps her hands for quiet.

"OK, guys. Before we embark on our journey through the eighties, I need to remind you about the auditions coming up next week."

A cymbal clash couldn't've silenced the room so effectively. My nails gouge into my palms. This is it.

"Here's how it's going to work," Calypso says. "You'll each perform two songs for the panel of judges, which includes myself and my gran, Leticia. Monday through Wednesday, between two-thirty and six, we'll be holding solo auditions. This is your chance to shine, to really show us who you are as an artist, so choose your piece wisely."

Sure, no pressure. At once, I skip through my mental playlist of original songs. How to know which one to pick, which will earn me the most points.

"Then, on Thursday afternoon," Calypso continues, "you'll perform a song with your band, just so we can see how you excel as part of a team. On Friday, the judges will meet to discuss all the week's performances, and shortly after that, you'll each receive an email informing you whether you've been offered the scholarship."

A gasp ripples through the room, the audible equivalent of a Mexican wave. I hug my knees so tightly every muscle pulls taut.

Calypso laughs. "I won't tell you not to be nervous. I know what a big deal this is. My best advice would be to have fun with it, enjoy the opportunity. You should get an email today with the audition schedule, but if you have any questions, see me after the session. Now, though, let's dive into the realm of eighties rock."

She launches into her introduction, something about the rise of heavy metal. I scarcely hear her. Everything has been leading up to this. In just over a week from now, I'll be getting ready to perform my arse off. It has to be good enough. I've already vandalised the truest friendship I've ever had. If I don't win the scholarship, this summer will've been a total washout.

42. MINA

GEORGIE'S AVOIDING ME.

After Calypso's workshop, I expected we'd all head over to the dining room for coffee as usual. Instead, Georgie went back to the house so Star could have a drink, refusing my offer to go with her. Now, when I look for her so we can walk to lunch together, she's nowhere to be found. Since I have no appetite anyway, I spend the lunch hour wandering through campus, Georgie's absence a cramp in my belly.

Not that I blame her. Given the way I'd abandoned her the previous evening, and my clumsy attempts this morning to act like everything's normal, I'd fervently love to avoid myself. I hoped, if I pretended nothing had happened, we could simply return to our easy friendship of before. One glance at Georgie's closed expression was enough to shatter that idea.

I arrive at our practice room to find Gareth and Art already there. Just last Friday, I'd barged in on them kissing, Art straddling Gareth's lap, their hands buried inside one another's clothes. Now, Gareth's seated alone at the piano while Art stands behind his drum kit, sticks tapping out a soft rhythm. At least they're speaking, although they break off when I come in.

"Hey, mate." Art's pale beneath his tan, his smile a few watts dimmer than usual. Wary of his reception after Saturday night, probably.

"Hey." I drop into a chair and unpack my banjo, too weary to mask my coolness towards him. I like Art, I truly do, but if he ends up breaking Gareth's heart, I'll never forgive him.

"We were debating which song to do for our group audition." Gareth props his elbow on the lid of the piano, eyes tired and sad. "Art thinks last week's was more original, like, but I think we sang the first one better. Any thoughts?"

I shrug. Twenty-four hours ago, this would have seemed like the most important decision of my life. In this moment, however, all I can focus on is the hollowness inside me.

I make an effort to sound as though I care. "You both have a point. Let's see what the others think, shall we?"

If they even show. Given Georgie's distance this morning, it's likely she'll skip our session altogether. Why would she want to be in the same room as me?

I'm wrong, as it turns out. Georgie enters a few minutes later, accompanied by Star and Zephan. I should have known the scholarship's too important to let her feelings about me get in the way. At the sight of her, expression creased with strain and fatigue, it's all I can do to stop myself running to her and wrapping her in my arms. But I can't. It wouldn't be fair when I'm unable to give her what she wants.

"Hi." Good grief. I'm doing it again, speaking in that falsely bright voice. You'd think I were auditioning to present *Strictly Come Dancing*. Cringing, I pat the seat beside me so Georgie can follow the sound. "We were discussing the group audition, which song we should perform."

Georgie nods, but otherwise makes no comment. She sits, Zephan dropping into the chair next to hers, and the two of them begin unpacking their guitars. Gareth casts me a commiserating look, while Art glances between Georgie and me, forehead creased. A stranger would've picked up on the atmosphere.

I reach for something to say. "Really brought it home, didn't it? Calypso talking about the auditions."

Maybe if I behave as though the tension between us is merely a result of nerves, the others will play along.

"Definitely." Art accepts the baton and runs with it. "Feels so much more real now. In less than two weeks, we'll know who's won the scholarship."

Gareth groans, his skin taking on a greenish tinge. "Don't remind me. This is my one chance. What if I completely blow it?"

"You won't," Art says, voice brimming with conviction.

Gareth blushes and stares down at his hands. "It's just, if I don't win, that's it for me. My family could never afford to send me here."

"My dad can afford it, but there's no way he's paying for me to study music." Art's mouth twists in a wry grin. "All that sex, drugs and rock 'n' roll. Way too many opportunities to fall into sin."

"I'm surprised he let you do the programme." From what I've learned of Art's father, he doesn't seem the type to be easily swayed.

Art shrugs. "Dad accepted some big construction project in London. It means he'll be away a lot over the summer. Reckon he figured I'd be less likely to get into trouble here than at home with my stepmother."

"Yeah, how's that working out?" Zephan mutters.

"My parents are the same," I say. "Not the falling into sin part, but they'd much rather I chose a more stable career path."

"Bet you don't have that problem, eh, Zeph?" Gareth asks. "Your whole family are artists. They must be right behind you."

Zephan plucks the D string of his guitar, twiddling the peg to tune it. "They are, but it's not like they have much spare cash."

"How about you, Georgie?" To my relief, my tone comes out sounding more normal. "You're from a musical family."

Georgie stoops to stroke Star, who's sprawled across her feet. "Dad really wants this for me. My brother, too. Mum, though… Well, she's had to watch my dad pining for a music career that didn't work out. I think she'd like to protect me from all that."

We grow quiet. I glance around at my bandmates, all equally talented in their own way. They each need this opportunity every bit as much as I do—more so, if I'm honest—and any one of them would be a worthy winner.

My gaze settles on Georgie and my stomach twists into a thousand tiny knots. We can't go on like this. Somehow, I have to put this right. At the start of the summer, I believed my toughest challenge would be winning the scholarship and persuading my parents music could be a viable career. Now, however, the task of finding the words to mend things with Georgie feels infinitely more difficult.

43. GEORGIE

WHEN THE KNOCK comes that evening, I'm ready. Crouched on the tiled floor of my en suite, I grip Star's collar, barely breathing. The bedroom door's locked. No one can get in. Still, a single whine from Star will give us away, and I beg her telepathically to stay quiet.

"Georgie?" Mina knocks again.

At the sound of her voice, Star strains against my grasp. I squeeze the leather so hard it digs into my fingers. Star must sense my urgency, because she stays silent.

"Georgie, are you in there?" Mina asks. "I wondered if you wanted to walk over to dinner."

Her tone…so so uncertain, it almost has me unlocking the door. I bloody hate this. Avoiding Chanelle and co was bad enough, but this is agony.

A pause, before Mina retreats. I count to a hundred, just to make trebly sure she's gone. Then I release Star and open the bathroom door. She darts out ahead of me, running circles around my legs. How simple to be a dog. To her, this has all been some strange new game.

"Ready for dinner?" I ask, and Star thumps her tail.

Once I've sorted her out, I throw together a ham sandwich and take it into the garden. Can't stomach shutting myself in my room all evening. With Star's lead secured to the picnic table, I swing my legs over the bench.

It's quiet out here, nothing but the maraca rustle of leaves. The aroma of coconut and spices wafts from the dining room. Damn, I'm missing Rick's curry.

I chew a bite of sandwich. The bread turns to grit in my mouth. It's as though I've travelled back to the start of the summer, to those hours of lonely meals and isolation. Only, this is far worse. Now I know what it's like to have friends, to be part of something. The loss of it pinches like a stitch in my side.

I can't hide from Mina forever. Sooner or later, I'll have to toughen the hell up and face her. She clearly wants to talk; her knock earlier proves that much. It's just…what's the point? There's no rewinding the clock. We can agree to be friends, but it'll still be there, the knowledge that I feel more for Mina than she does for me. It's bound to drive a wedge between us.

"Georgia, hi."

Crap. The second-to-last person I want to see right now.

Chanelle plonks her bum onto the bench beside me, facing outwards. She lights up with an audible flick. "So, how's it going?"

"Fine." *Yeah, Georgie, so convincing.* Not that it matters. Doubt Chanelle's here to ask how I am.

"Cool." She blows smoke into my face. "Did you ask Zephan about me?"

So that's it. Should've been obvious from the moment she sat down. I scuff the concrete with my trainer. It would be easy to hedge, to pretend I haven't managed to pin Zeph down, but, shit, I'm not in the mood.

"Yeah." I fiddle with my barely touched sandwich. "I talked to him."

"And?"

"He's not interested."

"Oh." Chanelle couldn't've sounded more shocked if I'd told her Zeph's taken a vow of celibacy. "What makes you say that?"

I resist an eyeroll. *The fact that he ducks out of sight whenever he hears you coming might be a clue. Or the way he pretends not to be in every time you knock.*

Before I can cobble together an answer, Chanelle carries on. "Is he even straight? I mean, he hangs out with Art and Gareth a lot, and at least that would make sense."

Is she for real? The only reason Zephan wouldn't fancy her is that he's gay? He might be, for all I know. It isn't like we've indulged in long heart-to-hearts about his sexuality. Still, this girl's arrogance is off the scale.

"Yeah, that must be it," she says with obvious relief. "No wonder he's been ignoring my signals. Thanks for helping me figure that out, Georgia."

Trust me, Chanelle, you got there all by yourself. I focus on peeling the crust off my sandwich. *God, leave me alone.*

Chanelle's quiet, puffing on her cigarette. Then she says, "I see you and Mina Farhan together a lot."

The sandwich slips from my fingers. She can't know how much her words sting, but that doesn't stop me loathing her. "We're friends."

"Sure you are," she says, as though humouring a toddler. Chanelle stands and grinds her dogend beneath her foot. "Mina's a sweet person. It's kind of her to take you under her wing."

What did she say?

Cheeks burning, I twist on the bench to glare at her. "Rather than palming me off on someone else, you mean?"

"I'm sorry?" Chanelle had started to walk away, but she halts.

I scoff. "I heard you, Chanelle, our first night here. I came to Himari's room, and I heard what you said."

"You...what?" She's doing a decent job of playing dumb, but her voice falters. "Georgia, I—"

"Oh, and my name's Georgie, not Georgia. Just in case you actually give a damn."

Chanelle's silent. No witty comeback. Then she's marching inside, heels clomping a rapid retreat. Clearly can't wait to get away. I smirk. About time someone called her out on her bullshit. This girl might've held the power to hurt me once, but not anymore. Not now I have real friends.

Yeah, although you've gone and lost one of them.

I pick up my sandwich...drop it again. No point trying to eat, and I'm too riled up to sit in my room. I could take Star for a walk, but...too risky. Sod's law I'd run into Mina.

What about our practice room?

I unclip Star from the table leg, pick up my plate, and head indoors. With my solo audition scheduled for next Tuesday, I really should work on my piece. I'm toying with performing 'Girl Like You', the song I wrote the first weekend here, but is it good enough? What I need is an honest opinion.

I toss the remains of my sandwich and have to stop Star from launching herself into the bin after it. Together, we head along the hall to knock on Zeph's door. "Only me."

Plodding footsteps, then the click of the lock.

"Hey," I say once he has the door open. "Want to go into hiding with us?"

44. MINA

I SHOVE MY LUNCH plate away, the lasagne untouched. All around me, the dining room echoes with conversation and the clatter of cutlery. It only makes me more aware of the empty chair beside mine, the one where Georgie should be sitting.

"You have to talk to her." Gareth isn't eating either. He's seated across from me, elbows resting on the table.

It sounds so simple, doesn't it? I'm desperate for the chance to explain, to try and make Georgie see why I ran. The problem is, she clearly has no desire to talk to me.

"I'm serious, hun," Gareth says. "You can't go on like this. Anyone can see it's making you both miserable."

I let out a long breath and drop my head in my hands. He's right, I know he is, and not just because of how Georgie and I feel. With the auditions looming, allowing this awkwardness between us to drag on would be unfair to the rest of the band. It's just…how to pin someone down when they're doing everything they can to avoid you?

Gareth reaches over to squeeze my shoulder. "Do it later, yeah? After practice."

"Yes. Yes, I will." The cowardly part of me wants to crawl under the table and hide, but I straighten my spine. I can do this. I have to do this.

"He ever planning on joining us, you reckon?" Gareth has his arms folded, gazing at a point behind me.

I swivel in my seat to look. Art's a couple of tables over, perched on the corner, his foot propped on the chair belonging to a cute boy with cornrows. As I watch, Art leans in to say something in the boy's ear that makes him laugh.

I turn back to Gareth, keeping my tone light. "Well, we can't expect him to spend all his time with us. He does have other friends."

"Yeah, those two definitely look friendly." Gareth snorts, but his derision can't disguise the pain underneath.

"Gaz…" What can I say? Everything about Art's demeanour—the prolonged eye contact, his foot resting against the boy's thigh—screams flirty. It might not mean anything, might simply be Art's way. Still, I have the urge to pick up my full plate and chuck the contents in his face.

By the time Art ambles over, Gareth's gripping his upper arms hard enough to bruise.

"Hey." Art smiles between us as he sets down his plate, pulling out the chair next to mine. "No Zeph or Georgie again?"

Gareth shakes his head, the movement jerky. You'd have to be an extraterrestrial not to realise something's wrong.

Art's smile fades. "Everything all right, mate?"

"Sure," Gareth says, but his tone implies the opposite.

"Look." Art's forehead creases. "Sorry I was late. Was just catching up with some mates."

"Catching up? Is that what we're calling it now?"

"'Xcuse me?"

Gareth huffs. "Forget it. If you can't see the problem, there's no point me trying to explain."

"No, go on." Art picks up his knife and fork, then drops them with a clang. "If you have an issue with me, spit it out. I'm not allowed to talk to other guys, that it?"

"Talking? Art, you were practically sitting on his lap."

"Christ, don't be pathetic."

Gareth laughs, though there's no humour in it. "Don't hold back, will you? Is that what you think? I'm so pathetic I'll just sit here while you chat up other guys in front of me?"

"Yeah, you know what? I'm not hungry." Art scrapes back his chair and stands, expression blank. "Catch you later."

He saunters out of the dining room, thumbs hooked into the waistband of his jeans. An outsider would think he didn't have a care in the world, but I won't believe it, don't believe it. His feelings for Gaz were—are—real, and if he's as unaffected as he pretends, I'm a heavyweight boxing champion.

Gareth sinks his head in his hands, tears glistening on his lashes. "Shit. What've I done?"

I gnaw on my lower lip, wishing I knew how to help. Eventually, I get up and touch his shoulder. "Come on. We may as well wait in the practice room. You can patch things up with Art when he gets there."

We take a meandering route in the August sunshine, stopping by Osborne House to pick up my banjo. Neither of us speak, but I link my arm through Gaz's, reassuring him I'm here.

In the practice room, Gareth slumps over the piano and buries his face in his arms. I unpack my instrument and go through my usual tuning routine. With my solo audition set for the following Wednesday, this would be the ideal opportunity to fit in some extra rehearsal. Instead, I run my fingers over the strings, scarcely aware which chords I'm playing. Two-thirty comes and goes, and still there's no sign of our bandmates.

"They're not coming," Gareth says, the wood muffling his words, "are they?"

I sigh and bend to replace my banjo in its case. "It doesn't look like it."

Gareth straightens, twisting on the bench to face me. His expression holds apprehension, but also a steely resolve— the same emotions which have my own stomach in a vice. When our eyes lock, understanding leaps between us. We both know what has to be done.

45. GEORGIE

I LEAN MY ELBOWS on the picnic table, its slats baking in the afternoon sun. Unable to stomach the dining room, I've spent the lunch break in the garden of Osborne House with Zeph. Over several mugs of tea, I fill him in on my class-A blunder.

"Talk to her already," he says once I've finished.

I snort. "Rich coming from the guy who'd rather eat dung than discuss his feelings."

"Leave me out of it. This is about you."

He's right, damn him.

Me and Mina can't go on like this. For one thing, the tension's bound to affect our music. It could screw up our chances of landing the scholarship. For another, the thought of limping through the last weeks without Mina's friendship…God, it would be torture.

"So, you know I love playing agony aunt," Zephan says, "but lunch ended half an hour ago."

"Shit." I scramble off the bench. Much as I'd like to skip rehearsal, it wouldn't be fair on our bandmates. We need all the practice we can get.

As I clip Star into her harness, I reach a decision. After our jam, I'll grasp the guitar by the neck and ask Mina for a private word. We need to sort this out.

Great minds think alike, apparently. The three of us are leaving the flat, about to head over to the rec building, when we bump into Mina.

Before I can apologise for being late, she clutches my arm. "Georgie, can we talk?"

"We don't have to." It's a doomed attempt, gutless. With Mina right here, though, my resolve slinks into a corner. I'm not ready.

"We do. I want to. Please."

She sounds so desperate. A heart of granite couldn't've held out against that.

In my room, we perch on the bed while Star settles in for a nap. I lean against the wall, arms strangling my shins.

Hey, asteroids, if you're there, now would be a great time to fall out of the sky and squash me. Anything to put off the most cringe-inducing conversation of my life. Maybe it would be better to jump in first.

"I'm so sorry," I blurt, just as Mina says the same.

She exhales a shaky breath. "Silly girl. What've you got to be sorry for?"

"God, don't pretend." I bury my face in my knees. "I feel bad enough as it is."

"Why, though? I was the one who ran. You didn't do anything wrong."

I scoff.

"No, really. You...well, you never did anything I didn't want you to." Mina brushes my shoulder. Her fingers send a shiver down my arm.

I hug her words to my chest. "You mean that?"

"Come on. You must've guessed how I feel about you."

"Not totally. I kind of hoped, but then you ran."

"I know, I know. I just panicked."

"Why? Because of the Catholic thing?"

"Partly." Mina sighs. "I know my parents will struggle with the idea, but also… I've told you about my sister, haven't I?"

"The champion swimmer?"

"Actually, she was a champion at pretty much everything she did. Prefect, head girl, top student. Whereas I have to work my socks off to stay near the top of my class, May would get 'A's without even trying. She won a place at Cambridge and was all set to follow our parents into medicine."

"Yikes." I wrinkle my nose. "She sounds irritating."

Mina laughs. "She is a bit. Then she got pregnant during her second year of uni and she wasn't so perfect anymore."

"Wow, bet that went down well."

"Exactly. To be fair, Mum and Dad were incredibly supportive, paying for the wedding and helping May and Tom put down a deposit on a flat. Still, it can't be what they wanted for their golden daughter. Now there's only me. Not that I could ever be as brilliant as May, but I have to try."

I pick at the frayed cuff of my denim shorts. It makes sense, Mina wanting to live up to her parents' expectations now her sister can't. It's the sort of person she is. Still, the whole thing jars like a wrong note in a favourite song.

"It's not the same. Your sister made a mistake, but you didn't choose to be gay. This is who you are."

"I realise that, really I do, and they'll have to know someday. Just not yet."

"Don't tell them then." It's a no-brainer. Our parents don't need to know everything about us. Much better for them if they're kept in the dark.

"I don't know, Georgie. I think maybe I'm just not ready for a relationship."

The fight gusts out of me. Just my luck. The first person who's ever returned my feelings is too bogged down in family loyalty to act on them.

"I'm sorry." The misery in Mina's voice matches mine.

I nod; it's all I can manage. *Don't cry. Mina likes you. She as good as said, if things were different, you'd be together.* I swallow the tears; they stick like a gobstopper in my throat.

"Friends?" she asks.

An hour earlier, I would've given both thumbs to go back to how we were. Now, though, this reeks of second best.

"Friends," I say, and try to ignore the ache in my gut.

46. MINA

THE MOMENT WE stumble into our weekly recital for Calypso on Friday afternoon, it's clear something's off. We've given 'That's Entertainment' by The Jam a country makeover, and technically there's nothing wrong with the performance. Our harmony's in tune, every note and drumbeat on point, but it lacks any spark.

Well, what did I expect? Although we've all turned up to the last few practices, no one's heart has been in it. With Georgie's and my friendship so fragile, and tension quivering between Gareth and Art, creative energy has been thin on the ground.

All the same, when our woeful performance staggers through its final chord, Calypso rewards it with a round of applause. "Fantastic job. Love the whole Lady A vibe."

Her praise drops into an incredulous silence.

"Come on, guys." Calypso leans forward in her chair, smile coaxing. "I admit you've played better, but cut yourself some slack, yeah? You're just nervous. It's natural with the auditions coming up."

Lord, like I needed reminding. I've saved the schedule to my phone and highlighted my slots in shocking pink, a bold colour designed to fill me with confidence. So much for that. Given how my stomach plummets at the mere mention of the auditions, an ominous black would've been more appropriate.

"You'll be fine," Calypso says with the assurance of a veteran tightrope walker about to send us across a hundred-foot ravine. "The fact you're here means every one of you has what it takes. Relax and do your best. That's all any of us can ask."

Put like that, it sounds so simple. If only I didn't feel as though everything else in my life were slipping like newly polished piano keys from my fingers.

Once Calypso's gone, the air hangs heavy with disappointment. For a brief time, we'd glimpsed the promise of something special, the beginnings of a real band. Now, the five of us sit separate from one another, no longer a cohesive whole. I could cry.

Without a word, Zephan stows his guitar in its case and walks out. Well, after that lacklustre performance, what is there to say?

"Right." In the quiet, Art's voice sounds forced. "Gonna love you and leave you. I have a pool tournament to win. Hopefully, I'll show more prowess with a cue than I did with these today."

He drops his drumsticks in disgust and heads for the exit. Gareth casts him a hopeful look, but either Art doesn't see or he chooses to ignore it.

Once the door closes behind him, Gareth sags over the piano and buries his head in his arms.

"Gaz," I ask, "what's happening with you two?"

He huffs. "Nothing, clearly."

"But you made up the other day. You said—"

"Oh, Art was cool about it, like, told me not to worry, but you've seen how he is. When he can stand to be around me."

I bite my lip, twiddling one of the tuning pegs on my banjo. Beside me, Georgie cradles her guitar and strums a series of minor chords. We've all noticed the change in Art; it would've been impossible not to. He's still friendly enough, but there's less joking around, more reserve.

"What am I meant to do?" Gareth's voice cracks. "I've tried to give him space, but he just pulls further away."

I can relate to that. My gaze slides to Georgie, lost in her melody, and all at once this room feels claustrophobic. I stow away my instrument and stand. "There's no point the three of us moping around indoors. "Let's get a drink and sit outside."

Gareth nods and clambers off the bench, shoulders bowed.

"Georgie?" My nails dig into my palms. *Please say yes.*

She shrugs, expression neutral. "Sure."

I let out my breath. Not overly enthusiastic, but anything's a win at the moment. While she packs up, I watch her with an ache in my chest. Gosh, I hate this. We might be back on speaking terms, might spend our free time together, but it isn't the same. The laughter and intimacy has gone, dispersed like smoke on the summer breeze.

And it's all my fault.

47. GEORGIE

WHO KNEW? TURNS out you can feel happy and absolutely bloody miserable at the same time.

After that soggy biscuit of a performance, we grab drinks from the student centre and find a shady patch of lawn. It's a sultry afternoon, the air sluggish with the smell of dry soil. The jukebox plays Louis Capaldi, his vocals merging with splashes and shouts from the pool.

I snap open my can and take a swig. Lemon Tango fizzes down my throat, tart and sweet, bitter with regret.

"You know what?" Mina's voice radiates zeal. It's like she thinks her optimism will stitch our wounded group back together. You have to love her for trying.

I lean against the tree, grass tickling my bare legs. "What's that?"

"We should perform something at the open mic tomorrow. As a trio."

Prone on Mina's other side, Gareth groans. "After what just happened in there? You have to be kidding."

"But that's the point," Mina says. "We could all use a confidence boost. You'd be up for it, wouldn't you, Georgie?"

Hell, no. The idea has me wanting to crawl inside my instrument case and stay there. Mina's so keen, though; she's making such an effort.

"It'll be fun." She pounces, sensing weakness. "I have the perfect song."

A frenzied clicking as Mina taps away on her phone. I press my palm into the grass between us. So much space. Probably only a foot but may as well be the Atlantic. Before I went and complicated it, our relationship was made up of a thousand tiny touches. Mina would rest her head on my shoulder while we talked, or I'd nudge her knee to get her attention. Now, there's this no-go zone we're too nervous to cross.

At least Mina still wants to be friends. Another girl might've cut me dead. And she likes me. She likes me the way I like her. So what if she won't do anything about it? I should be pumped, and part of me is. It's just…getting to be with Mina, and yet being unable to hold her?

It sucks donkey's balls.

"Found it." Mina shifts closer, although not close enough for our arms to brush. "You like Train, right?"

"Yeah." I swallow. She's so warm. The scent of her coconut shampoo fills my nose.

"That's what I thought. So, there's this country singer I like. Ashley Monroe. I was looking through some of her videos on YouTube and she did a song with Train. As soon as I heard it, I thought…we'd be great singing this. Listen."

Mina hits play and the funky guitar spills from her phone. It's super cheesy but has one of those tunes you can't help humming. Despite everything, I smile.

"You know it?" Mina asks. "What do you think? Could we put something together by tomorrow evening?"

I focus on the chord sequence. "Don't see why not. If we practise our arses off."

"Yay! Knew you'd be up for it. How about you, Gaz?"

"Really, hun, I'm not in the mood." Gareth's words are muffled, like he has his face mushed into the ground. "It'll work better as a duet, anyway."

We fall quiet, and I sip my Tango. Poor Gaz. It's crappy, knowing how down he is. His and Art's public displays might've made me want to vom, but they were better than this.

I crush the empty can in my fist. "Why don't you just talk to him?"

His snort would've shamed a wild boar. "Because he doesn't want to talk to me. He's made that pretty damned clear."

Figured he'd say that. Gareth wouldn't go into the student centre where the pool tournament's happening, instead waiting outside with me while Mina got the drinks. Not that I blame him. Art's been tougher to pin down than a moth this week. They were so cute together, though. Crazy to throw that away without a fight.

Mina must be thinking the same, because she says, "You can't just give up on him. What you had was too special."

"Yeah." Gareth scoffs. "That's what I thought. Seems Art doesn't see it like that, though."

"He does. You just have to show him what he's missing."

"Right. And how do I do that, like?"

Mina's quiet, fingers drumming a soft tattoo on her thigh.

"OK," she says at length, "here's what we're going to do."

48. MINA

I F I FAIL at a music career, perhaps I could make it as an actor. By nine that evening, the three of us are living it up on the dance floor of eighties night…or pretending to. It's difficult to tell when I can't see myself, but I'd say I'm putting on a passable performance of having a good time. Madonna vibrates through the soles of my sandals and I leap about with my usual graceless enthusiasm. Who cares if my soul's weeping great hiccupping sobs? No one watching would ever guess.

I twirl, head thrown back. LED bulbs bathe the dancers in flashes of alternating colour—pink, amber, fiery orange—and glow-in-the-dark parrots soar across the ceiling amidst garlands of orchids. It's like I've stepped into a tropical sunset. Is this really happening, or am I experiencing some strange psychedelic dream? I look at Georgie, doing a half-hearted shuffle next to me. No, this is real. Painfully, unmistakably real.

I lean closer to shout in Georgie's ear. That scent, a heady mix of apples and White Musk. "Having fun?"

Georgie nods, but she isn't fooling anyone. To judge by her grim expression, you'd think she were dancing for her survival.

Madonna implores us to open our hearts, and her words reach inside me, into my chest, and squeeze. But that's what Georgie had done, isn't it? Laid herself bare, confronted her feelings head on and followed through. That girl has more backbone than a giraffe, far more than I do. I don't even have the courage to meet her halfway.

Madonna melds into 'Club Tropicana', and I launch into another spin, catching Gareth's eye. He grins and gives me a thumbs up. It took him a while to shake off his gloom, but gradually, the music worked it's magic. Now he's lost in the rhythm, eyes alight with a happiness that hasn't been there in days. What does it matter if every second of this hurts like nails digging into a fresh cut? Insisting we come tonight was the right thing to do.

Gareth's also under strict instructions to avoid so much as glancing in Art's direction. "If he thinks you're over him, it'll make him want you all the more."

How ironic, me dispensing relationship advice. Still, Gareth's gone along with it so far, dancing as though he's the only person in the room. Art's on the far side of the dance floor, visible amidst a small crowd that includes Chanelle Clarke and the boy with the cornrows. Every so often, Art looks Gareth's way and I give myself a mental pat on the back. It's working.

An orange strobe illuminates Georgie's face. She's pushing the hair off her forehead and sweat clings like raindrops to her skin.

"Timeout?" I call.

She nods, clearly relieved. Gareth refuses the offer to come with us, so we leave him to it, weaving an erratic path towards the refreshment tables. Georgie's so close, her forearm pressed into the sensitive crease of my elbow. The satin heat of it sends shockwaves to the tips of my fingers.

Rick stands behind a makeshift bar, serving non-alcoholic cocktails. I read the menu to Georgie and we both opt for a virgin daiquiri, a fruity mix of Seven Up, lime juice and fresh strawberries. Plastic glasses in hand, we head for a couple of seats between an artificial palm and a giant inflatable guitar.

On the dance floor, Art has acquired a blow-up microphone that's as tall as he is. He's holding it as though it's his male partner in a waltz, twirling and dipping while his admirers double up with laughter.

"Please tell me this plan's doing the trick." Georgie leans towards me to be heard.

"Seems to be. Art's definitely noticed. Ooh, yes, he's going over to talk to him."

I follow Art's meandering progress, microphone still cradled to his body. When he reaches Gareth, he raises himself on tiptoe and says something that makes Gareth laugh.

"What's happening?" Georgie asks.

"They're talking. That has to be a good sign, right?" If only I could hear what they're saying.

They chat for a minute or so, then Gareth nods, his beam more radiant than the lights flashing all around him.

"I'm glad," Georgie says when I describe his smile. "At least this hasn't been a complete washout."

Ouch. Her tone holds no malice, but still… Has spending this evening with me really been such a trial? How different from last Friday, that giddy night of tentative touches and almost confessions. Tears scald my eyelids and I blink them back. *It's no use crying. You have no one to blame but yourself.*

Art re-joins his friends, and shortly afterwards, he and cornrows boy exit through the French windows. A few minutes later, Gareth drops into the chair on my other side.

"What happened?" I clutch his arm, almost spilling my mocktail.

He brushes the damp curls off his brow, scattering joy like glitter. "Said I looked hot…and that he'd see me later."

My shriek has Gareth's grin breaking free, his irises luminous in the dimness.

"Want a drink?" I ask. "Rick's mixing up all sorts over there."

He shakes his head. "Think I'm done here, if that's OK with you guys."

Neither Georgie nor I protest. It isn't as if we have any desire to be here, and Gareth's plainly desperate to find Art. So, after gulping down our daiquiris, the three of us make our escape.

Away from the sunset glow inside, the twilight is calm and ocean deep. The noise of the disco recedes and the air wraps itself around us, balmy and soft.

"Thanks for making me come tonight." Gareth bounces ahead of us, glancing at me over his shoulder. "You were right."

Warmth blossoms in my chest. I've done a good thing. "You two are made for each other. Art just needed reminding."

As Gareth plans what he'll say to Art, speaking more to himself than to us, I cross my fingers in the pocket of my dress. *God, if you're listening, please help him and Art sort things out. Then perhaps we can be a proper band again, and if we practise our bums off, maybe, just maybe, we'll put in a worthy performance at the group auditions.*

At Osborne House, Gareth pushes open the door to Flat Two, stopping so abruptly Georgie and I collide with his back.

"Gaz, what…?" The words stick in my throat.

Oh, no. I clap a hand to my mouth. This can't be happening… but it is. Art has cornrows boy shoved up against the wall outside his room and…and they're kissing.

49. GEORGIE

T HE SILENCE STINKS worse than the toilets at Glastonbury. It would've told me something was up even if I hadn't just whacked my forehead on Gareth's shoulder blade.

"Hey, guys." That's Art. He couldn't sound more awkward if he tried. "So, this is Andre."

The puzzle pieces slot together. Hell, this isn't how it was supposed to go.

"How…?" Gareth chokes on the word. "How could you?"

"Babes…" Art says, but Gareth cuts him off.

"No. No way. You don't get to call me that. Not anymore." He sobs, stumbling forward a pace.

I don't want to be part of this. It's too raw, too private. Sliding my arm from Mina's, I edge past Gareth into the flat. No one stops me. Not sure they even notice.

"I'm sorry," Art's saying, "but, mate, you knew things were over between us."

I slink along the wall, feeling for the door to the living area. Here, I cross to my room and fumble with my key.

Gareth's raised voice chases me inside. "I didn't know. I thought you, like, needed some space."

As soon as I have my door shut, Star presses herself into my legs. She hates rows.

"It's all right, girl. No one's cross with you." I kneel on the floor to hug her. She nestles into me, chin on my shoulder.

I want to stick my fingers in my ears, to block out the argument in the hall. Instead, I run soothing fingers through Star's fur.

"I thought we had something." Gareth's properly crying now. His syllables bleed together like wet paint. "I thought you cared about me."

"We did. I do. It's just—"

"You just decided to mix things up a bit and snog someone else behind my back. Well, fuck you, Art. Fuck you to hell."

Running feet, the slamming of the outer door, then… nothing. Star and I stay where we are, waiting. It feels like a year. Eventually, though, someone I don't know—probably Andre— says he'll see Art tomorrow. Once his footsteps have faded, a latch clicks home and Art moves around in the next room. A moment later, there's a tap at my door.

"Hey," Mina says, coming in. Her greeting wobbles.

"Hey." I scramble up to sit on the edge of my bed. "Where'd Gaz go?"

"Not sure. I'm going to find him. Will you be OK?"

"'Course. You should be with him."

I mean it. Gareth needs her right now. All the same, when she's gone, the house feels way too quiet. I thought I was done with loneliness. Stupid.

Star settles into her corner with the usual rustling and sighing. I huddle on my side, folded in on myself. I wish Mina were here. I wish we could go back to those nights before the kiss, nights spent lying on my bed, legs all tangled up, talking till our tongues dropped off. God, I want to go home.

Something hard's pressing into my hip. My phone. I dig it out to check the time. Ten thirty-six. Not too late.

Dad answers on the second ring. "Watcha, George Porge."

"Watcha, Dad." His voice is so familiar, conjuring up silly jokes and bedtime stories. My chest sort of tightens and eases at the same time. An audience laughs in the background. *"Only Fools and Horses?"*

"Yup. Your mum's at another of her piss-ups and Jake's with Kirsten, so I'm having a quiet beer in front of the telly."

It's like I'm there, Dad and me snuggled at either end of the sofa, Doritos on the cushion between us. If I imagine hard enough, maybe I'll teleport right into our living room.

"What's up?" Dad asks. "Not partying on a Friday night?"

"Just got back from the eighties disco." No need to tell him what an absolute bloody disaster it turned out to be.

"Ah, you must've loved that."

"Sure. Such an eighties fan, me."

Dad chuckles. "Can't believe you've been there three weeks. Bet it's flown by."

"Yeah." I can't tell him the truth. Some days have gushed like a waterfall through my fingers, while others have dragged on forever. That would take too much explaining, so I say, "Auditions start on Monday."

"Your big moment." Dad grows serious. "Don't overthink it. Just do your best. Whatever happens, we're proud of you."

"Cheers, Dad." I swallow.

"And," he adds, "we can't wait for next Sunday."

At first, I think he means they're looking forward to having me home. Then I remember. Damn. The end-of-camp concert. It's only a bit of fun, a way to mark our last day at Dukes. Any campers who want to perform can get up on stage. No pressure, thank God.

At least Dad's words have brought home one fact. There's no way to know how the following week will pan out. I could win the scholarship, or have my dreams blasted to bits. Mina and I might salvage our friendship or leave and never see each other again. Whatever happens, this roller-coaster summer is almost over.

50. MINA

B Y THE TIME I creep downstairs, the house is heavy with that dead-of-night hush. Despite the lateness, light seeps from under Art's door. My knock prompts a weary "Come in," and I slip inside.

Art's lying on his bed, still wearing the jeans and vest from earlier. The glow from the bedside lamp illuminates his eyes, red and swollen from crying.

"If you're here to have a go, don't bother," he says, voice raw. "You can't make me feel any more of a shit than I do already."

I sit in his desk chair and spin it to face him. "That's not why I came."

I conceal my crossed fingers in the folds of my skirt. *Please, God, forgive me that teensy white lie.* After hours of holding Gareth while he wept into my shoulder, I'd wanted nothing more than to give Art a sizeable piece of my mind. Now, though, seeing the state he's in, I can't bring myself to do it.

Art scoffs. "Really?"

"Really." My gaze locks with his. "I just want to know why."

He stares up at the ceiling as though there's a riddle etched into the paintwork. At last, he says, "I can't be who he needs me to be."

"What sort of flimsy excuse is that? Gaz thinks the world of you. You're everything he's ever wanted."

"I'm not. He wants a boyfriend, a guy who's in this for the long haul. I...I can't be that guy."

His words break, but that doesn't prevent my anger from resurfacing. I fold my arms, cheeks hot, and glare at him. "So why start something? It must've been obvious Gaz was looking for a proper relationship. Why get his hopes up?"

"I didn't know. I swear I didn't." A tear slides down Art's cheek and he bats it away. "I thought he just wanted a fling. I heard him say as much to you that day at the picnic."

I open my mouth to deny it, then stop. My memory rewinds to orientation, to the moments directly before Art joined us, Gareth teasing me about having an admirer. Oh, no. "He...he was talking about me."

"What?"

"He was winding me up, joking that I should have a fling."

Art's face disintegrates. "Fuck."

I watch his distress, chewing on my lower lip. It isn't that I don't feel sorry for him—of course I do—but I'd be a lot more sympathetic if he hadn't broken my best friend's heart.

"I don't understand. You obviously care about Gaz. You wouldn't be this upset if you didn't, so why ruin things between you?"

"I don't have a choice." Art rolls onto his side, hand straying to the spot on his lower back. His gaze finds mine. "You saw, didn't you? That day in the practice room."

All at once, it's a struggle to force the words past the tightness in my throat. "Did...did he do that to you? Your dad?"

"The night before camp started. Caught me packing the nail varnishes I'd bought."

"Your dad beat you because of some nail varnish?"

"Yup, so imagine what he'd do if he discovered I had a boyfriend. He'd kill me. Gaz, too." Art laughs, a mirthless sound that makes it clear he isn't joking.

I shiver, hugging myself against the sudden chill. That any parent could do such a thing to their own child…it's abhorrent. "You could go to the police."

"Nah. Dad's this pillar of the community, Catenian president, member of the local parish council. His best mate's a police officer, for fuck's sake."

"But what about your family? Is there no one you can trust?"

He shrugs. "I could talk to Aunt Anna, Mam's sister. I know she'd believe me. I'm just not sure she has the legal clout to do anything, and if I'm honest, I'm scared what Dad would do to me if I tried. No, I need to put up with it for one more year. Then, whatever happens with the scholarship, I'm out of there."

We're quiet for a while. My chest aches for the boy across from me, the incredible drummer and insatiable flirt, who has suffered more than anyone should ever have to. Yet, no amount of sympathy can erase the picture of Gareth curled in a foetal position, tears trickling from beneath sodden lashes even as he slept.

Art glances at me. "You're still pissed off, aren't you?"

"Not exactly." I pleat the material of my skirt. "I just wish… I wish you hadn't led Gaz on."

"Yeah, well, we don't always do the right thing when we like someone. You should get that more than most."

"What's that supposed to mean?"

He snorts. "Come off it, mate. Anyone can see how you feel about Georgie."

"I don't…" My cheeks flame. Am I really that transparent? Panic sends my pulse beating allegrissimo. "That's not the same."

Art rolls his eyes.

My eyelids sting. "It isn't. I wouldn't hurt Georgie for the world."

"Sorry," Art says, though he doesn't sound it. "So you're not shying away from a relationship because you're afraid how your parents will react?"

One moment I'm sitting in Art's desk chair, the next I'm heading for the exit. I won't listen to this. The implication that our situations are in any way similar is ridiculous. My parents have rarely even raised their voices to me, let alone beaten me badly enough to leave a mark. How dare he lecture me after the way he's treated Gaz? Besides, his accusations aren't true. I never gave Georgie a reason to believe there was anything other than friendship between us.

That isn't entirely true, though, is it? the rational part of my brain whispers in my ear.

I close the bedroom door with a snap, but Art's words pursue me into the darkened hall. *"What're you scared of, Mina?"*

51. GEORGIE

OVER A BREAKFAST of tea and toast, I catch Zephan up on last night's drama. Around us, the back garden of Osborne House snoozes in the mid-morning sun.

"What an arse," Zephan says.

I prop my elbows on the picnic table between us. "Still can't quite believe he did it. Gaz deserves better."

"Damned right." Zephan's tone crackles with anger. Can't blame him. Art binned Gareth's heart as if it were an empty Coke can. No one should be treated like that, especially someone as sweet as Gaz.

I lean my chin on my palms. My eyes droop, lids gritty with tiredness. After getting off the phone to Dad, I put my audiobook on, hoped it would lull me to sleep. An eternity later, I was still wide awake when I heard the tap on Art's door.

Mina. Didn't matter that her voice was muffled. I'd know it anywhere. I lay there, ears strained. A low buzz filtered through the wall. I couldn't make out the words, but you didn't need to be a genius to suss what they were talking about.

A decade later, Art's door clicked open. I held my breath. *Please knock for me, just to see if I'm awake.* Before that kiss, she would've done. We would've snuggled under my duvet, Mina's cheek against my shoulder, rehashing the whole mess until we drifted off.

She didn't come.

I massage my aching brow, take a sip of tea.

"Hey."

I shake my head. *Snap out of it, George. You want more than anything for her to be here, so your brain's conjured her up.*

The bench dips as someone sits beside me. Man, that scent. Sunshine and lemon meringue. I'm not going mad. She's real.

"Hey." My throat cracks and I swallow a mouthful of tea. "Uh, how's Gaz?"

"Sleeping. He's worn out, poor thing."

I nod, unable to speak. Maybe it's my sleepless night, I dunno, but this feels especially hard today. Mina's so close. I want to reach for her, to take away some of the anxiety coming off her in waves.

But I can't.

"Georgie?" My name sounds awkward on her tongue. Can she sense what I'm feeling?

I grip my mug, bracing myself. She's going to say she can't perform with me at the open mic tonight, that she needs to be there for Gareth. Well, that suits me fine. It's not like I'm in any hurry to be holed up in a secluded space with Mina. The intimacy will only highlight how far apart we've drifted. Right now, that's more than I can stand.

She sucks in an audible breath. "Come for a walk with me?"

52. MINA

EVERYWHERE IS TOO crowded. Musicians are scattered about campus, some sitting on benches with paper cups of coffee, others winding along the paths in small groups. Music flows from open windows, Billie Eilish blending with Bastille and something with squealing guitars. Everything feels blurry, distorted, as though I'm trapped behind a pane of frosted glass.

"What're you scared of, Mina?"

I inhale, trying to calm my nerves, but a leaden weight crushes my chest. I can't breathe, can barely think.

What precisely am I scared of? Admitting the desire that skulks like a naughty schoolgirl in my heart? Enduring my parents' disappointment when they learn I'm not the daughter they believed me to be? Compared with the violence Art's suffered, my own fears seem petty, childish.

Gosh, I need to get away from all these people. I veer off the main path, leading Georgie along the shortcut between the rec building and study block.

"Mina?" She squeezes my arm.

The gesture brings me back to myself. "Sorry. I'm… I'm not sure how to do this."

Georgie's quiet, chewing on her lip. The walls cast her face in shadow and the circles around her eyes stand out against her pallor. When the alley opens up, the lawn between us and the pool house stretches sun-glazed and deserted. I draw Georgie off the path, into the shade of the study block.

She lets go of my elbow and wraps both arms around herself. "You don't have to say anything. I get it."

"You do?" The weight on my chest lightens a fraction. Can she really sense what I'm feeling? What a relief, not to have to find the right words. I scan her expression, but it reflects none of my own tentative hope.

Georgie ducks her head, parting the grass with the toe of her trainer. "I mean, if this is too difficult, if you can't be friends—"

"What? No!" I rush to reassure her. "That isn't it at all."

"It isn't?"

"Not even close. Kind of the opposite, actually."

Georgie frowns, but a spark of something glimmers beneath her confusion, something bright. Blood fills my ears with white noise. I can't do this. I'm not brave, not like Georgie. But she's turned towards me, uncertainty and anticipation playing across her wonderfully expressive features, and I can't *not* do it.

Fingers trembling, I reach for Georgie's hand. Her palm grazes mine, callused and warm. She doesn't pull away, but neither does she return my pressure. Well, I've already rejected her once; why would she risk that a second time? No, this is up to me.

I hold her hand tighter. If I grip firmly enough, maybe I'll convince her how sincere I am. My voice emerges as a croak. "I…I don't want to run away anymore."

That smile. It's beautiful—the most beautiful smile I've ever seen—wide and infectious and brimming with joy. With that smile, everything becomes absurdly simple. I release her fingers and cup her face.

"You sure?" Georgie asks.

Her question whispers against my lips. It's gentle as a butterfly's wings, powerful enough to rob me of speech, and so I answer the only way I can.

I lean in and kiss her.

Georgie's hands slide around my waist to settle on the small of my back, and I tangle my fingers in her springy curls. Her lips are like silk, her tongue a teasing caress. I press my body into hers, every one of her curves melding with every one of mine, and Georgie lets out a soft moan. Or maybe it's me. I don't know anything except that this is everything I ever dreamed it would be and so much more.

WEEK FOUR

Love is a friendship set to music.

– Joseph Campbell

53. GEORGIE

"FINALLY." I GRIN at Mina as we enter the Dukes Building on Monday morning. "Some decent music."

Mina's laughter mingles with 'Under the Bridge' by the Red Hot Chilli Peppers. It fizzes in my chest like the champagne I drank at Mum's best mate's wedding.

Is this really happening?

The hours since yesterday's kiss have been a blur. They've rushed by in a haze of lips and hands and tumbled words. Even as I unclip Star's harness and slide my arm through Mina's, I can't believe it's real.

Mina peers into the reception room. "The boys're already here."

"How does Gaz look?"

"Tired. Sad. Gosh, I'm a terrible person. I've totally neglected him."

Ouch. It smarts, the idea that she might regret a single second of our time together. I squeeze her elbow. "Don't worry. Zeph's been taking care of him. The two of them were talking for ages last night. Well, Gaz was. Zeph was mostly listening."

Mina exhales, her shoulder relaxing against mine. Star pulls on the lead, and we let her drag us over to our corner.

"Here come the lovebirds," Gareth says as we settle onto cushions. He's pleased for us; it's clear even through the scratchiness in his voice.

"Oh, shush," Mina protests. She leans towards him, tone softening. "You OK?"

While they talk, her fingers lace through mine. It's the most natural thing in the world, like we've been doing this forever.

"Look any smugger," Zephan drawls in my ear, "and I'll vomit down the back of your T-shirt."

I grin...and don't stop grinning until Calypso calls us to attention.

"Morning, guys. Before we start, a quick reminder that the first auditions will be held this afternoon."

Quiet drops as though she's hit a mute button. I can almost taste the tension, metallic on my tongue. Shit. My grin vanishes. It isn't that I've forgotten. How could I? It's just, in the buzz of being with Mina, my nerves over the auditions have slunk into the wings. Now, they strut back on stage in all their gut-churning glory.

Less than thirty-six hours to go. It's nowhere near long enough. I'm not ready. By tomorrow afternoon, I'll have either convinced the judges I deserve the scholarship or tossed my dreams on the bonfire.

"Try not to stress out about them, yeah?" Calypso goes on, which is easy for her to say. "Just do your best and enjoy it. The performance technique sessions after break are still running but aren't compulsory. Feel free to use that time to put in some extra practice."

She launches into her introduction to nineties rock, something about the surge in female stars—Tracy Chapman, Sheryl Crow, Alanis Morissette. This is the workshop I've been looking forward to. I try to focus, but the prospect of the auditions steals my concentration. They loom huge in my mind, tougher to scale than Everest.

"How's everyone feeling?" Mina asks.

It's morning break and we're seated at a picnic table in the sunshine. I grimace, dropping the shortbread I'd been about to dunk in my tea.

Gareth groans, voice muffled in his arms. "Like I want to emigrate to Australia."

"Aw, but your song's incredible. You've been practising since we got our acceptance letters." Mina reaches past me to pat his shoulder.

Gareth huffs. "'S'all right for you lot. At least you won't chuck up over the priceless Steinway."

Zephan snorts.

My fingers curl around my mug. "You don't know what I'll do. I've never performed on my own before."

"And I might not normally suffer from stage fright," Mina says, "but this will be the biggest performance of my life."

We lapse into taut silence. From nearby tables, snippets of intense conversation leap out at me—utterly terrified, forgotten lyrics, must choose the right song. Doubts jostle me like fans at a Sarel concert.

A few days ago, performing 'Girl Like You' seemed the obvious choice. Now, though… On the one hand, it's probably the truest thing I've ever written, but is it too much? Manipulative, even? What if the judges think I want them to feel sorry for me?

"So," Mina's voice breaks into my thoughts, "since none of us are auditioning today, shall we skip PT and get in some extra rehearsal? Then, after lunch, we can sort out what we're doing for our group audition."

"Assuming Art shows, like," Gareth says. "Pretty sure he's avoiding me."

"He'd bloody better show," Zephan growls. "He's not screwing the rest of us over because he can't keep it in his boxers."

Gareth chokes, the sound somewhere between a laugh and a sob. His shoes scrape as he stands. "Come on, let's get practising."

54. MINA

I'M PART WAY through getting ready next morning when there's a soft knock at my door. My smile breaks loose. That'll be Georgie, come to see if I want to join her and Star on their pre-workshop walk. I pull a dress over my head and rush to answer it.

"Oh." I fold my arms, frowning. "What happened to you yesterday?"

Art drums a nervous rhythm on his leg, dark rings around his eyes. "Yeah, sorry about that, mate. Can we talk?"

I sigh, stepping aside to let him in. After everything he confided in me, I owe it to Art to hear him out. Still, he doesn't rank among my favourite people right now. I sit on the bed and do my best to channel the sternness Mum turned on May or me whenever she suspected a feigned illness. "So?"

Art perches on my desk, grimacing. Given the awkwardness between him and Gareth, no one was surprised when he didn't materialise for the previous afternoon's rehearsal. All the same, with our band audition mere days away, the least he could've done was make an appearance.

"Wasn't sure Gaz was ready to see me," he says. "Wanted to give him some space. Then I kind of got caught up in my audition."

"Ooh." For a moment, I forget my antipathy. "How did it go?"

"You know me. Put on a good show for them." He mimes wielding invisible drumsticks, arms flailing in a parody of his flamboyant style.

I giggle, then immediately feel disloyal.

Art's self-mocking grin fades. "Look, I really am sorry about missing rehearsal. I'm, well, I'm going to talk to Gaz, tell him what I told you."

"That's a good idea," I say. "He thinks it's his fault you broke up."

Art groans, pressing a palm to his forehead. "Shit, I never wanted any of this. I really care about him."

And I believe he does. His hunched shoulders and shadowed expression prove his regret more than any words.

"Is that what you came to tell me?" I ask.

"Huh?" Art blinks, thoughts clearly elsewhere. "Oh, no. I actually wanted to apologise."

"To me? What for?"

"For the other night. What I said about Georgie. It was out of order."

My cheeks catch fire. "Don't worry about that. Truly, you did me a favour."

I mean it. Without Art's intervention, I might never have found the courage to act on my feelings. I might never have discovered the joy of being with Georgie, instead allowing our wounded friendship to stumble on until it collapsed and died. It's unthinkable. No, whatever Art's mistakes, I'll always be grateful to him.

By lunchtime, Georgie's a quivering ball of nerves. She toys with her Bolognese, pushing the spaghetti around and around her plate.

I stroke her leg under the table. Her muscles are wound so taut they vibrate against my palm. "You really should eat something."

"Bad idea." Georgie shoves her food away. "Unless you want me to puke in your lap."

She looks as though she might, too. Her skin's clammy with perspiration and she's turned greener than the avocado on her plate. According to Zephan, though, she hadn't eaten breakfast either. Surely, she shouldn't face the most important moment of her life on an empty belly.

I pat her thigh, coaxing. "Just a few mouthfuls? We can't have you fainting in front of the judges."

"I dunno. It would make my audition stand out."

Zephan snorts into his water glass. Even Gareth manages a weak grin, although he's barely touched his own food. All morning I've cradled my conversation with Art to my chest, wishing I could tell Gaz none of this is his fault, but it isn't my secret to share. He needs to hear it from Art.

I wind a strand of spaghetti around my fork, but my stomach constricts in protest and I lay it down. For pity's sake, this is silly. Zephan's already polished off his lunch and the rest of us aren't making any headway. There's no sense in us sitting here, stirring our food into mush.

I brush Georgie's shoulder and glance over at the boys. "Anyone fancy a walk?"

The three of them push back their chairs without a word. As I get to my feet, every molecule of me aches. We spent the better part of yesterday and several hours this morning cooped up in our practice room, perfecting our audition pieces. After countless wrong chords and fumbled lyrics, song changes and frustrated outbursts, the four of us are as prepared as we can be. There's nothing more we can do—nothing except hold it together in front of the judges and pray they like what they hear.

We wander out into the afternoon sunshine and away from the rec building. Georgie's biting her cuticles, something I've never seen her do before, and the arm looped through mine is rigid with tension.

I press it into my side, injecting my voice with all the confidence I have in her. "You'll be fine. More than fine. You'll be incredible."

"Incredibly bad, maybe." Georgie shows me her trembling fingers. "Doubt I'll even be able to play at this rate."

"Of course you will. Just perform it like you did for us. You'll have Calypso and the others falling at your feet."

She'd blown us all away during rehearsals—that song, so haunting and raw, and delivered with Georgie's yelping huskiness. It put my own upbeat ode to friendship to shame.

"How about you?" Gareth nudges Zephan. "Ready to show 'em what you're made of?"

"Nope." His body hunches in on itself, as if he's hoping to disappear.

"Aw, hun, you'll be fantastic. You have more gravel than bloody Steven Tyler. Oh, that's me." Gareth's phone pings, and we all slow while he retrieves it.

I lean in to peer at the screen. "Who's texting?"

"Get out of it, Miss Nosy. It's Art."

"And?"

"He wants to talk, asked me to meet him by the fountain." A light glimmers in Gareth's eyes, the faintest spark of hope. "Zeph, don't look at me like that. I have to hear him out."

Zephan crosses his arms, expression transmitting his disapproval.

"Good luck, guys." Gareth claps first Georgie on the back, then Zephan. "You'll do amazing."

Smile wide, he veers onto a dissecting path and hurries towards the centre of campus. It's obvious what he's thinking, that Art's texted him to patch things up. Poor Gaz. He needs to know, but still. I watch him go, wishing I could spare him this pain.

55. GEORGIE

How come, when you wish time would dig in its heels, it sprints ahead like bloody Usain Bolt?

Since Zeph's audition is right before mine, Mina suggests we all walk over together.

"Don't need a damned entourage," he grumbles.

We ignore him, first swinging by the house so me and Zeph can grab our instruments. With some gentle prodding, I coax Star out of bed. I need her for moral support.

My fingers fumble with the harness. For a moment, I rest my cheek against Star's soft neck, head spinning. I can't do this. I can't.

As if it's been lying in wait, my nightmare of last night ambushes me. I stood before the judges, alone on that famous stage, ready to give it my all. My lips parted, fingers forming the opening chord, and…nothing. The concert hall echoed with a horrible silence.

Then the jeering started.

Oh, God. I bury my face in Star's fur and she nuzzles my ear. I'm going to screw up. I'm going to screw up in front of Calypso and Leticia and all the other industry greats and destroy any hope I have of coming to Dukes.

I don't realise Mina's there until she rests a palm on my back. "Hey, you're OK."

"I can't do this."

"You can. Slow, deep breaths."

I try. In...out. In...out. It's so hard, like there's a slab of concrete crushing my chest. In...out. In...out. Mina traces soothing patterns along my spine, talking quietly. Gradually, my breathing steadies and I'm calm enough to re-join Zephan.

Mina stays close the whole way to the Dukes Building. Outside, we sit on the bench to wait while Zephan goes in.

"Good luck," Mina calls after him.

"Yeah," I add, "break a finger, or whatever the musical equivalent is."

Zephan chokes out a laugh before the door bangs shut behind him. Once he comes out again, it'll be my turn. I'm not ready. Nowhere near. I draw my feet onto the bench and strangle my knees. If I keep perfectly still, maybe time will just...stop.

Mina keeps up a flow of chatter, a blatant effort to distract me. She tells me about her sister's crippling nerves before a major swimming competition, her black mood that would darken the house for a week if she didn't perform to her own high standards.

I half listen, my brain scrabbling for the lyrics to 'Girl Like You'. What the hell is the first line? *For Christ's sake, you can't've forgotten. You've sung it a hundred times over the past couple of days. Shit, shit, shit.*

The main door clunks and trainers plod towards us. Oh, no. He's finished already.

"How did it go?" Mina asks.

"We'll see," Zephan grunts. He thuds onto the bench and prods me in the ribs. "You're up."

I stumble to my feet. My legs shake so much I'm sure they'll collapse beneath me. How does anyone do this? How do artists find the guts time and time again to go out on stage and perform for hundreds—sometimes thousands—of strangers? It'll be a miracle if I take a step without faceplanting into the concrete.

"I'll walk you in," Mina says.

I loop the strap of my guitar case over my shoulder. Somehow, with one arm through Mina's and the other hand gripping Star's harness, I make it to the main entrance without tripping.

"Break a finger," Zephan calls.

The foyer is cool after the August heat. All the same, sweat slicks my forehead and armpits. At the doors to the concert hall, Mina wraps me in a tight hug. It's awkward, what with the bulk of my instrument and us getting tangled up in Star's lead. Still, I melt against her, inhale her lemon meringue scent.

Mina's lips brush my ear. "Go be amazing. I'll wait for you outside."

I can't speak. Not with my heart trying to force its way up my windpipe. I simply nod and grip Star's harness. *Come on, George, you can do this.* Hand trembling, I knock on the double doors and step inside.

"Georgie." Leticia Dukes' rich voice greets me. "Lovely to see you. How're you doing?"

"Um…OK, thanks." My tongue snags on the words. It must be obvious to everyone that whatever I'm feeling, OK isn't it.

Calypso bounds towards me. "No need to look so terrified. We're all fans here. Hey, Star, fancy being an honorary judge?"

No, don't take her away. She's my mascot, my lucky charm. Biting my lip, I hand the lead to Calypso and she escorts Star over to the other judges. Then she's back, guiding me up the steps onto the stage.

"Sit or stand?" she asks.

"Sit." If I don't take the strain off my legs, I'll end up in a blob of jelly on the wooden boards.

Calypso shows me to a chair and re-joins her fellow judges. Suddenly, this is real. I'm here, on the very stage where Sarel once performed. Somewhere below is the audience who have the power to change my future.

"So, what're you going to play for us?" Leticia's words float up to me.

"I, uh…" My throat rasps and I cough to clear it. "I'm going to sing an original song."

"Fabulous. We can't wait to hear it."

Right. No pressure.

I bend to unpack my Fender, fighting with the zip. My head swims worse than it did on Art's vodka. Guitar clutched to my body like a shield, I settle back in my chair. I do a quick tune-up, strum a few experimental chords. My fingers slip and judder on the strings. It's as if they belong to someone else. And I'm supposed to play an entire song?

"There's no rush," Leticia says. "Whenever you're ready."

Shit. I'm taking too long, holding them up when they have loads of auditions to get through. Unseen eyes weigh on me, their expectation like a too heavy-coat. Without giving myself a chance to prepare, I rush into the first chord sequence. A toddler couldn't've made such a racket. The clash of notes rings through the hall, harsh and discordant.

"I'm so sorry." How humiliating. My body floods with red-hot lava. I knew this would happen, knew I wouldn't be able to hack it. *God, let me die.* Tears scald my eyelids. *Don't you dare cry, Georgie Wilde.*

"It's fine," Calypso says. "Happens to the best of us. Just take a breather and start again."

I blink away the tears and straighten my spine. *You can do this. You know you can. Ignore the judges. Pretend you're in the practice room, performing for Mina and the others.*

I suck in air until my pulse slows. I'm ready. Positioning my fingers on the strings, I play the opening chord.

56. MINA

Is she OK? Georgie looked so petrified as she went in, face set, fingers clutching Star's harness as though it were the sole thing keeping her upright. I dither in the foyer, hand pressed to the double doors. The hum of voices vibrates against my palm, but I can't distinguish the words.

Faith burns like a prayer candle in my chest. Georgie will be fine. With that talent, that song, how can she not be? Still, it requires all my self-control to resist bursting into the concert hall and giving her one last hug.

I tear myself away and wander back outside. In my absence, Gareth has joined Zephan on the bench. He's talking quietly, wiping a forearm across his eyes, Zephan listening with a rare softness to his expression.

Protectiveness spurs me towards them. "What's happened? Gaz, what's wrong?"

"I'll leave you to it." Zephan stands, moving as if to rest a hand on Gareth's shoulder. He settles for a wave, then turns to walk across campus.

Gareth stares after him. "Nice guy. Once you get past the grouchiness."

"He is." I sit beside him, leaning my shoulder into his. "You OK?"

"Kind of. Not really. Art told me all this stuff. It's messed up." Gareth shakes his head, running a hand through his hair.

Haltingly, he relays everything Art told me the other night, fresh tears spilling from beneath his lashes. "He showed me his back. It's why he always kept the lights off. Didn't want me to see."

"That's…" I falter, searching for a sufficiently strong adjective. Best not to let on that I've heard it all before. It might upset him, discovering Art confided in me first, and Gaz has been hurt too much already. "His dad's a monster. He needs to be locked up."

"That's what I said, but apparently, he's this respected figure in the community. Art doesn't think anyone would believe him, like."

"So that's why he broke up with you? He's worried about his dad finding out?"

Gareth nods. "Wish he'd been honest with me from the start, made it clear this could only be a summer thing, but I get it."

"I'm sorry." I squeeze him in a half hug. "For what it's worth, I think he really likes you. If things were different—"

"Yeah." Gareth drapes an arm over my shoulders, his lips wobbling into the saddest smile I've ever seen. "And it helps to know it wasn't anything I did."

We fall quiet, staring out across the jigsaw puzzle of lawn and tree-lined paths. *Thank you, Art Dabrowski, with all my heart.* It may take Gaz time to heal from his first foray into love, but at least he knows its failure wasn't his fault.

"I completely bombed," Georgie says in the practice room a while later. She's hunched over, head buried in her drawn-up knees.

It's horrible seeing her like this, so dejected. I edge my chair closer and rub her back. "I'm sure it wasn't that bad."

"It was. All that rehearsal and I screwed up the opening chords. Total disaster."

"Aw, don't sweat it, hun." Gareth twists on the piano bench to face us. "You were nervous, like. Bet the judges see it all the time. Hope so, anyway, because I'll be a jibbering wreck tomorrow."

"Better a jibbering wreck than a cocky arsehole," Zephan mutters, and behind the drum kit, Art flinches.

Georgie straightens with a shaky laugh and brushes the tangle of hair out of her eyes. "You really think I still have a chance?"

"Of course," I say, and I mean it. "The judges would've thought it was weird if you weren't nervous. They'll take that into account."

Her features relax. I slide my arm around her, pulling her into me, and she rests her cheek against the bare skin of my shoulder. In the brief silence, my gaze connects with Gareth's and his expression mirrors my anxiety. Like me, he'll be tracking the time between now and tomorrow afternoon when it will be our turn.

For a few shining moments, I picture myself standing on that stage, fingers flying over the strings of my banjo while my voice bounces off the high ceiling in a cascade of shimmering notes. After I've left, the judges will turn to each other in wonder. "*That's the one,*" they'll say. "*That's our winner.*"

Art's voice, unusually tentative, breaks into the quiet. "Do you think maybe we should decide on our piece for the group audition?"

I blink and the golden fantasy bursts in a shower of glitter. I'm getting ahead of myself. There'll be plenty of time for daydreaming once the auditions are over, but now we have work to do, hours of rehearsal to catch up on.

"Right, yeah." Gareth glances at Art and then away again, blushing. He swings back to the piano and plays a confetti of notes. "What's everyone thinking?"

Georgie sits up, bending to unzip her guitar case. "Not sure. Should we attempt something new or stick to one of the tracks we've already learned?"

"Well," Art ventures, "I know I said the song we did the second week was more original, but Calypso really liked the first one."

It's true, but things were different then, no bruised feelings or complicated dynamics. We'd been embarking on something new, exciting, and the summer stretched ahead, brilliant with possibility.

Aloud, all I say is, "I could go for that idea, if everyone else is OK with it."

Georgie and Gareth both nod. Zephan merely shrugs, but he stoops to unpack his bass, which Art clearly takes as agreement. He leaps into action, sticks twirling with some of his old energy.

"Righty then," he says, eyes flashing. "Let's do this."

57. GEORGIE

"How did it go?" Dad asks when I call home that evening. He sounds so excited, so sure I have good news for him.

Seated cross-legged on my bed, I pick at a loose thread on my shorts. How can I tell him the truth? He has such high hopes for me, wants so much for me to have the career Uncle Sean's death snatched from him. I can't admit I crumbled at the first hurdle. It would crush him.

"It went all right," I say instead. "I think the judges liked the song."

"'Course they did. Bet you dazzled them."

A lump sticks in my throat. I've let him down. Somehow that's harder to bear than my own disappointment.

I swallow. "Thanks, Dad. Is Jake there?"

"Sure, sure. Just let me know as soon as you hear the results. Not that you have anything to worry about. I have a good feeling about this."

We say goodbye, and I drum my fingers on my thigh, waiting. As soon as Jake comes on the line, I say, "Can you go somewhere Dad can't hear?"

"I'm going upstairs now." The murmur of the telly recedes, replaced by my brother's heavy footfalls. A door closes. "OK, I'm in my room. Everything OK?"

"Not really. I couldn't tell Dad, but I sort of botched the audition."

"Botched it how?"

With a sigh, I flop onto my pillow and recount how my nerves got the better of me. Reliving it, my body flushes with fresh humiliation. Man, this will haunt me for the rest of my life.

When I've finished, Jake says, "I honestly wouldn't worry about it. You're hardly the first person to have a wobble on stage."

"That's what my friends said."

"There you are then. And you played the song fine the second time, right?"

"I s'pose." There had been no missed chords on my next attempt, no forgotten lyrics. All the same, the pressure had got to me. I wasn't at my best, and to win the scholarship, only the best would do.

THE FOLLOWING AFTERNOON, we're back on our bench outside the Dukes Building. Any minute, Gareth will come out and bring Mina's turn that bit closer. Kai's a short way off, surrounded by well-wishers. Their encouragement and back slaps drift across to us.

"I can't sit still." Mina shifts beside me, her leg jiggling against mine. "I'd be fine if the judges were expecting me to dance for them."

"Trust me, no one wants to see that." I nudge her, grinning.

Mina laughs. For all her fidgeting, she seems more psyched than scared, eager to get out there and perform. Doubts swim about inside me. Maybe that's how it's meant to be, all keyed-up anticipation. Maybe my attack of nerves yesterday proves I'm not cut out for this, that I'm deluding myself.

"Ooh, here he comes." Mina's excitement hauls me from my thoughts. She half stands, waving. "Gaz, how did it go?"

Gareth flops on my other side. He's shaking so much the bench quakes. Over by the main doors, the group wishes Kai good luck with a slew of audible high-fives.

"Glad that's done." Air puffs from Gareth in a rush.

Mina leans across me, seizing his arm. "But how did it go?"

"Well, I got through it without regurgitating my paella. That has to count for something, right?" Gareth laughs. He sounds relieved, giddy, lightyears away from how I felt after my audition.

The two of them chat across me, Mina insisting on a blow-by-blow account. I scarcely hear them. Before facing the judges, Gareth had been a wreck. He spent half the morning crouched over the toilet, could hardly speak for trembling. If even he can get through a live performance without making a hash of it, maybe I really don't have what it takes.

The door to the Dukes Building thuds open and Kai reappears to a tumult of whoops.

"I'm up." Mina's on her feet at once, reaching down to clasp my hand. "Come with me?"

Gareth stands to give her a hug. Then, as she did for me yesterday, I walk Mina into the foyer.

Outside the concert hall, I squeeze her fingers. "Good luck. You'll be awesome."

"I hope so." One last shuddering breath and Mina's gone, the double doors thumping shut behind her.

Left alone, I rest my cheek against the doorframe. I should probably go. Mina might not like me eavesdropping. Not that I can hear much. Whatever's going on, it's too muffled to make out.

Until the music starts.

First there's only the banjo. Though it's muted, the waterfall of notes is as sharp and bubbling as old-fashioned lemonade. Joyful. That's the word for it. I'm smiling before I even realise I'm doing it. God, she's amazing. I listen, transfixed. Couldn't tear myself away if I wanted to.

When Mina's vocal joins in, it's utterly bloody stunning. My chest constricts. I've never been prouder of anyone in my life. I honestly couldn't feel more proud if it were me up there, being incredible, blowing the judges' minds. At the same time, I've never been so sure of my own shortcomings.

58. MINA

I'M SOARING.

It's as though my body has taken control, fingers flying over the strings of their own volition, lyrics pouring from me in a heady torrent. I'd been anxious as I climbed the steps to the stage, reliving all those moments during rehearsals when I'd plucked a wrong note or a phrase darted out of reach. The instant I started playing, though, my worries were swept away. This is what I was born to do.

The final chord fades and my senses return to find all four judges on their feet, giving me a standing ovation.

"Bravo, Mina," Leticia calls. Beside her, Calypso beams and offers me a thumbs up. "A truly wonderful performance. Congratulations."

"Thank you for the opportunity." After the way my vocals had filled the large space, my words sound insubstantial. I stow away my banjo and float from the concert hall on a carpet of marshmallow.

Georgie's waiting for me in the foyer, leaning against a pillar. I crush the impulse to run to her, to seize her hands and swing her in circles. She's been so downcast, the last thing I want is to rub her nose in it.

As soon as the doors thud behind me, a smile illuminates Georgie's face. "You were... I mean, how did it go?"

"Georgie Wilde." I advance on her, eyebrow raised. "Were you eavesdropping on me?"

Her grin turns sheepish. "Maybe. Just a bit. Couldn't resist."

I laugh and give her my arm. At the main doors, we almost collide with Himari.

"Good luck," I tell her. Not that she appears to need it. Compared with the jitters I've observed from most of my campmates, Himari is the epitome of composure. She might be on her way to buy a pint of milk.

She acknowledges us with a wave and we wander out into the afternoon warmth. In my post-performance buzz, everything seems painted in vibrant colour—the sun brighter, the grass more green, the sky a deeper shade of blue.

Gareth leaps up from the bench and hurries over. "How was it?"

"OK, I think." I bite my lip against the huge smile trying to break free. "The judges seemed to enjoy it, at least."

Georgie scoffs. "She's being modest. She was bloody brilliant."

"That's my girl." Gareth punches me on the shoulder. "Knew you'd smash it."

Now there's no stopping the smile. Their praise fills me up like sherbet, the tingle spreading to the tips of my toes. It makes me want to turn cartwheels on the lawn until I'm too dizzy to stand.

"I fancy a swim. How about you guys?"

"Sure," Georgie says at once.

Gareth shakes his head, though. "Not me. Think I'll see what Zeph's up to."

THE WATER LAPS against my skin, cool and delicious, soothing the tautness from my muscles. Campers splash one another and organise races, but the area around us is calm, so that we drift alone in our own private sea.

I rest my folded arms on the inflatable doughnut and gaze across it at Georgie. Gosh, she's beautiful, the bronzed curve of her shoulders visible above the surface, damp curls pasted to her cheeks.

"You OK?" she asks. "You're kind of quiet."

Oh, I'm fine. Just thinking how much I'd love to kiss you right now, but I can't because I'm not that brave yet and I have this ridiculous idea that someone here will see us and report back to my parents before I have a chance to tell them I'm gay.

Rather than attempt to explain any of this, I extend my feet under the water to find Georgie's. Our legs entangle and the silky warmth of her skin against mine sends pleasure zinging up the insides of my thighs.

"Yeah, I'm OK." I trail a toe along Georgie's calf. One day, when this isn't so scary and new, I'll feel able to kiss Georgie and not care who sees. At least, I hope I will. For now, though, this is enough.

59. GEORGIE

HERE WE GO again.

On Thursday afternoon, the members of Wildest Dreams head across campus for our group audition. I adjust the strap of my guitar case, which the heat has glued to my skin. My stomach roils. Not sure I can face another humiliation.

"So, our last chance to impress," Art says. "How's everyone doing?"

Gareth utters a strangled sound. He's walking on my right, as far away from Art as he can get. They might be speaking again, but there's this reserve between them.

I shrug. "At least we get another shot. My first performance wouldn't've impressed a class of five-year-olds."

"Oh, shush." Mina bumps my hip. "Only positive vibes allowed today."

"You're being very mysterious, Zeph." Art says. "You haven't told us a thing about your audition."

"What's the point? It's done now. Nothing I can do about it." He stomps ahead, putting some space between himself and Art. Seems Zephan Oduro doesn't forgive easily.

We walk the rest of the way in silence. Poor Art. It's kind of sweet, how Zeph's so angry on Gaz's behalf. Still, he should cut Art some slack. Sure, what he did was wrong, but there was no malice in it.

As we near the Dukes Building, the main doors fly open. Excited chatter spills out. Chanelle and her posse. The girls take no notice of us; they're too busy giggling and talking over each other. Their audition must've gone well.

"Just look at them," Mina sighs once they're out of earshot. "They're so…relevant. Then there's me with my country music and patterned dresses. How can I compete?"

I give her a gentle shake. "Hey, Miss Standing Ovation. Only positive vibes allowed, remember?"

Mina laughs. She squeezes me tight for a moment, body soft and warm against mine.

In the foyer, Art pushes himself between Mina and me, flinging an arm around each of our shoulders. "Group hug!"

"Over my rotting remains." Zephan couldn't have sounded more horrified if Art had suggested he do a striptease for the judges. "I'm serious."

"Aw, hun, it's only us," Gareth says.

Zephan shifts, trainers squeaking on the wooden floor. His brain must be whirring, seeking a way out.

"Fine," he snaps. "Let's get this over with."

We converge in a huddle, shoulders knocking, holding on to one another. Nerves and anticipation quiver around the circle. There's no getting away from it. We aren't the seamless whole we were a couple of weeks ago. You can trace the cracks, like a mug that's been smashed and stuck back together. We're in one piece, though, and that's enough.

"Well, here goes nothing," Art says when we break apart. Then he pushes open the doors to the concert hall.

THE HIGH FROM our group audition lasts into the evening.

Mina nuzzles into me with a sigh. We're pretzeled on my bed, The Cranberries spilling from my Bluetooth speakers. I draw her closer. She's so slight in my arms, so soft. My whole body hums with her nearness and the echo of my earlier adrenalin.

Wildest Dreams really came together this afternoon. Not that the anger and bruised feelings have magically gone away. We just left it all outside the concert hall and focused on what needed to be done. The result? Our tightest performance of the summer.

There's nothing else I can do. No more rehearsals, no more chances to convince the judges. God, all that pressure, the pressure I put on myself. Without that weighing on me, I feel tons lighter.

Mina traces my lips with a finger. "You look happy. Are you?"

"Yeah." I shiver at her touch. "I'm also wondering…"

"What's that?"

"Well, the other day in my audition, I was…man, I was a hot mess. I'm amazed I managed to perform at all. Today, though… I was still nervous, but nowhere near as bad. I really enjoyed it, playing with you guys."

"So you're thinking…what? That you'd like to be in a band? Like your dad?"

I hadn't thought of it like that, but she's right. I would be following in Dad's footsteps. Makes sense. Sure, he's an incredible guitarist and a decent songwriter, but Uncle Sean was the star of the Wilde Landers. Dad would be the first to admit he'd never have made it solo, however hard he dreamed.

I nod. "It's just an idea, but maybe I'm more suited to being part of a band."

"Or maybe you need to build up your confidence. That was the first time you've ever performed in front of anyone other than your family. Maybe you just need practice."

"Yeah, maybe."

"You have plenty of time to figure it out." Mina tucks a curl behind my ear, fingertips grazing my cheek. "We all do."

Next September, when we return to Dukes for real. The silent hope floats between us, delicate as a soap bubble. It would be so easy to pop it. There's no guarantee any of us will be coming back the following year, least of all me.

Instead, I cup the nape of Mina's neck and kiss her.

Her mouth parts. She tastes sweet, like the strawberries and ice cream we had for pudding. Lips…tongues…exploring hands… My world shrinks until nothing exists but her. God, I never knew it could be like this, like a new kind of music. Our bodies fuse, move in harmony, creating something miraculous and all our own.

60. MINA

"I'M GOING TO throw up." Gareth moans as the two of us make our way to Calypso's final workshop.

"Me, too." I press a palm to my belly. In the hope that it would give me courage, I'm wearing one of my favourite dresses, cream with a pattern of butterflies. Now, it's as if the butterflies have come to life and are flapping up a storm inside me.

Campers mill about, many with their arms around each other, although no one appears as nervous as Gareth, who's greener than the Incredible Hulk.

"Promise me something," he says. "If I throw up in Calypso's session, just kill me on the spot."

I laugh and take his hand. "You'll be fine, and whatever happens later, remember you're still amazing."

"Cheers, hun." He squeezes my fingers, managing a wan smile. "So are you. Don't you sort of wish, though, that we could just stay like this forever? In this moment, I mean, not knowing whether we've won or not."

"Totally," I say, although I'm no longer thinking about the scholarship. Just imagine it, the summer stretching brilliant and endless ahead, day after sun-gilded day to spend with Georgie, discovering everything there is to know about this incredible girl who has spun my world into an entirely new orbit.

And there she is, standing with Star and Zephan outside the Dukes Building, waiting for me. My heart performs a joyful somersault at the sight of her, and I rush to join them.

"Hey, you." I lay a hand on Georgie's back, her skin warm through the fabric of her Oasis T-shirt. "How're you feeling?"

"Absolutely bloody terrified. You?"

"Same. How about you, Zeph?"

"You know me." The corner of his mouth lifts in an ironic smirk. "Cooler than a penguin's butt crack."

Laughing, the four of us and Star head inside and across the foyer. Like I don't have enough reasons to be happy, as we enter the reception room, 'This Flower' by Kasey Chambers is pouring from the speakers.

"I love this song." I beam, drawing Georgie onto our usual cushions.

She frees Star from her harness, tilting her head to one side the way she does when she's listening. "Great voice, but the lyrics are a bit soppy."

"Says the girl who spends her life reading teen romances."

Georgie sticks her tongue out at me and we crease up, holding on to one another. Her breath tickles my neck and it's all I can do not to kiss her right here in front of everyone.

Gareth raises his eyebrows at Zephan. "Nice to know our friends are so mature."

"Hey, they're all yours. Nothing to do with me," Zephan says, only making us giggle harder.

"OK, guys." Calypso walks in with an armload of paper and pens, which she begins passing among us. "Since this is our last session, I thought we'd do something fun. If you'd like to sort yourselves into teams, I've organised a little music quiz."

Her announcement sparks the inevitable mix of grumbling and cheers. All across the room, our fellow campers rearrange themselves into huddles, while the four of us shift our cushions into a horseshoe so we can confer more easily.

A few groups over, Patrice raises her hand. "Do you know when we're likely to get our results?"

At once, the noise level sinks several decibels and the air quivers with expectancy. Calypso nears our corner, handing me a pen and a sheet of paper on her way past.

"I can't give you an exact time, I'm afraid," she says. "The other judges and I will be getting together to discuss the auditions after morning break and there's no telling how long the meeting will go on. To judge by past years, though, I wouldn't look for an email until mid-afternoon at the earliest."

A collective groan travels through the assembly, and several people, Gareth among them, drop their heads in their hands. Gosh, as long as that? If I survive till evening with my sanity intact, it will be a miracle.

61. GEORGIE

THE MORNING DRIFTS by like I'm in someone else's dream. At lunch, the atmosphere in the dining room is more posh restaurant than summer camp. The chatter's muted, any laughter quickly snuffed out. The four of us don't talk much. In a daze, I fork up mouthfuls of what the menu called salmon fishcakes. For all the notice I take, they could be made of woodchip.

Afterwards, Mina and I go for a walk, just for something to do. The air hangs sluggish and thick, the sun bouncing off the path in physical waves. At least the trees offer pools of shade.

"Still nothing." Mina has her phone out, keeping a constant eye on her emails. "You?"

I fish out my mobile and swipe through the messages— Audible, Apple, some spam promising to enlarge my manhood. "Nothing."

When the heat becomes too much, we collapse in the shadow of a beech, the fountain splashing nearby. We lie side by side in the grass, fingers entwined. Mina tells me about her niece, Aaliyah, her sister's unplanned but adored baby girl. I tell her about growing up around the record store, playing hide-and-seek amidst the shelves. And every few minutes, we check for messages.

"Should we wait, do you think?" Mina asks. "If one of us gets an email first, I mean. Then we can read them together."

Shit. The moment I've been putting off. What if I hurt Mina's feelings? I could just agree. It's not like I've been shy about sharing stuff with her up to now. My dreams and insecurities, grudges and favourite jokes. This girl knows more about me—the real me—than anyone alive. I could learn my fate with Mina right there beside me. She'd see every emotion play out over my treacherous face. My insides shrivel. I can't do it.

"Unless…" Mina's tone falters. "Unless you'd rather be alone."

"Would that be OK?"

"Of course, silly girl. I totally get it. Shall we wander back to our rooms? It can't be much longer."

Mina's upset. She's pretending not to mind, but I can hear the cracks in her words. As we take the twisting path to Osborne House, I scour my brain for something to say. Can I backtrack, tell her we should definitely find out our results together? Would it really be that big a deal?

Yes.

This is too huge, too personal. I have to be by myself. Good news or bad, I'll need time to absorb it, come to terms. Mina will understand. *God, please let her understand.*

So, I say nothing until we're in the lobby. There, I take her hand and squeeze. "Good luck."

"You, too." She holds on for a long moment, then releases me. "See you in a while?"

"'Course. I'll keep everything crossed for you."

I head through the swing door and along the hall to my room. I'm digging out my key when someone enters the flat behind me.

"Hi, Georgie." Chanelle sounds less sure of herself than usual, more subdued.

Damn her. I touch the phone in my pocket. It's like the email from Dukes is singeing a hole in the denim. On the plus side, talking to Chanelle will let me cling to the hope a bit longer, and at least she actually got my name right.

Chanelle leans against the wall opposite. "Got your results yet?"

"Not yet. You?"

"Yeah, the whole of my band just found out. None of us got it."

"Ah, hard luck." I mean it. If someone had predicted on the first night of camp that I'd wind up feeling sorry for Chanelle Clarke, I'd have told them to get a brain transplant. Still, crazy as it seems, I do.

"Thanks, Georgie," Chanelle says. "The rest of the girls are having a meltdown, so I thought I'd chill in my room for a bit."

I nod. No surprise there, Blair and co falling to pieces. If anything, I would've imagined Chanelle wailing right along with them. Those girls have always seemed so self-assured, like they each knew they were destined to come out on top. Deep down, I think we all thought one of them would win.

"Listen." Chanelle halts, then goes on. "I've been meaning to talk to you about…about what you said."

I duck my head, fiddling with the key ring. "It's fine. Don't worry about it."

"I am worried, though. I've been worrying about it for days. When I realised you'd heard…well, we should never have said those things in the first place, but knowing you were there… That must've been so hurtful."

I shrug. What can I say? Not like I'm going to let her off the hook. Because of a few careless words, I considered giving up this entire summer. I could've missed out on it all—my first real friendships, being with Mina.

"I'm so ashamed," Chanelle says, her voice more sandpaper than chocolate. "I was ignorant and stupid and...well, I was a selfish cow, basically. I'd slice out my own tongue and give it to you on a necklace if it would convince you how much I regret it."

Laughter snorts from my nose. "Thanks, but no thanks. I believe you."

She laughs, too. It's a nice moment, the kind I never would've dreamt of sharing with Chanelle.

"I'll leave you to it," she says, "so you can check your emails. Good luck, Georgie."

Chanelle continues along the hall, and I let myself into my room. Star thumps her tail but doesn't bother getting out of bed. I haul in a deep breath. No point putting it off. Not knowing won't change the outcome. I curl up on the floor beside Star, drawing courage from her drowsy warmth, and pull out my phone.

62. MINA

I SIT ON MY bed, phone in hand, finger hovering over the email from Dukes. A single tap and my hopes will either be realised or lie in tatters at my feet. Somehow, I can't bring myself to do it.

From along the hallway comes the sound of sobbing. It's clearly bad news for at least one of my flatmates. Georgie's voice floats into my mind, pragmatic with a twist of irony. *"One competitor down, fifty-eight to go."*

Gosh, I wish she were here, steadying my nerves with her presence. Of course, I completely understand her need to be alone when she reads her results. It's a life-altering moment, finding out whether your dreams have come true, and sometimes you don't want to share your first reactions with the world. All the same, I could have done with her to hold my hand.

I switch to my messages, but there's still nothing from Gaz. I'd texted him on the way to my room, asking if he wanted to read our results together, and it's unusual for him not to respond. Either he, too, would rather be alone, or he's mired too deep in disappointment to climb out. I need to be there, to comfort him if it's bad news.

Before that, though... *Come on, Mina, time to put on your big girl pants and discover your fate.* I grasp my courage by the neck and open the email.

Dear Mina,

First, I'd like to thank you for participating in our summer music programme. In the years since I set up the academy, having the opportunity to develop and nurture young talent such as yours has given me endless pleasure.

As you know, each year Dukes offers a scholarship to one musician we feel would particularly benefit from a fully funded place on our course. I must tell you that your audition left both my fellow judges and myself deeply impressed. We found your country style modern and refreshing, and I'd be delighted to welcome you to Dukes next September should you choose…

Sweat slicks my palms and I barely prevent the phone from sliding from my grasp onto the carpet. Dukes would be delighted to welcome me. The judges were deeply impressed. Pulse cantering, I continue to read.

…should you choose to apply. However, it's with regret that I have to inform you that we're unable to award you the scholarship. Please accept my assurances that this in no way…

The words blur and fracture before my eyes. Phrases jump out at me — *high level of competition…no reflection on your talent…mustn't be discouraged* — but they scarcely register. I haven't won. All that dreaming, the planning and praying and practising until my fingertips were raw, it's all come to nothing.

I drop the phone and hug my legs to my body, cheek resting on my thigh. What now? Do I give up, resign myself to following my parents into medicine? That had been the deal, after all, the deal I'd struck with myself. My future opens in front of me, dizzying and infinite, a steady slog of studying, patient appointments and medical conferences. A fulfilling life, perhaps, a good life, but all so safe and predictable.

No.

My spine straightens. I can't abandon my dream without a fight. Persuading my parents won't be easy, but if there's one lesson this summer has taught me, it's that I have to pursue my music, that I'll never be happy unless I try.

Of course, not everyone has the luxury of a comfortably off family. For them, losing out on the scholarship will feel like the end of everything. I check there's still no word from Gareth, then go in search of him.

Normally, the hallways echo with activity—mingled voices, doors banging, distant snippets of music. Yet, as I climb the stairs, an eerie hush cloaks the house.

There's no response when I tap on Gareth's door. I press my ear to it, listening, but nothing stirs inside.

"Gaz?" I call. "It's me."

No answer. Could he be with Zephan? Those two have become pretty friendly this past week. But, no, he wouldn't share his results with anyone before me…would he? Then again, I've been caught up in Georgie these past days, so perhaps Gareth's felt neglected. Brushing my hurt aside, I return downstairs.

Georgie's in the kitchen, emptying dry food into Star's bowl. Zephan's leaning against the worktop nearby, but there's no sign of Gareth.

"Hey." I glance between them, trying to read their expressions. "What did…? Have you heard anything?"

Georgie turns on the cold tap to add a splash of water to the dog food before setting the bowl on the floor. Star falls on her dinner and begins gobbling it up as though it's the first meal she's seen in days.

"It was a no," Georgie says, while Zephan shakes his head once.

"Oh." I cross the kitchen, taking her hands in mine. "I'm so sorry. Me, too."

"Well, we always knew it was a long shot, right?" Georgie squeezes my fingers, her touch conveying more sympathy than words ever could. She flashes me a lopsided smile, putting a brave face on her disappointment.

"Have either of you seen Gaz?" I ask. "He's not in his room and isn't answering my texts."

"Nope, and he hasn't texted me back either." Zephan pulls out his phone, checking the screen.

Sugar. If Gareth received the same email as the rest of us, there's no telling what state he'll be in. He might be huddled in some secluded corner of campus, alone and grieving, struggling to reconcile himself to a future without Dukes.

Georgie's thumb traces soothing circles on my palm. "Maybe he's gone over to the barbecue. Let me take Star out to the loo, then we'll go and find him."

Five minutes later, with Star snuggled in her bed for a post-dinner nap, Georgie, Zephan and I wander across to the area outside the dining room. The atmosphere is quieter than usual, campers talking in small groups on the lawn or at the picnic tables, others forming an orderly line for the barbecue. I scan the gathering, seeking a glimpse of fiery hair, but Gareth's nowhere to be seen.

63. GEORGIE

THE BARBY HAS a weird, end-to-the-holidays kind of vibe. Mina and I are seated cross-legged on the grass, apart from the crowd. I twirl the kebab skewer between my fingers. An emptiness gapes in my stomach, but it's not the sort food can fill.

"How're you feeling?" Mina plays with her fork, metal chinking against china.

I chew on my lip. How do I feel? There's a definite post-Christmas lull, but I'm relieved, too, like when you step into the sunshine after your final exam. "Not as bad as I expected."

"Same. I thought, if I didn't win, it would be the end of the world, and yet—"

"Here we are, and the world hasn't exploded."

We fall quiet. Neither of us needs to put the jumble of emotions into words. I'm gutted; no way around it. All the same, it isn't the crushing thing I thought it would be.

"Wonder who it is," Mina says. "No one seems to be celebrating."

I shrug. If I had to bet, I'd put my money on Art. With his confidence and lightning-fast drumming, he would've knocked the judges dead.

"Still nothing from Gaz?" I ask. Soon as we arrived at the barby, Zephan had grabbed a burger and gone to track Gareth down. That was half an hour ago.

"No, nothing." Worry coats Mina's words. "I hope he's OK. If it's bad news, he shouldn't have to deal with it on his own."

"Maybe it isn't bad news."

"Then he needs to get himself over here so we can celebrate. Are you eating that?"

I drop the skewer. "Not really."

"Come on then." Mina scrambles to her feet. "Let's go and find him."

Once we've scraped our untouched food into the bin, we dump our dirty plates and stroll arm in arm through campus.

Hard to believe the summer's almost over. No more snaking walks or dipping our fingers in the cool water of the lily pond. No more afternoon practice sessions or lounging on cushions by the pool. No more time to spend with Mina—kissing, talking, being in love. Man, I'll miss this.

"There he is," Mina says. "Zeph's with him."

She tugs on my arm. We break into a run, shoes pounding the concrete. By the time we skid to a stop, we're both out of breath.

Mina releases me to brush the hair from her face. "Gaz, where have you been?"

"Hey." He sounds like someone's dragged him from a deep sleep. "Zeph said you were looking for me."

"Well, of course we were. I was really worried when we couldn't find you."

"Sorry, hun. I didn't mean to… Just needed to clear my head, like."

"I get it," Mina says. "We're all kind of reeling. You OK?"

Gareth expels what must be every atom of carbon dioxide from his body. "Yeah, I… I'm not sure how to… Christ, Zeph, you tell them."

"He won." Zephan's drawl carries an unmistakable note of pride. "He fucking did it."

My mouth drops open. What the...? Did he just say...? He didn't. But he did. I let out a whoop, punching the air.

"Oh my gosh!" Mina flings herself at Gareth. "You did it. You actually did it. Wow, I'm so, so happy for you I could cry."

"Keep it down. Everyone will hear." Gareth's tone veers between elation and embarrassment.

"Let them," I say. "They should know how awesome you are."

Gareth laughs. He grabs my hand in his large one and pulls me into their hug. Then the three of us are jumping up and down, holding on to each other and cackling like a pack of hyenas who've won the wildlife lottery.

If it couldn't be me or Mina, at least it's Gaz. The judges couldn't have picked a more worthy winner.

64. MINA

By the time dusk settles over campus, the expanse of lawn behind the study block and the rec building has been transformed into a beachside dance floor. Glass torches flicker and spark at the fringes, casting the inflatable palm trees in shifting shades of azure and turquoise. Campers sway and mingle on the grass, some bare foot, many with swimming costumes peeping from beneath dresses and T-shirts. A cluster has formed around the circular bar at its centre, slurping Slush Puppies through helter-skelter straws.

The entire glass wall of the pool house has been folded back, allowing the party to spill into the water. Beneath its surface, the florescent sea creatures glimmer through the twilight, splashing the skin of the swimmers in jewel-bright colour.

We're sprawled on one of the stripy towels laid out around the edge of the dance floor—Gareth, Zephan, Georgie and me. Star's seated like a queen in the centre, observing the writhing bodies with fascination. In contrast, Zephan has one of his Agatha Christies open on his lap. Given the aversion he's shown towards parties throughout the summer, it's a miracle Gaz persuaded him to join us at all.

"I feel kind of guilty," Gareth says.

"Why would you?" I ask. "You haven't done anything wrong."

"I dunno. It's like, everyone here is so incredible. You guys are so incredible. I can't help wondering…why me?" He fiddles with the hem of his shirt. Despite his words, his expression shines in the dimness.

My heart swells with pride and love until I'm afraid it might burst. There's regret there, too, a yearning in my soul. I'd so wanted it to be me, to prove to my parents that I can do this. Already, that brilliant future, the one where I swap textbooks and diagrams of the human body for the chance to study music, feels that much further away. Yet, I can't begrudge Gareth a single second of this triumph.

Zephan snorts into his book. "Because you're too bloody talented for your own good, maybe?"

"Aw, get out of it." Gareth blushes.

"It's true," I say. "You're an amazing pianist, you have the voice of an angel, can dance like Ashley Banjo…"

"You can swear in Welsh," Georgie adds, and Gareth and I collapse with giggles.

"Exactly," I say. "And you actually iron your own shirts without burning holes in them."

"Plus, you make a mean cup of tea."

"And your hugs are the best."

"Stop!" Gareth falls backwards on the towel, hands over his face. "Just…stop before my head explodes."

What with our laughter and the pounding music, none of us notice anyone approach until Star lumbers to her feet, tail wagging. Then he's right there, standing beside our group, thumbs hooked into the belt loops of his skinny jeans.

"Hey." Art smiles around at us, a cautious smile.

It's the first time we've seen him since our band audition. We murmur a muted hello, all apart from Zephan who has lowered his book and is glaring at Art as though he'd like to re-enact one of Christie's murders. Gareth stares up at Art from his supine position, his expression a heartbreaking mix of hope and sadness.

Art's smile dims. His eyes, earnest in the gathering dusk, find Gareth's. "I just heard. Well played, mate."

"Oh." Gareth sits up, arms wrapped around himself as if to hold his emotions inside.

"Knew it'd be you." Art's mouth quirks, all bravado gone. "I'm glad. You deserve it more than anyone."

Gareth's cheeks glow pink in the gloom. When he speaks, his voice is choked. "Thanks."

"I mean it." Art glances around at the rest of us, a united front flanking Gareth, and his posture sags. "Anyway, that's all I wanted to say. I'll leave you guys to it."

Gareth watches him walk away, graceful as a ballerina, narrow hips swaying. The longing in his expression makes me wish I could travel back in time. I'd persuade Gaz against going to the welcome party, think up something fun to do instead, just the two of us. Art would have set his sights on some other boy and my best friend wouldn't be hurting right now.

Zephan reaches over to tap Gareth's knee. "So, when do I get to witness this famous dancing?"

"Oh, God." Gareth turns to him, face relaxing. "Well, only if you show me some of your moves."

"Seriously. That's something no one wants to see."

"Ah, come on. You can't be worse than us. Can he?" Georgie nudges me and I agree, grinning.

Zephan arches an eyebrow. "Wanna bet?"

"You're on," I say. "Let's see what you can do."

"Oh, no, I'm not making an ass of myself until I know what I'm up against. Me and Star will watch. Right, Star?" Zephan extends a hand to her and she trots over, nestling into his side.

Gareth's already on his feet, gaze bright with the prospect of dancing. He smirks down at Zephan. "Fine, but don't think we'll let you off the hook."

Zephan merely waves us away.

"Ready to strut our stuff?" I ask Georgie.

She nods and interlaces her fingers with mine. I pull her up with me, the tingling warmth of her palm pressed to mine. Then we're following Gareth onto the dance floor, the three of us becoming submerged in the sea of music and twilight and undulating bodies.

65. GEORGIE

I LIE ON THE towel, head cushioned against Star's fur. Gareth's finally dragged Zephan onto the dance floor and Mina's gone to the bar. The night is a blur of sound, people splashing and shouting to one another while Damon Albarn sings about park life.

It's weird. I never would've thought I'd be this happy after losing out on the scholarship, my one surefire way back to Dukes, but I am. More than happy. I'm drunk. Drunk on dancing and laughing and being with Mina and our friends.

"Hey, Georgie," Calypso says above me. "And hey there, gorgeous girl."

"Hey." I beam, scrambling to sit up. Star, the humongous flirt, rolls over for a belly rub.

Calypso flops down beside me. "Having a good time?"

"Yeah, really good, thanks." 'Wonder Wall' is playing now, and I smile. "Loving the music."

"Still a staunch nineties fan, huh?"

"Always have been, always will be."

Calypso sighs. "I was sure at least one of you would see the error of their ways and realise the seventies is the only true path."

I laugh. Amazing to think how in awe of this young woman I was at the start of the programme. Well, I'm still in awe of her talent, but I've also come to know her as the funny, bubbly, kind person she is.

"I've been meaning to tell you," Calypso says. "Your audition the other day totally rocked."

"Thanks. Not sure I was at my best, honestly."

"You kidding? That was just nerves, completely understandable. I loved the hell out of that track."

I can't help it. My mouth stretches in a grin so wide it could swallow my guitar, case and all. For Calypso, the award-winning singer and composer, to compliment one of my original songs… it's everything.

"Dukes would be lucky to have you," she goes on, oblivious to the fact that I'm having an oh-my-God moment. "Hope you'll apply for next September."

"I definitely want to." Understatement of the millennium. Now I know Gaz will be coming, I want it even more. I doubt Zeph will have trouble convincing his musical family this is the place for him, either, and if Mina can persuade her parents… The future tugs at me, rich with friendship and kisses and new discoveries. If only I can argue my case with Mum…

Oasis melds into 'Head Over Feet' by Alanis Morissette. Man, I love this song. The lyrics match so exactly how I'm feeling, they could've been written for me.

This summer's been unexpected in the best possible ways. Making true friends in Zeph and Gaz, the sort of friends I've always dreamed of finding. Discovering how much I love playing as part of a band. Late-night chats and drinking games and laughing till my stomach hurts.

And Mina.

Never, even in my wildest fantasies, did I imagine meeting a girl like Mina. A girl who's sweet and smart and riddled with contradictions. A girl who genuinely seems to like me every bit as much as I like her.

Who knows? Given all the incredible things that've happened, maybe Mum will surprise me.

"So, you and Mina, huh?" Calypso teases.

Damn, my expression must've given me away again. My cheeks heat up and I duck my head.

Calypso nudges me. "Hey, I think it's adorable, and of course I have to take some of the credit."

"What?" I snort through my embarrassment. "You knew we'd get together?"

"Not exactly, but I was the one who suggested you guys team up, so that makes me indirectly responsible, right?"

The air grows chill against my skin. It freezes the words in my throat so that they crack like frost. "That… That was you?"

It isn't true. It can't be. Calypso's made a mistake. I told Mina everything. Perched on the wall of the lily pond that first day, I told her about Emma and Chanelle, and she said nothing. Nothing about asking me to join her band being someone else's idea. But she wouldn't have kept that from me. Not once I confided in her. She wouldn't.

"Well, sure." Calypso falters. "I mean, you didn't have a band yet, and Mina was a bit down. It seemed the obvious… Are you OK?"

I'm not OK. Not even close. With clumsy fingers, I reach for Star's harness and lurch to my feet. My legs shake under me. I shiver, my skin clammy like I'm coming down with a virus.

"Star, up stand." My voice sounds strange, thick and raspy.

"Georgie?" Calypso gets up, too, tone warm with concern.

"I'm all right." Can't stay here. Need to get away. I fumble Star into her harness and try to speak calmly. "Have a headache. Think I'll go back to the house."

"Oh, poor you. Should I find Mina?" Calypso asks.

"No!" It comes out harsher than I intend. I take a deep breath. "No, I...I don't want to ruin her night. Could you just let her know I've gone to bed and not to worry?"

"Of course. Sure you'll be OK?"

"Yeah. Yeah, I'll be fine."

I can't think straight. Mina could get back any second, and I don't want to be here when she does. Before Calypso can say anything else, I seize Star's harness and flee.

66. MINA

"No, no. Like this." Gareth's laughing so hard he can scarcely stand. Somehow, he manages to repeat the steps, moving with deliberate slowness so Zephan can follow.

On my way around the dance floor, a raspberry Slush Puppie in each hand, I can't resist pausing to watch.

Zephan rolls his eyes heavenward, then imitates Gareth's movements with all the grace of a waxwork come to life. Gareth doubles up, clutching his stomach. And I thought I was bad. I'm giggling so much, electric-blue liquid sloshes onto the grass. Zeph can't really be this awkward, can he? It must be an act to amuse Gaz. Either way, it's lovely to see my best friend laugh.

I leave the boys to it and thread my way back through the dancers—back to Georgie. We have so little time left. What with fretting about my auditions and the scholarship, I couldn't see beyond the results, but now it hits me. In forty-eight hours, Georgie will be a hundred miles away, an image on a computer screen, a voice on the end of the phone. I won't simply be able to reach out and touch her, to feel her warmth, smell the apple sweetness of her hair.

Well, there's no sense in missing Georgie while she's still here. Leaving on Sunday will be like tearing off a piece of myself, but we have the rest of this evening to enjoy and the whole of tomorrow. I'll need to rehearse for the concert, hopefully persuade Georgie to duet with me, and we'll have to make a start on our packing. In between all that, though, there'll be time for us—time to retreat to that private world of kisses and whispered promises.

I peer through the tangle of limbs and scan the towels spread out around the makeshift dance floor. We'd been sitting just over there, I could swear to it. Am I misremembering? Mum's always doing that, thinking she's put her car keys on the kitchen worktop, only to discover she's left them in her handbag. This isn't something I'm usually guilty of, but I must be. Georgie wouldn't have left without telling me.

Calypso waves to me through the crowd and I hurry towards her as fast as I can without spilling the drinks. "Calypso, hi. You haven't seen Georgie, have you?"

"Uh, yeah." She fiddles with a silver stud in her earlobe. "I was just with her. She said not to worry, but she had a headache and was going back to the house."

"Oh." The shimmering night I'd imagined—the two of us dancing and talking into the early hours—floats away like a helium balloon with its string cut.

Calypso bites her lip. "Thing is, I think I said something I shouldn't."

"Really? What?" A dread I can't put a name to stirs in the dark recesses of my brain.

Calypso's words sound far away, as though travelling along a bad phone line. "Not sure, exactly. I was joking about taking some of the credit for you guys getting together, seeing as it was me who suggested you ask Georgie to join your band, and… she went kind of odd. Have I put my foot in it?"

Oh, no. No, no, no, no, no. I'm going to throw up. My hands shake, ice chips rattling against the sides of the plastic cups. This can't be happening. It can't.

Calypso's expression crumples. "God, I have, haven't I? Me and my big mouth."

"It's not your fault," I say. After all, how could she have known? Calypso would have assumed she was telling Georgie something she was already aware of, something the two of us have laughed about while wrapped up in each other's arms. *Just think, if Calypso hadn't come up with the idea of us forming a band…*

And maybe we would have, if I'd been honest from the beginning. But how could I have been, knowing what I did about Georgie's past experiences? She would surely have jumped to conclusions, assumed I was merely asking her out of obligation, and I couldn't have borne that.

I need to find Georgie, to explain. *Stupid drinks.* I stare around wildly, looking for somewhere, anywhere, I can deposit them.

"I'll take those." Calypso removes the cups from my grasp. "You go. I really am sorry."

I barely register her apology, barely hear the muffled curses as I shove a path through the dancers. *Must get to Georgie. Must fix this before it's too late.* The campus opens up in front of me, dark and alive with shadows, and I run.

67. GEORGIE

"*I* WAS THE ONE *who suggested the two of you team up…*"
Calypso's words chase me along the path, whispering poison in my ear. I urge Star to go faster. She must pick up on my mood because she abandons her usual plodding walk, launching into a trot.

And you know the worst thing? Calypso tossed it out there so casually, like she had no idea she was ripping my happiness to shreds. Not that any of this is her fault. She isn't the one who's been lying to me. She hasn't spent the summer acting out a friendship that never existed.

I catch my toe on an uneven paving slab, almost go down. Tears burn my eyelids. *For Christ's sake, George, don't cry. You haven't got time for this. Just keep moving. You're almost home.*

"Georgie!"

I freeze, one hand on the door to Osborne House. *Please, God, no.* She wasn't meant to get here so quickly. I should be in my room, duvet over my head, lock firmly in place. I can't deal with this—with her excuses, her apologies. Not now. Maybe not ever.

Mina's ballet pumps slap behind me. "Georgie, wait. Please."

That voice. It's traced promises on my lips late at night, breathed ticklish laughter against my neck. These past days, it's become the most important voice in the world to me. The sound of it twists me up inside.

I don't wait. In a violent motion that sends the door crashing against the brickwork, I yank it open and hurry Star inside. Tears clog my throat. Stupid. How had I not seen this coming? I should have. After Emma, after Chanelle, after every little disappointment in between. I should've realised this was too good to be true. *Stupid, stupid, stupid.*

Outside my room, I fumble the key from my pocket. I'm so jittery it jumps from my grasp onto the floor. *Shit.* I drop to my knees, Star's lead clutched in one hand, feeling around with the other. *Come on, come on, come on.*

My fingers close on cold metal. *Thank Christ.* I snatch up my key and jam it into the lock.

"Georgie." The outer door bursts open and Mina's beside me, breathless and urgent. "We need to talk."

My heart drops. I turn the key and let the door swing inwards. Looks like we're doing this, after all.

"What's there to talk about?" The question comes out taut with unshed tears. I won't cry. I bloody well won't.

"How can you say that?" Mina asks. "After everything."

I snort. Like that meant a damned thing. Released from her harness, Star ambles into the room ahead of us.

"Georgie?" My name trembles on Mina's tongue.

Don't say it, not ever again. You have no right. That's what I want to snap. More than that, I want to escape this whole conversation, to shove her into the hall and slam the door in her face. I want to crawl into bed with Star, curl myself around her and block out the world.

I can't do any of that, though. Instead, I round on Mina, hugging my chest to stop myself from crumbling. "You lied."

"I didn't. I'd never do that to you. Never."

"Right. You just forgot to mention that you only asked me to join your band because you were told to, that it?"

"Georgie," Mina says, then falters. The door clicks shut and she moves towards me, shoes scuffing the carpet. I flinch and she halts. "Look, Calypso might've given me the idea, but that doesn't change anything."

"It changes everything!" The shout rips from me, jagged and raw. "This whole thing...our friendship...us...none of it has been real."

Mina starts to cry. Her hitching sobs dig razor claws into my soul. "How can you think that? You know how I feel about you."

"I don't know anything anymore. You fucking lied to me, Mina. You lied to me, and now I can't tell if any of it was true."

"Of course it was true. All of it. You really think I'd pretend to be your friend, pretend to fall for you?"

"Then why didn't you tell me the truth?" I hurl it at her, the anger and disappointment. "After I confided in you about Emma, about Chanelle. Why didn't you just tell me?"

"Because I knew you'd assume I was just like the others." The sobs nearly swallow Mina's reply. "And because I didn't want to hurt you."

"Wow, epic fail. Congratulations."

"I'm sorry, Georgie. I'm so, so sorry. If I could go back and do it differently..."

I massage my forehead; a dull ache beats against it like a metronome. I'm too tired for this. "Just leave me alone."

"But—"

"Please, Mina, there's no point. I...I can't trust a single thing you say."

She doesn't apologise again, doesn't try to change my mind. Maybe my stance is enough to convince her it's pointless. Maybe, deep down, it's a relief that she can finally drop the pretence. Either way, she flees without another word.

As soon as her footsteps have faded, I lurch over to the door and lock it. Then, flinging myself on my bed, I bury my face in the pillow and howl.

FAREWELL
WEEKEND

*Music is the divine way to tell beautiful,
poetic things to the heart.*

– Pablo Casals

68. MINA

A HARSH RINGING BLASTS in my ear, penetrating the boggy layers of sleep. My phone. I kick free of the duvet, sweaty and disoriented. It must be the crack of dawn, for pity's sake. Who would be calling me?

The truth has me struggling to sit up, groping for my mobile on the bedside cabinet. It'll be Georgie. She's had time to cool off and realises she got it all wrong. Her accusation, hurled with so much anger and betrayal, slinks back to taunt me.

"This whole thing…our friendship…us…none of it has been real."

My heart twists, but she didn't mean it, not really. She knows I'm incapable of that kind of deceit and wants to talk, to make up.

My fingers close around my mobile at the precise moment it stops ringing. *Blast it.* I snatch it up and squint at the display. A blade of sunshine pierces the curtains and into my eyes, blinding me. I blink to clear my vision and glance at the time. Eleven seventeen. Wow, I've never slept this late in my life, not even after the family New Year's Eve party, which invariably goes on till three in the morning.

My lock screen shows one missed call. Home. The disappointment is so acute it wrenches a sob from my chest. Of course it isn't Georgie. Why would she have any desire to talk to me when, as far as she's concerned, I'm a liar and a fraud?

I let my head fall against the wall behind me. This day has only just begun and I wish it were over. I need to call back, but how can I speak to my parents, act as if everything's normal? Gosh, every part of me aches. My head throbs and my eyelids feel as though someone's attacked them with the rougher side of a nail file.

The ringing starts up again. I stay motionless, phone held loosely in my hand. It would be so easy to ignore it, allow the call to go to voicemail…but no. Dad's danger detector, always on high alert where his daughters are concerned, would trigger in an explosion of sirens and hazard lights. He'd get straight onto the phone to the college, a member of staff would be despatched to check I haven't been kidnapped in the night, and the whole thing would be toe-clenchingly embarrassing.

Arm weighed down with cement, I lift the phone to my ear. "Hello?"

"Mina, sweetheart, how are you?" Mum's voice wraps around me, full of tender understanding.

I swallow against the rush of tears. "I'm OK."

"Of course you're not," Dad says. He must be on the extension in their bedroom. "You're disappointed. That's natural. We both know you had your hopes pinned on winning the competition."

It takes my brain a moment to grasp his meaning. Since the fight with Georgie, I've thought of nothing else. Incredible as it would have seemed twenty-four hours earlier, the scholarship no longer feels important. Still, it doesn't matter that their sympathy is aimed in the wrong direction; the fact that they care has emotion clogging my throat. For a moment, I consider letting it all spill out—my sexuality, my feelings for Georgie, how I'd ruined everything. My insides curl into a protective ball. I will tell them, but not over the phone.

"We're so proud of you," Mum adds. "So very proud."

I open my mouth to reply, to say how much their support means to me, and burst into tears.

If they were here, I know my parents would have enveloped me in a group hug, Mum on one side of me, Dad on the other. They're not here, though, so all they can do is comfort me with their words, assure me everything will be all right.

"No problem is insurmountable." Dad's tone transmits absolute confidence. "There's always a solution. We just have to find it."

"Really?" I sniff, wiping my eyes, and the tiniest flame of hope kindles inside me. Does he mean…? Is he saying there might still be a chance for me to attend Dukes?

"Always," Mum agrees, "but we can discuss it properly when we see you. We can't wait for the concert."

"And watching our girl steal the show," Dad says.

I've forgotten I'd signed up to sing tomorrow. That feels like a lifetime ago, back when Georgie and I were happy and I still clung to the hope of winning the scholarship. Now, the prospect of climbing on stage has weariness dragging at my limbs. I'm tempted to go to Calypso, inform her I have to pull out, but I can't let Mum and Dad down.

After we hang up, I prop myself against the pillows, Dad's mantra playing on repeat in my mind. *There's always a solution.* It's something I've grown up believing. Whenever I had a problem, I'd go to Dad and he'd help me fix it, although this might not be so simple. It's more than a broken bicycle pedal or a minor falling out with Allie. Maybe there's actually no way to mend this.

I chew my lip, staring down at the phone in my hand. Perhaps this is that thing Dad doesn't believe exists—a problem without a solution. Still, just because it might not work, does that mean I shouldn't even try?

Another of Dad's mantras is that anything worth having is worth fighting for. I've never wanted anyone as much as I want Georgie. Surely, I'm not going to give up on us without at least attempting to repair the damage. Before I can argue against it, I tap out a text.

69. GEORGIE

WHY CAN'T EVERYONE *leave me alone?*
I drag my carcass out of the shower to a small pile-up of texts. One each from Mum and Dad, two from Jake. I skim the opening sentences. Just my family checking up on me, making sure I'm not too bummed over the scholarship. Like that's the only thing I have going on.

I toss my phone onto the pillow. It bounces off, falling to the floor with a muted thud. *Hell.* I slump onto the bed and bury my face in my knees. The towel strokes my cheek, raw from having the water cranked too hot. How can I talk to my parents, to Jake? Dad's disappointment would've been tough to take as it is. On top of everything else... I can't fake it for them, can't act like my heart isn't in bits.

Star shoves her head under my arm, nudging me to sit up. I give myself a mental shake and ruffle her fur. "OK, OK, I'm coming."

I finish drying off and pull on yesterday's clothes. Reaching for Star's lead, I pause. Should probably message my family back. They'll only wear my battery flat with anxious calls. Better to fob them off. I feel around on the floor until I find my phone and dictate a group text.

> *All good here. Just grabbing some breakfast. Can't wait to see you tomorrow.*

Tomorrow. I grimace. There'll be no avoiding my family when they arrive to watch the big end-of-summer concert and take me home. I'll have to talk to them then, and thanks to my expressive face, they'll know something's up. Something more than disappointment.

Star, impatient with this delay, prods me with her nose. I drop my mobile on the bedside cabinet, scoop Star's lead off the desk, and follow her across the hall. In the kitchen, I measure out her food and pop the kettle on.

While the water boils, I take Star out into the garden. It's cooler than the past few days. A breeze runs light fingers over my skin, the sun gently warm. How dare the weather be so bloody perfect? It has no right. Not when my world's imploded.

We return indoors to find someone's invaded the kitchen. Drawers rattle, mugs clink, metal meets china with a musical *ching*. Just what I need. Why couldn't whoever it is have waited until I was back in my room? Maybe if I walk fast enough, I can slip out into the hall without being noticed. I swallow. Christ, I'm thirsty. Still, a parched throat is better than having to make conversation. I'm scarcely halfway to the door, when…

"Good morning to you, too."

Damn it. Of the four flatmates I could've run into, it had to be the one most likely to see through my bullshit. I continue towards freedom, my tone falsely upbeat. "Hey, Zeph."

"Whoa." His arm shoots across me so that I walk straight into it. "Sit."

I retreat a pace. "Huh?"

"Sit," Zephan repeats. He shunts me backwards until the creases of my knees collide with a chair.

I drop into it with a huff and fold my arms. "I'm not a dog."

Star lowers herself onto her haunches beside me, head swinging as she glances between us. I glower at Zephan, but he's already returned to the kitchen area.

"Tea." With a *thunk*, he sets a mug on the table at my elbow. "Now, talk."

"What about?"

"Hmmmm. For starters, how about where you buggered off to last night."

"I had a headache. Went to bed."

"And second, how come you look like someone's smashed your Fender with a sledgehammer?"

I grip the mug so it scalds my palms. It doesn't matter that I can't see it; Zeph's gaze drills into me. I duck my chin, hair falling forwards to hide my face. "Reckon someone spiked your Slush Puppie last night or something."

Zephan snorts. He pulls out a chair with the screech of wood on wood and sits across from me. "Try again."

I gulp a mouthful of tea and almost sear off my tongue. *Shit.* Tears build behind my eyelids. Tears that have nothing to do with the pain. *You have no business crying. It's your own fault for being so gullible, so desperate to believe in something real.*

"It's Mina," Zephan says, his voice gruff, "isn't it?"

I take another too-big slug of tea, welcoming the burn. "Don't want to talk about it."

Zephan's quiet. I can feel his stare, excavating me from the inside out. At length, he says, "You should. If not to me, then to her."

"Seriously." I set down my mug too quickly and hot liquid splashes my wrist. "Give it a rest."

Zephan doesn't speak, but his silence stinks of judgement. Anger shoves me to my feet. How dare he judge me? It isn't as if he knows a damned thing about what's gone on. Besides, who is he to lecture me about talking when he's so crap at it himself?

"Come on, Star." I stalk across the living area, Star at my heels, and reach out to locate the doorframe. Zephan doesn't apologise, doesn't call me back. Still, his disapproval pursues me into the hall.

I'm pushing open the door to my room when my mobile pings. Probably a reply to my group text. I release Star and cross to pick up my phone. The message isn't from any of my family. I read it, heart banging like a bongo.

I'm more sorry than I can say. Can we talk? Please?

I curl in on myself, phone slipping from lifeless fingers. *God, Mina, I miss you. I miss you so bloody much.* How can anything hurt this bad and not kill me?

It isn't that I don't believe her. Of course she's sorry. Mina's no monster. Hurting me would've been the last thing she wanted, but that doesn't change the fact that she lied. She lied to me and now I can't tell what was true.

Somehow, I straighten against the ache in my gut and fumble for my phone. Mina needs to understand where we're at. Voice ragged with grief, I choke out a text.

70. MINA

*T*HERE'S NOTHING TO *say.*

Huddled in bed, I stare down at Georgie's reply. How can there be nothing to say? We've shared so much in such a short space of time, cracked open our protective shells to show each other the secret pearls within. I made a mistake, I realise that, but after everything we've been through, to deny we have anything to talk about...

Hot tears spurt down my cheeks. It seems I have an unlimited supply, and I couldn't stop them even if I wanted to. As it is, I don't even try. I merely roll into a ball and pull the pillow over my head.

Hours later—or has it only been minutes?—someone taps on my door. I smother my sobs in the duvet. *Please go away.* I can't speak to anyone, don't have the energy to slot the shattered pieces of myself back together.

The knock sounds again. "Hun, it's me. You OK?"

I burrow deeper under the covers. Gaz has his own heartache to deal with and doesn't need me heaping mine on top.

"Hun, I know you're in there." Gareth rattles the door handle. "If you don't unlock this door by the time I count to five, I'll bloody well smash it in. One...two..."

The idea of my gentle giant of a best friend breaking down my door is so absurd, it almost coaxes a smile from me. I scrub the tears from my eyes and build a hasty dam against the ones waiting to spill. It requires far more strength than it should to shove the duvet off me, but I stagger out of bed and across the room.

"Five," Gareth says just as I pull the door open. He falls silent, studying me.

I tuck the sleep-dishevelled hair behind my ears and glance down at myself. What must I look like, nightshirt crumpled and sweat-stained, my face swollen from crying?

Gareth holds out his arms, eyes soft, and I stumble into them, my feeble defences collapsing. He guides us to sit on the bed, stroking my back until my sobs fade to hiccups. His familiar bulk is so comforting, the cotton of his shirt soft against my cheek. My insides feel hollow, scraped out, as if someone has scoured them clean with a spatula.

Gareth eases me away from him and peers into my eyes. "Better?"

"A bit." I sniff, sounding like I have a severe cold. "But I don't know what to do. Georgie—"

Gareth touches my shoulder. "We'll sort it, promise. First, though, you're going to get dressed. Then we'll go for a walk."

FIFTEEN MINUTES LATER, we're wandering along a path flecked with sunlight and shade. A drowsy languor has settled over campus, musicians clustered on benches and on the grass, talking softly.

"You gonna tell me?" Gareth drapes an arm across my shoulders. "Zeph says Georgie seemed off earlier. Did something happen?"

Just the sound of her name causes a sharp pain in my heart. Memories close in from every direction—strolling arm in arm with Georgie along these same paths; the way her expression came alive when she laughed; nighttime kisses stolen in the shadow of a beech tree.

I sigh. "I messed up, Gaz. Really messed up."

Haltingly, I recount the events of the previous evening, by some miracle managing not to cry. Perhaps I truly have used up my reserves. Gareth listens, his face serious, letting me pour it all out without interruption.

Once I've finished, he shakes his head. "She seriously thinks you've been pretending this whole time? That makes no sense."

"It does, sort of." I repeat everything Georgie confided in me, about Chanelle's casual cruelty and the misguided kindness of the girl in her English class. Gosh, I'm so ashamed. Perhaps, if I'd been up front from the start, we could have avoided this hurt.

"That's shitty," Gareth says. "Explains why she was a bit wary around us at first, like. I still can't believe she'd think that of you, though."

I hug my elbows to my body, teeth worrying at my lower lip. Nor can I, if I'm honest. We may not have known each other long, but the ease with which Georgie jumped to the worst conclusions cuts me to the soul.

Gareth tightens his arm around me, pressing me into his side. "We can fix this."

"You really think so?"

"'Course. What you and Georgie have is too special."

Gareth's warmth seeps through my numbness, steady and reassuring. I take a deep breath and my spine straightens. He's right; Georgie and I have something precious, something worth saving. I have to believe that. The question is, how can I convince her to believe it, too?

"What you need," Gareth says, answering my unspoken question, "is some way of telling Georgie how you feel that she can't just dismiss. Like that scene in *10 Things I Hate About You*. The one where Heath Ledger's character hijacks the mic at the football game and serenades the girl he fancies in front of the whole school."

"Gaz, you know I don't watch movies unless at least one character gets disembowelled."

"Right, sorry. I was forgetting my best friend's a bloodthirsty philistine."

I give him a playful shove. Already, though, an idea is beginning to form in my mind. The question is, am I brave enough to go through with it?

71. GEORGIE

THE AFTERNOON DRAGS.

I lug an armful of T-shirts over to the bed and dump the whole lot into my suitcase. Look at me being all organised. Chucking my stuff together at the last minute's more my style. Still, not like I have anything better to do.

I head back to the wardrobe to empty another drawer. Radiohead's *OK Computer* blasts from my Bluetooth speakers. Thom Yorke's doleful vocals suit my mood and the pounding guitar makes it hard to think.

Star barks and runs to the door, panting. I pause, my arms full of jeans. A knock, barely audible under the music. Without Star's warning, doubt I would've heard it. Damn my dog and her superhuman ears. *God, please don't be Mina. I can't be near her right now.*

The knock comes again, louder.

"Hang on," I call. Well, it's not like I can pretend no one's in, is it? Dropping the tangle of clothes into the case, I reach for the remote and turn down the volume. "Who is it?"

"Only us," Gareth answers. "Can we come in?"

I hesitate. "Mina with you?"

"Nope, only me and Zeph."

Star whines, snuffling at the door. I don't move. Has Mina told them about last night? I huff through my nose. Of course she has. That's why the pair of them are outside my room. Gaz will've taken Mina's side, being her best mate an' all. He probably hates me. Zeph, too. On top of losing Mina, I've probably lost the only friends I've ever had.

"We have tea," Gareth adds.

I hover by the bed. He doesn't seem angry or like he loathes my guts. It could be a trick. He'll get me to open the door, then lay into me. I shake my head. Not Gaz's style. Plus, he has tea. When could I ever resist a cuppa? Sighing, I unlock the door and retreat to collapse into my desk chair.

"About time," Zephan grumbles. "Felt like a groupie waiting backstage at a bloody Harry Styles concert."

Gareth laughs, setting a mug on the desk beside me. "Here you are, hun."

"Thanks." I curl my fingers around the mug, blinking hard. You'd think I was a neglected puppy, grateful for the smallest kindness.

Bedsprings creak as the boys perch either side of my half-packed suitcase. I spin to face them, gripping my tea like a shield against whatever they've come to say.

"You doing all right?" Gareth asks.

His tone's so gentle. No accusation, no judgement. It would've been easier if he'd shouted. I swallow, shaking my head.

"Mina told me," Gareth says. "Hope that was OK."

I shrug. What does it matter? It's not like anyone can change what happened. I gulp a mouthful of tea. It scalds my tongue but can't numb the pain of hearing her name.

"She's really cut up, like," Gareth says.

I trail a foot over the carpet, the pile parting for my bare toes. "She doesn't need to worry. I know she meant well."

Zephan scoffs. "What? You think you're some charity case? That Mina adopted you like some stray kitten?"

I hide behind another sip of tea. Truth is, I might not've put it quite like that, but...yeah. Mina found out from Calypso how

I was struggling to fit in and came to my rescue. Being the person she is, how could she have refused?

"You can't be serious," Gareth says. "Hun, you might not be able to see the way Mina looks at you, but I can. She's besotted."

Zephan grunts. "It's enough to make you puke."

A noise spews from me, half laugh, half sob. Are they right? They seem so sure. I clutch their certainty close the way I used to cling to Patch, my stuffed panda. I want so much to believe them, want it more than anything in the world.

Gareth rests a hand on my knee and squeezes. "Honestly, I wouldn't lie to you. I've never seen Mina like this before, so... herself, and it's all down to you."

ONCE THEY'VE GONE, I draw my knees to my chest. How did I get it so wrong? Well, that's a no-brainer. I jumped to conclusions, let everything that happened to me in the past muddy the now. I shoved Mina away, didn't even given her the chance to defend herself. And the things I said to her... As if Mina could ever be anything like Chanelle. I should've known she'd never lie to me. I did know it, deep down. It's just that Calypso's revelation spun me around until I was too dizzy to think straight.

Will Mina forgive me? I scoff. Of course she will. That girl probably doesn't know how to bear a grudge. If I went to her, grovelled at her feet, she'd welcome me back with open arms. But would a part of her still blame herself? It tears me up, the idea of her clinging on to a guilt that was never hers in the first place. What I need...

My brain kickstarts into action. What I need is to show her how sorry I am in such a way that she's in no doubt. Maybe then she'll believe me when I tell her none of this is her fault, that it's all on me.

72. MINA

B Y MID-MORNING ON Sunday, the car park is crowded
with vehicles, gleaming Bentleys rubbing shoulders with
battered Fords. I sit on the front steps and watch the activity.
Boots gape open so suitcases and instruments can be stowed
inside, ready for their owners to head home after the concert.

The concert. I scan the front gates for a glimpse of Dad's
Audi, stomach knotting. Mum texted me before I walked over
here to let me know they were only minutes away. Part of me is
desperate to see them, to let them snuggle me up in their love
and reassurances, but another part wishes I could postpone the
moment forever. Anything to avoid having to watch their worry
and disappointment. At least the purple dye has almost washed
out, and with my hair in a French plait, you can barely see it.

A car turns in through the gates, sunlight flashing off metallic
silver. At the sight of that familiar figure behind the wheel, my
nerves retreat into the wings. In a single bound, I'm down the
steps and racing across the concrete.

"Mina, galbi." The driver's door opens and Dad climbs out,
beaming. "We made it."

I fly into his arms, bury my nose in the clean cotton of his
shirt and cling to him as if I'll never let go. Then Mum joins us,
and the whole reunion descends into a wonderful confusion of
hugs and laughter and the unmistakable scent of home.

"You look tired, sweetheart." Mum tucks the hair behind my ear, studying me with her professional gaze. "Did you not get much sleep?"

"A bit." I was up into the early hours putting the finishing touches to my plan, falling into an exhausted coma at around four.

"Too many late nights." Dad pokes me in the ribs, eyes twinkling. "You know what that means. Early to bed for the rest of the holidays."

I roll my eyes, suppressing a smile. Another time, his overprotectiveness might have exasperated me, but not today. Today, it feels good to be cosseted.

Mum slips her arm around my waist. "Going to show us around?"

We amble indoors, me sandwiched between my parents. The foyer is deserted and the pillars throw bars of shadow across the chestnut floor.

"This is the concert hall." I usher them over to the double doors. "It's where we'll be performing later."

"We're looking forward to it," Dad says.

He beams at me, expression glowing with pride. Will he still look at me like that once he knows? I need to tell them. It's important they hear the truth from me before I declare it in front of the entire audience, but not yet. Let me enjoy this time with my parents, free from complications and judgement.

"Beautiful piano," Mum says, nudging me. "Bet you couldn't wait to try that out."

I grin through the ache in my heart. How is it my parents can know parts of me so well whilst being utterly clueless about others?

We continue outside where the golden morning is alive with the chatter and laughter of family reunions. Zephan's surrounded by a boisterous crowd of young people who range in age from early teens to mid-twenties. The Ghanaian Von Trapps, presumably. He's slumped against the trunk of a nearby beech, shoulders hunched, looking as though he'd like to sink into its roots and disappear. Poor Zeph.

I take my parents on a magical mystery tour of the grounds, showing them the lily pond with its statue of the young guitar player and the glass-fronted pool house. Once we've explored every meandering path, I let them peer in through the windows of the study block before leading them into the rec building.

They admire it all—the corridors of practice rooms and the store cupboards crammed with spare instruments, the airy dining room overlooking the patio. In the student centre, Dad can't resist demonstrating his prowess at the pool table. The more my parents enthuse, the brighter my hope flares. Surely, they wouldn't be so positive if they couldn't entertain the possibility of me coming here. Or maybe they're simply relieved the camp is ending and they can whisk me home again. What's the sense in hoping, anyway? Whatever they feel now, when I sit them down and reveal the piece of myself I've kept hidden for so long, everything will change.

As we emerge from the student centre, a boy gives me a faint smile. I return it, then do a double take. His hair's plain brown now, smoothed flat against his head, and he's swapped the vibrant vests for a white T-shirt. He's trailing after a powerfully built man with a shaved head, his posture stooped, all the energy and self-assurance drained out of him. If Art hadn't caught my eye, I wouldn't have recognised him.

"And who might that young man be?" Dad taps me on the shoulder.

I jump. Did he see me exchange smiles with Art? But, no, Dad's pointing in the opposite direction, to where Gareth's seated on a bench between a man with his broad frame and a woman with red curls. He waves to me, our agreed signal. This is the day for finally being honest with my parents, and that includes sharing my most important friendship.

Despite my brave intentions, my reply comes out strangled. "That's Gareth. One of my bandmates."

"Bandmate, eh? Is there something you'd like to tell me?" Dad raises an eyebrow, expression beady.

"Dad." I cringe. "We're just friends. Gareth won the scholarship."

"Did he now? Well then, you'd better introduce us." Dad steers me forward with a palm on my back. "I have to meet the scoundrel who beat my daughter."

"Samir," Mum reproves.

Laughing, I allow myself to be guided over to the bench. Gosh, I love my dad. He might've had doubts about me attending the summer camp, but that doesn't stop him from getting all protective on my behalf.

Gareth flashes me a smile tinged with apprehension, then turns to his parents. "Mam, Dad, this is Mina."

The three of them stand to greet us and there's the usual round of handshakes and exchanging of names. Gareth's dad introduces himself to me as Lloyd, his work-roughened hand completely engulfing my smaller one.

"Here's what I want to know," he says in his booming voice. "How come my son hasn't asked you out yet?"

"Dad!" A blush spreads up Gareth's neck into his face.

His father claps him on the back. "What? It's a fair question. I would've snapped this one up when I was your age."

Lloyd winks at me and my cheeks flame. *Please, God, I know it's asking a lot, but the ability to teleport would be very much appreciated.* Gareth hunches in on himself beside me, an obvious attempt to disappear.

"That's a real gentleman you have there," Dad says, intervening with the tact he's learned from years of chairing Catenian functions. Honestly, I could kiss him.

Lloyd harrumphs, clearly wishing his son were rather less of a gentleman.

"And," Mum smiles at Gareth, "we hear congratulations are in order."

Gareth's dad brightens, rewarding his son with another hearty slap on the back. "Ah, thanks. Plays like an angel from heaven, our boy."

"We're so proud." Gareth's mum, Briony, gives him a squeeze.

Slowly, as our parents compete to see who had the worst journey getting here, Gareth's shoulders relax. I tap him on the arm and we wander a short distance away.

"Sorry," Gareth mutters. "He's a nightmare."

I want to hug him, but that would only equip his dad with more ammunition. "Really, don't worry about it. Mum and Dad didn't take any of that seriously."

In fact, it was far less painful than I expected, introducing my parents to my best friend, who just so happens to be a boy. Well, that first hurdle was always going to be the easy one. The sun flits behind a cloud and I shiver, goosebumps pricking my skin. I'm still faced with the hardest thing I've ever done in my life, and I have no idea where I'll find the courage.

73. GEORGIE

THE PICNIC STARTS at half twelve on the lawn outside the dining room. We arrive early, Jake snagging us a prime spot close to the patio.

"Perfect for grabbing seconds…and thirds," he says as we settle onto our blanket with plates of cold buffet. Star plonks herself in the centre of the blanket, the ideal vantage point to keep watch on the food.

I roll my eyes, nibbling on a cheese straw. "You and your stomach."

"This place is incredible, George." Dad's tone holds an ocean of wistfulness. "Wish Dukes had been around when I was your age."

"Neil…" Mum warns.

"What? Think of all the musicians who've studied here. I would've given anything for a chance like this. Georgie's lucky, that's all I'm saying."

"And I'm saying not now."

I pick up my slice of quiche, then put it down again. My appetite, what little I'd had, buggers off somewhere. They've been like this all morning—Dad overenthusiastic about everything, Mum reining him in. I'd hoped, once my parents knew how happy I was at Dukes, they might've come to some agreement. So much for that.

Jake nudges his knee against mine. "Nervous about the concert?"

"Shit scared, yeah." I dump my plate on the blanket and hug my knees to my chest.

"Your first time getting up on stage in front of a proper audience," Dad says. "That's a big deal."

"Yeah, Dad, thanks for reminding me." Nausea roils in my gut.

Dad mushes my hair. "Aw, don't sweat it. Nerves are par for the course. I remember when the band landed our first gig at The Royal Oak."

"Please. That's hardly the same thing, singing for a load of drunks," Mum says.

"You can mock, but drunks are the worst. Much more likely to heckle you if they don't like what they hear. Seriously, George, your uncle Rob nearly missed the show because he was too busy chucking up in the gents.'"

"Really?" I can't imagine it. Uncle Rob's always been the life and soul of the party, bit of a practical joker. If he was able to get over his stage fright and perform, maybe there's hope for me, too.

"Star, no," Jake cries, jerking me from my thoughts. He lurches forward, but…too late. Star's already demolishing her prize with a satisfied smacking of lips.

"Uh-oh." I grasp her collar. "Bad girl."

Jake flops back beside me. "Sorry. Never knew Star could move that fast. You didn't want that quiche, did you?"

ONCE WE'VE EATEN, Dad and Jake head off to load my stuff in the car. Mum suggests me and her go for a walk, let Star stretch her legs before the concert. Arm in arm, Star out in front, we mooch along the path that winds away from the rec building.

Soon, the chatter from the picnic fades behind us and there's only the coo of pigeons.

"This campus really is stunning," Mum says. "It must be an amazing place to study."

"Yeah." *Calm down, George.* I avert my face to hide the longing that must be written there. Am I reading too much into this? Could Mum actually be warming to the idea of me coming to Dukes?

Mum squeezes my elbow. "So, how're things with Mina?"

"Oh, God." I loop Star's lead over my wrist and knuckle my tired eyes. "They're a bloody disaster."

As we walk, I fill her in on the whole saga—the mistimed kiss, Mina's worries about upsetting her Catholic parents, the painful week while we skirted the awkwardness between us. When I get to Mina's change of heart and describe the magic of those few days together, my throat closes. By the time I've relayed Calypso's revelation and the shitty things I said, we're nearing the tinkle of the fountain.

"Oh, George." Mum draws me onto the wall of the lily pond and hugs me to her side. "What am I going to do with you?"

I lean my head on her shoulder. It's a relief to pour it all out, the way you feel better after throwing up. Star rests her chin on my leg and I stroke her sun-warmed fur. "I seriously messed up, didn't I?"

"A bit, but it's nothing that can't be fixed. Mina knows you've been hurt before. She'll understand."

"Hope so. I've, well, I've written this song. For Mina. It's what I'm performing at the concert."

"Wow, get you. That's incredibly brave."

"I don't feel brave. More like a jibbering wreck."

"You'll be fab," Mum says with the confidence of someone who's never suffered a quiver of nerves in her life. "And it'll all be worth it when you and Mina patch things up."

I nod, toying with one of Star's silky ears. Mum's so definite, so certain things will work out. Wish I shared her optimism. Behind me, the fountain plays its bubbling tune. If I never get to come back, this could be the last time I sit here, listening to the music of the water. Man, I'm going to miss it.

Mum shakes my shoulder. "Speak to me."

"It's just…" I scuff the sole of my trainer against the concrete. "I'm not sure there's much point."

"How do you mean?"

"Well, if I'm not allowed to come to Dukes, we might never see each other again."

Mum expels an irritated breath. She withdraws her arm from around me. "Georgie, no one's saying you're not allowed."

"Really?" I sit upright, twisting to face her. "But you're not keen on the idea."

"Obviously. You're my daughter. I'd hate to see you disappointed, but that doesn't mean we can't have a discussion about it."

A smile fights to break free. For the first time since I lost out on the scholarship, a future at Dukes feels at least possible. Before I can thank her, Star makes a choking sound. The next instant she spews her breakfast and the stolen quiche in a sticky mess all over me.

74. MINA

Time is slipping away. However hard I will it to slow down, the minutes unspool like a Slinky through my fingers.

We set up our picnic blanket next to Gareth and his parents. I wasn't sure how our families would hit it off, given we inhabit such different worlds, but Mum and Lloyd discover their shared passion for gardening, while Dad and Briony bond over a love of cooking.

I filled my plate along with everyone else, although I only toy with my egg and cress sandwich. If I can't get Mum and Dad alone soon, I'll lose my opportunity to speak to them before the concert.

"Not hungry, sweetheart?" Mum breaks off from discussing her vegetable patch to touch my shoulder.

"Ah, she's just nervous about getting up on stage." Dad casts me a sympathetic smile. "Right, galbi?"

"A bit." My throat rasps and I cough to clear it. At this rate, I won't be able to sing at all.

Mum rubs my back. "This isn't like you. When have you ever been nervous about performing?"

She's right. The stage is my happy place, and I'd never normally pass up the chance to play for an audience. Then again, I've also never apologised to a girl I like in front of an entire hall of spectators. Gosh, what am I doing?

"I'm sure you'll be fine," Briony tells me with a warm smile. She's so kind, Gareth's mum, it makes me want to cry. That must be where Gaz gets his sweetness.

Mum nudges me, gesturing to the far side of the lawn. "Is that your friend? The one with the guide dog?"

My stomach lurches, but I drag my gaze from my plate. Georgie's sitting between a stunning blonde woman and a young man with muscular arms covered in tattoos. Not trusting myself to speak, I only nod. *Please don't suggest we go over and say hello. The awkwardness might actually kill me.*

"Gorgeous dog," Dad says, unable to disguise his longing. "Mina, you must introduce us before we leave."

I hum a noncommittal response. At least he hadn't insisted on meeting them right away, and by the end of the concert, he'll have more pressing matters to worry about.

Calypso appears beside our blanket, Dutch at her elbow. They're dressed more smartly than usual, Calypso in black leggings and a floaty top, Dutch wearing jeans and a short-sleeved shirt. Calypso's carrying an upside-down bowler hat, which she extends to me.

"Pick a number," she says, shaking the hat so its contents rustle. "It's to decide the order you'll perform in."

Oh, lord. I lower my hand into the sea of folded paper like someone reaching into a shark tank. My fingers feel clumsy, the shiny scraps darting from my grasp. At last, I grab hold of one and unfold it. *Please let me be in the second half.* That way I might be able to talk to my parents during the interval.

"What've you got?" Calypso shifts from foot to foot, eyes dancing.

I swallow and do my best to keep the panic from my voice. "Two."

"Ooh, right near the beginning of the first half." Calypso nods at Dutch, who makes a note on his iPad. "OK, your turn."

She proffers the hat to Gareth, and I twist to gape at him. Since when has my best friend got so brave?

Gareth fishes out a piece of paper and gulps. "Five."

"Excellent." Calypso beams. "The concert's due to start in around thirty minutes, so you'll probably want to collect your instruments and head backstage soon, tune up and whatever. Good luck."

"Yeah, good luck, guys." Dutch offers us each a thumbs up, and then the two of them wander over to where Chanelle's being used as a climbing frame for two little girls.

After they've gone, Dad begins taking requests for teas and coffees, and I turn to Gareth. "I didn't know you were performing."

"Nor did I till yesterday afternoon." Gareth shrugs, expression sheepish. "Zeph and me are duetting."

"I don't believe you. There's no way you persuaded Zeph to sing."

"I know, right? I asked him if he was finally going to get up on stage, just as a joke, like, and he said he would if I did."

"Wow." I shake my head. "You clearly have some secret superpower. I can't wait to hear it."

Gareth's skin takes on a greenish tinge. "Actually, I kind of wish I hadn't agreed to it."

"Nonsense." Lloyd, catching these last words, claps his son on the back. "You'll be amazing as always. You too, Mina."

I try to smile, but my mouth feels like dried-out clay. Gareth's parents have been so welcoming to me, but how will they react once they know? From what Gareth's told me, the community he's grown up in still holds on to its traditional values. What if they discourage Gaz from being friends with me? I put down my plate, abandoning any pretence at eating.

Gareth pinches a cocktail sausage. "Want to head over a bit early? I could do with running through my lyrics."

I hesitate, chewing my lip. If I catch them now, there'll still be time to talk to my parents before the concert. But Dad's already vanishing inside to fulfil the drink orders and Mum's laughing with Briony. It's no use. I can't ask them for a private word, not in front of an audience.

My heart settles in my chest, heavy but resolute. I have no option, other than abandoning the plan altogether, and it's too important for that. No, I'll have to steam ahead with it and explain afterwards.

I drain my Tango and stumble to my feet. "Let's go."

75. GEORGIE

Ugh.

I sit on the wall of the lily pond while warm gunk seeps through my jeans. This did not just happen. I'll wake up in a second and it'll all be some hellish dream. Sensing she's done something wrong, Star whines. I stroke her head. Poor girl. Not her fault.

"Hey, it's all right," I tell her, even as panic froths in my gut. What to do? The concert will be starting soon and I can't turn up covered in dog sick.

Mum lays a hand on my back, keeping an arm's length between us. "Relax. You're not on till the second half. We have plenty of time."

"But my friends are doing a duet. I don't want to miss it, and Dad's probably already loaded my stuff in the car."

"Then we'd better go and find him, hadn't we? No point getting yourself in a state."

"I can't walk past the concert hall. Everyone will see me."

Mum gets to her feet. "We're early yet. Looks like most people are still at the picnic. Come on, let's get you cleaned up."

Mum's not big on hugs and sympathy; that's more Dad's style. Still, her briskness is what I need right now. She guides me along the path to the Dukes Building, Star trotting ahead on her lead. Nothing keeps that dog down for long.

My clothes paste themselves to my skin. They make this gross squelching sound with every step and I cringe. *Please, please, please don't let us bump into anyone.* Getting up on stage will be tough enough as it is. I'll never live it down, being the girl caked in vomit. But Mum's right, thank God, and this part of campus is deserted.

We cross the foyer and emerge through the front entrance. Mum halts us at the top of the steps, twisting to scan the car park. "Blast. We must've missed them."

My heart divebombs into my stomach. No way I'll make it now. "What're we going to do? I really wanted to see Zeph and Gaz perform."

Mum's off again, rushing me down the steps and over the concrete. She lays my palm against the sun-baked metal of the car. "You wait here. I'll track them down and be straight back."

"Be quick," I urge her, but she's already hurrying away, heels clopping.

Star tries to follow, but I call her back. Once she's lying down, I huddle into the side of the car and rest my forehead against the window. Everyone will be filing into the hall for the concert. No reason for anyone to come out here.

The thought has barely formed when…voices.

"Dad, come on. I'm supposed to be backstage."

That's Blair. I press myself further into the shelter of the car. *Please don't notice me. You've done a fantastic job of ignoring me all summer. Why stop now?*

"You're the one who insisted on bringing two suitcases." Her dad's accent is even broader than Blair's. "Come on, pet. Chuck your stuff in the boot and we'll get you inside."

I stand stock still, muscles rigid. If this were a game of Musical Statues, I'd win hands down.

There's a grunt of effort from Blair, followed by two heavy thuds. The boot slams, and Blair calls to her dad to hurry up. They retreat indoors, their conversation fading, then Star and I are alone.

76. MINA

IN THE CORRIDOR behind the concert hall, I steel myself to pull open the stage door. Damp with sweat, my palm slips on the shiny metal handle. This is madness. I can't go out there, can't expose my secret self in front of all those people.

Gareth squeezes my shoulder. "You're almost up."

He's right. Any second now, Nazneen will come to the end of her song and it'll be my turn. My feet glue themselves to the oak flooring. "I can't do it. What if Mum and Dad hate me?"

"Hun, your parents adore you. I only had to see you together for five minutes to know that."

"But they'll be disappointed in me. And Georgie—"

"Will love it." Gareth nudges me forward with a gentle shove. "Go, go, go."

Before I realise what's happening, I'm through the door and stumbling up the stairs into the wings. I've barely made it in time. Nazneen rounds off her performance with a flurry of chords and the audience goes wild. Concealed beyond the curtain, I steady myself against the wall. If only I could melt away, disappear into the velvet drapes. My pulse races, matching the erratic rhythm of the applause.

As Nazneen saunters off stage left, guitar held aloft, Calypso bounds from the wings and turns to the audience.

"Thank you, thank you." She waits for the applause to die down. "How sensational was that? And there's plenty more to come. Please put your hands together and give a huge welcome to Mina Farhan."

Calypso offers me a thumbs up and scampers once more into the wings. This is it. The spotlight blazes down on the now deserted boards, waiting to engulf me. I take a halting pace towards it. My body feels stiff and jerky, like a crudely programmed robot. Once I speak into that microphone, there'll be no going back. Whatever the outcome, nothing will ever be the same.

My steps falter. I'm not ready for this. I can still change my mind. Everything will continue as it always has, me acting out the role of the perfect Catholic daughter, my parents content in their ignorance. And Georgie? Georgie might never believe just how incredibly sorry I am.

No. That isn't the future I want for myself. I don't want to pretend anymore, can't risk this chance to win Georgie back. After gulping in a deep breath, I gather the tattered scraps of my courage. Then, shaking so hard I can scarcely stand, I straighten my spine and advance onto the stage.

77. GEORGIE

*F*OR CHRIST'S SAKE, *where are they?* I fidget from one foot to the other. How can it be taking so long for Mum to track them down?

The drone of a crowd drifts from the Dukes Building, friends and relatives assembling in the hall. *Shit.* The concert's about to start and I'm stuck here in the car park, drenched in puke. *Shit, shit, shit.*

I kick out, the toe of my trainer connecting with the nearest tyre. The most frustrating thing? It's all my fault. I should've kept closer tabs on Star at the picnic. She was bound to try her luck with all that food under her nose. If I'd just held her collar, I could've stopped her wolfing my quiche, but no. I'd been too lost in my nerves. Now I could miss my one chance to hear Zeph sing.

My brother's carrying laugh reaches me first. *About bloody time.* I shoot upright, waiting for my family to join me.

"Wow, Star definitely did a number on you, didn't she?" Jake says.

"Shut up." I fold my arms and glare. "Where the hell have you been?"

"Finally found them coming out of the loo by the student centre," Mum says. She's breathless and sounds abnormally harassed.

"Don't worry, George, we'll get you fixed up." Dad squeezes my shoulder on his way to the boot. The lock releases with a clunk. "Let me move Star's bed."

"Be quick." I dance on the spot. The soft strum of a guitar wafts across the car park. *Damn it.* The concert's begun without me. Who's up first? I strain my ears to listen. The voice is female, but I'm too far away to make out anything else.

Dad opens my case, zip rasping. "Anything in particular I'm looking for?"

"Doesn't matter. Just not the jeans I spilled chocolate sauce down."

"Gotcha. Ah, here's a nice top. And some matching shorts."

"For God's sake, Neil, those are pyjamas. Shift over." Mum brushes past me to take Dad's place. After a moment of rummaging, she thrusts a bundle into my arms. "You'd better change in the car. We'll shield you. Hang on, let me put a towel down. I don't want vomit all over the seat."

We always keep a towel in the boot in case Star gets muddy on one of her runs. I wait, stomach in knots. Eventually, once Mum's spent several centuries draping the towel over her precious leather, she lets me climb into the back.

With my family preserving my modesty, I undress. I'm peeling my soggy jeans down over my thighs when there's the clatter of applause. The first performance must've finished. If I get a shift on, I might catch whoever's on next. Stripped to my underwear, I hand the dirty clothes to Dad, who has a carrier bag at the ready.

Midway through pulling on the shorts Mum picked out, I pause to listen. Can't help myself. The tinkling notes of a piano float from the concert hall, faint but achingly sweet. Even though I can hardly hear it, something about that melody makes my heart hurt.

78. MINA

For a terrifying moment, the spotlight blinds me. The applause trickles away and a hush falls over the hall. It's a physical pressure, the weight of several hundred expectant eyes on me.

As my vision adjusts, I scan the audience, desperate for a gleam of honey-gold curls. Where is she? Georgie must be here somewhere, Star sprawled at her feet, but the brightness on stage makes it impossible to see beyond the front rows.

Someone coughs. Fabric rustles as people shift in their seats. A baby wails and is hastily shushed. What am I doing, standing like a petrified lemon in the middle of the stage? Flushing to the tips of my toes, I hurry over to the grand piano, almost losing one of my ballet pumps in the process. Only the piano bench prevents me from nosediving onto the wooden boards. I throw out an arm to stop my fall and collapse onto it. Humiliation averted.

A microphone perches atop the piano, relaying my every gasp and ragged breath to the audience. *Calm down, Mina, you've got this.*

"Uh, hi." My voice emerges half an octave higher than normal and I grip the edge of the piano, attempting to steady myself. "The song I'm going to sing, it's one I wrote for... for a very special person."

This gets their attention. The fidgeting quietens and the collective gaze of the audience bores into me like a search beam.

My parents are out there somewhere, watching me. I can picture their expressions, attentive but unconcerned, oblivious to how my next words will alter their perception of me forever. My heart cowers in my ribcage, but I give it a stern talking-to. *Don't think about Mum and Dad. Think about Georgie. She's the one you're doing this for.*

I clear my throat, so dry I'm afraid it will crack the instant I start singing. "This person…well, she knows who she is. This is for you, to say I'm sorry. That…that I love you."

Some idiot wolf whistles. My cheeks catch fire, but I force myself not to skim the audience for the culprit. Instead, I place my hands on the keys. They're smooth and shiny to the touch and I imagine them slipping away from me, spilling like a fistful of marbles from my grasp. *For heaven's sake, Mina, get a grip.* I flex my fingers, hoping to still their trembling, then position them for the opening chord.

The instant I begin to play, my entire body relaxes. Georgie, my nerves, the knowledge that I'm in the process of coming out to my parents—it all fades into the background and a sense of rightness settles over me. This is where I'm supposed to be, seated before the grand piano on Dukes' famous stage, notes pouring in a shimmering waterfall from my fingertips. For now, nothing matters but the music. I open my mouth, expand my diaphragm, and pour out the lyrics I'd stayed up most of the night composing.

79. GEORGIE

T HAT VOICE. I'D know it anywhere.
We shuffle into seats near the back of the hall as the third act gets underway. I whisper to Star to lie down and then settle back to enjoy the show. A melancholy guitar intro melds into lyrics charged with longing. Wow, those vocals, rich as tiramisu. Impossible not to be drawn in.

"Who's that?" Dad asks in my ear.

"Chanelle Clarke. She was in my flat."

"What a voice."

I nod. Before our talk, Dad's praise would've rankled, but not anymore. Plus…that song. It's poignant in a way that feels real, a love ballad about the pain of wanting someone who doesn't know you exist. Is it about Zephan? Maybe Chanelle's crush went deeper than I realised. Or maybe it's only a song.

Either way, how can I go up on stage after this? The effort I cobbled together during the early hours feels pathetic now. Panic froths in my gut. It'll be fine. Who cares what anyone else thinks? All that matters is that Mina hears it, that she understands.

God, is Mina performing today? Surely, she must be. This is what she thrives on, sharing her music with the world. She wouldn't pass up an opportunity like this, unless… Unless she's too upset over our fight to face it.

After Chanelle, an all-male band fronted by Kai has the audience stamping their feet to a rocked-up version of Pharrell Williams' 'Happy'. When the clapping and wolf whistles die down, Calypso announces Gareth and Zephan.

"That's them," I tell my family over the applause. "My friends."

"Hey, everyone," Gareth calls from the stage, and the hall falls quiet. "So, my mate Zeph here's a bit shy, like, so if you could give him an extra-big welcome…"

"Kill me now." Zephan mutters it under his breath, but his words carry clearly over the microphone.

Laughter ripples through the audience. Several people cheer and we all break into another round of applause. I clap so hard my palms sting.

"Yeah," Gareth continues, "he took a lot of persuading to come up on stage today. In the end, I think he only agreed because it would give him an excuse to slag me off in public."

More laughter and the scrape of the piano bench. Next moment, Gareth launches into the ominous chords of 'The Ballad of Tom Jones'.

Man, I love this song. It's one of our favourites to blast out on long car trips. Dad sings along with Space while I take the part of Cerys Matthews. We ham it up, completely murdering the Welsh accents, and by the end, all four of us are in hysterics.

The boys put us to shame, though. Zeph's really throwing himself into it, his Phil Phillips gruffness the flipside to Gaz's purer tone. As they get into character, trading insults like a jaded married couple, I laugh for the first time since the pool party.

80. MINA

As soon as Gareth and Zephan re-enter the performers' lounge, I leap off the couch to hug them. "You guys were incredible. That voice, Zeph. Where've you been hiding it?"

"Not hiding. Just…saving it for the right moment." Zephan gives me an awkward pat on the shoulder and disentangles himself. He crosses to set his guitar case in a corner before flopping into a nearby armchair.

The backstage lounge is the perfect space to unwind before or after a performance, bright and airy with comfy sofas clustered around shelves of books and board games. Speakers relay the audio from the hall so that Patrice's rendition of a Whitney Houston classic swells above the quiet conversation. A few girls are chatting over by the open window, while Kai sits cross-legged on the floor organising a round of cards.

"Want to watch the rest of the first half?" Gareth asks.

I shake my head. Much as I'd like to see my fellow campers perform, I'm not ready to face Mum and Dad. "You go, though, if you like."

"Nah. My family has the whole of the next year to spend with me. I'm not sure when we'll get to hang out again." Gareth puts an arm around me and we return to our couch.

I slip off my shoes and tuck my legs beneath me, resting my head on his shoulder. This summer may have had its ups and downs, but being able to spend this time with Gaz has been amazing. Soon, though, we'll have to say goodbye, revert to the days of texting and video calls. How will I bear it?

"I'm going to miss you," I tell him, swallowing the lump in my throat.

"Aw, don't. You'll have me bawling in a minute. We'll still talk every day, I promise."

I nod. It will be tough, only seeing him through a computer screen, but we'll always be there for one another.

Gareth tugs on my hair. "You must be proud of yourself. What you did, that was one of the bravest things I've ever seen."

My cheeks grow warm. The honest answer is that I'm not sure how I feel, my insides a jumble of conflicting emotions. There's a definite sense of pride, but it's all tangled up with disbelief that I'd actually gone through with it, and dread at how my parents will react. And underlying the whole mess… what if my efforts are too little too late?

At last, all I say is, "I just hope it'll be enough."

ONCE THE FIRST half is over, Gareth and I leave Zephan engrossed in his book and hurry from the performers' lounge. Surely Georgie will be waiting for me. She can't doubt how sorry I am, not now I've laid it all out there. Yet, when we emerge into the foyer, she's nowhere to be seen.

I pause, scanning the throng spilling from the concert hall and across to the reception room. When Gareth squeezes my shoulder and goes to join his parents, I scarcely notice him leave. Over and over, my gaze rakes the crowd. Where is she? Could she be waiting outside, figuring we could go somewhere more private to talk? Yes, that will be it.

"Mina?"

I'm part way towards the entrance to the grounds when Dad grasps my arm. His touch is gentle, but I flinch, spinning to find him and Mum behind me. *Oh, no. No, no, no.* I'd prayed I could slip past them, put off the inevitable a while longer.

"Galbi?" Dad studies my face as though it's an X-ray he's examining for fractured bones. "What's going on?"

"Is everything OK?" Mum adds. "Your song was beautiful, but we couldn't help wondering…"

She trails off, perhaps to give me the chance to fill in the gap. My fingers interlock, twisting together. I owe them the truth, but at the same time…

"I will explain," I say in a rush, "I promise I will, but I need to find Georgie. Is it all right if we talk later? Please?"

Mum takes both my hands in hers and looks into my eyes. "Do whatever you need to. We'll be here."

Dad drops a kiss on my forehead, frowning. "We'll go and get a drink. Join us when you're ready."

I watch them weave through the crowd, tears smarting behind my eyelids. Never before have I been so grateful for their trust in me, nor so conscious of the danger that I might lose that trust. Well, I can't worry about that now. Shaking my head to clear it, I head out into the afternoon sunshine.

A few people mill about with glasses of golden champagne in their hands, but Georgie isn't among them, so I extract my phone from my dress pocket. I'll text her, find out where she is. Only…the screen refuses to light up at my touch. *Sugar.* I never forget to charge my phone, but with everything going on, I must have.

Annoyed with myself, I look around and spy Chanelle Clarke and her friends squeezed onto the bench by the entrance.

It's a long shot, but I don't have any other ideas, so I wander over to them. "Hey, have any of you seen Georgie?"

Most of them shake their heads, but Blair gives a careless shrug. "You've missed her."

"I'm sorry?" What is she talking about? Has Georgie gone back to the house, assuming I'd follow her there?

Blair huffs. "I saw her waiting by the car before the concert. She'll be halfway home by now."

81. GEORGIE

THE ONE ADVANTAGE to arriving late to the concert? It's easy to make a quick exit.

The moment Calypso announces the interval, me and Star are outside and crossing the grounds to Osborne House. I need to run through my song one more time, get the lyrics straight in my head. This is my chance to put things right between us. I can't muck it up.

In our room, Star curls up in her corner. I unpack my guitar and perch on the mattress. Stripped of sheets, the duvet and pillows in a neat pile, the bed feels abandoned. How can the summer be over?

Sadness nips at me, but I shrug it off. A lot has happened within these walls; I've learned so much. I might never set foot in this exact room again, but maybe…just maybe I'll get to come back here. Right now, though, I have a job to do.

"Go KILL IT, George." In the foyer ten minutes later, Dad claps me on the shoulder. "We'll be right there cheering you on."

"Good luck," Mum says and ruffles my hair.

I nod, nerves clogging my throat. After bending to stroke Star, I hand the lead off to Jake. She'll watch from the audience with my family. Once they've gone, I stall for a few moments, adjusting the strap of my guitar case. *Come on. You can't hang around out here forever.* I take a deep breath, then feel my way along the backstage corridor to the performers' lounge.

"Georgie." Dutch greets me with his lazy drawl. "Come grab a seat. You're fourth on, I think, so you have a while to relax."

Relax? What a joke. Dutch offers his arm, guiding me over to a sofa. I collapse onto it and prop my instrument beside me. *God, don't throw up. I've dealt with enough sick today already.*

Laughter, conversation, the rattle of dice. No one else seems about to vomit. Well, why would they? None of them has so much riding on their performance.

"Hey." Zephan flops beside me.

I grin. In the rush of last-minute packing and giving my family the grand tour, I haven't seen him since our morning cuppa. "Hey. You were bloody brilliant. Can't believe Gaz finally got you on stage."

"You can talk. Since when are you so brave?"

"Brave? Hardly, but it's something I have to do." I fill him in on my plan. When I've finished, I let my head loll against the cushions. "I just need her to know she didn't do anything wrong. It's all my fault, me and my stupid pride."

Zephan's quiet for several seconds before he asks, "Mina didn't find you then? During the interval?"

"What? No, I went back to my room to run through my song."

"OK, but you know you don't have anything to sweat over, right? Fuck, the whole audience heard her."

I rub my forehead. He may as well be speaking Gnomish. "What're you going on about?"

"Shit." Zephan sounds like he's on the verge of solving a riddle. "You didn't hear it, did you?"

"Hear what?"

"Mina's song. The one she dedicated to you in front of a hall full of people."

What? Air snags in my chest. "I must've missed it. Star was sick all over me. I had to go back to the car and change. What… What did it say?"

"Oh, a shitload of mush. So sorry for hurting you, most important thing to me…blah, blah, blah."

Oh, God. How could I have missed it? If Mum had tracked Dad and Jake down quicker, if Dad hadn't buried my suitcase under all my other stuff, if I'd prevented Star from eating the quiche in the first place…

My eyelids burn. That was so brave. Mina's so scared of how her parents will react to her being a lesbian, doesn't want to let them down. Still, she bared her heart to me in front of everyone, and I wasn't even there.

Mina must've looked for me in the interval. She would've been desperate to know if her song had got through, if I'd forgiven her. Man, what had she thought when she couldn't find me? That I don't care, probably. *There's nothing to say.* That's what I'd texted her, wasn't it? Of course, when she hears my song…

If she hears it.

My breathing speeds up. What if Mina doesn't stick around? Doubt I would. If I were her, I'd want to slip away sharpish. For all I know, Mina could be headed home this very minute.

82. MINA

Mum and Dad find me wandering the patio outside the reception room, scarcely aware what I'm doing. Neither of them asks questions, which is just as well. I doubt I'd be able to speak without dissolving into an emotional mess at their feet. They simply take charge with their usual calm efficiency, whisking me away from the Dukes Building and across campus.

"Don't fret, sweetheart." Mum hugs me to her side as we walk. "Whatever it is, we'll sort it."

"There's always a solution, remember," Dad says.

He throws an arm over my shoulders so that I'm sheltered between him and Mum. It should make me feel safe, and it does, but in a bittersweet sort of way. What if this is the last time we exist like this, a united family unit?

As we wind along the main path, my parents keep up a flow of light chatter, telling me about Aaliyah's latest antics and a lovely restaurant where they thought we might stop for dinner on the way home. I barely hear them. Everything feels distant, unreal, as though I'm a ghost walking through the living world.

Georgie left. She left without saying goodbye, before she could discover how far I was prepared to go for her. I'd stood in front of everyone—in front of my parents—revealed the truths of my heart, and the one person I'd done it for hadn't even been there.

In the student centre, Mum goes into raptures over the hot drinks machine. "Look, they've even got pineapple and grapefruit, my favourite. Will you have your usual, Mina?"

I nod, too choked to answer, although I doubt the camomile will have much effect today. Dad ushers me onto the nearest sofa and sits beside me, rubbing my back. It's strange, the student centre being so empty. Apart from the whoosh and clunk of the drinks machine, the room is silent. It adds to my sense of unreality.

"Here you are, sweetheart." Mum presses a cup of tea into my hands. She passes Dad his Earl Gray and sits on my other side with her own drink. "So, are you going to tell us what's got you so upset?"

This is it, the moment that has loomed over my head for the whole of my teenage years. My gaze flicks from one face to the other, their identical expressions of love and concern. What if they never look at me like this again? What if they hate me?

"You know you can tell us anything," Dad says. "Anything at all. We won't judge."

He's so certain, truly believing nothing I say could change his opinion of me. Somehow, his unwavering faith only makes me feel worse. Still, what choice do I have? Not confiding in them will only cause them more worry. I open my mouth, no idea where to begin, and burst into tears.

83. GEORGIE

"HI, SO SORRY I can't take your call right now, but if you leave a message—"

I hang up without waiting for the beep. What's the point? She doesn't want to speak to me; the fact that she's switched her phone off says so loud and clear. For a moment, I rest my forehead in my palm. *God, Mina, I'm sorry. I'm sorry I wasn't there, that I made such a cock-up of everything.*

"Welcome back, everyone." Calypso's words pour from the speakers. "We have plenty more incredible acts for you, so let's do this. We're kicking off the second half with a group of young ladies who'll be performing an original song. Please put your hands together for the hugely talented Harmonia!"

I turn to Zephan, chest tight. "Voicemail. What now? I'm supposed to be on stage soon, but there's no point if Mina's already gone home."

"She won't have," Zephan says.

His calm annoys the crap out of me. "How do you know? Have you seen her since the interval?"

"Nope."

"Then how—"

"She'll want to watch the rest of the concert."

I scoff. "Why would she bother? She just sang a song for me, and as far as she knows, I've completely blanked her. Would you stick around?"

"Trust me," Zephan says, "this mess falls way outside my experience."

Can't argue with that. Before this summer, it would've been far outside mine, too. "OK, but pretend you're Mina. What would you do?"

Zephan's silent. The speakers spew out an upbeat pop/rock track, acoustic guitars accompanying a four-part harmony. It sets my teeth on edge.

At last, Zephan sighs and hauls himself to his feet. "I'll go hunt her down."

"Seriously?" My heart lifts, just a fraction. "Zeph, I love you."

"Shut it or I'll change my mind. Text me if you hear from her, yeah?"

"I will. And let me know as soon as you find her."

If he finds her.

I shove the thought away. Zeph'll track Mina down. He has to. My plan can't fail before I've even put it into action.

84. MINA

My parents are crying now, Mum wiping at her wet cheeks, Dad blinking against the dampness in his eyes. They hadn't interrupted as I talked, letting it all spill out between hiccupping sobs and sips of tea, but their tears say it all.

"I'm so sorry." I scrub at my face, puffy and raw. "You must be so disappointed in me."

Mum looks shocked. "How can you think that? We could never be disappointed in you for being the person you are."

"Your mum's right," Dad says, voice choked. "I don't know where we went wrong, how we could ever have given you that impression, but regardless, that's on us."

"Dad, no, it wasn't anything you did. None of this is your fault. I just thought, after everything with May…" I trail off. My parents are looking at one another across me, their expressions an identical mix of confusion and dismay.

Mum turns to me, brow creased. "Sweetheart, you've lost us. What does any of this have to do with your sister?"

It emerges from me in fits and starts—May's brilliance, Mum and Dad's hopes for her future, the shock of her pregnancy and dropping out of uni. With every syllable, my conviction ebbs. Surely, I shouldn't need to explain any of this, not if they feel the way I've always believed.

"So." Mum frowns, as though trying to get to the bottom of a complex diagnosis. "So, you believe your dad and I are disappointed in May?"

"Well, it made you so happy when she decided to study medicine. You were always saying what a great doctor she'd be one day. This can't be what you wanted for her."

"It's not what we would have chosen, perhaps, but that doesn't mean we aren't proud of the person she's become. The way she was so strong when she found out she was pregnant, how she's such a wonderful mother... I couldn't be prouder of her if I tried."

"And she's given us Aaliyah," Dad says, gaze soft. "Even if she'd become the top brain surgeon in the world, May couldn't have given us anything more precious."

85. GEORGIE

T HE MINUTES SPEED by faster than a cheetah on steroids. Harmonia leave the stage to thunderous applause and Andre takes their place. He hurls himself into an original track, hip-hop vocals over the screech of electric guitar. Man, the boy can rap. He's so fast I couldn't've kept up even if I weren't fixated on my phone.

Still nothing from Zeph. I shift on the sofa to ease my muscles. They're stretched tauter than the skin of a snare. Soon, Calypso will call my name and I'll have to walk out in front of all those people. Where's Zephan got to? Has he found Mina? Is she still here, or is she curled in the back seat of her parents' car, the distance between us growing with every second?

"All right, mate?" Art's voice pulls me from my thoughts. He sounds more subdued than normal, less sure of himself.

"Yeah," I lie, trying to smile. "Bit nervous."

"Tell me about it. I'm shitting myself."

"Come off it. You never get nervous."

He snorts a laugh. "Trust me, I do, especially when I have a certain someone to impress."

"Your dad's here then?" Poor Art. It must be hell for him, forced to conform to his dad's idea of masculinity.

"Yup, so no George Michael or Queen for me today. Nothing that'll get Dad started on one of his rants."

"Shit, Art, I'm sorry."

"It is what it is." His tone is matter-of-fact. "And who knows? If I impress him enough with my macho performance, maybe he'll let me come here next September."

For his sake, I hope so. Dukes might be my dream, but it's so much more to Art. It's his best chance of escape. From what Mina and Gareth have told me, the sooner Art can get away from his dad the better.

"Art, you're up," Dutch calls from his post by the door.

Come on, Zeph, where are you? Time's running out here. After Art, it'll be my turn. I have to know Mina's there in the audience, that this could still work.

Art punches me on the shoulder. "See you, mate. Good luck."

"And you," I manage. Then he's gone, and I'm alone again with my panic.

86. MINA

I SIT STILL, ABSORBING my parents' words. Sunshine spills through the window behind us and bathes me in golden warmth. How had I never realised? I'd been so fixated on May's mistakes, I'd completely missed the success she's made of this other life, unplanned but every bit as fulfilling.

"And all this time," Mum muses aloud, "you've been thinking you have to take May's place, step into her shoes."

I nod, staring into my empty mug. "Only, I can't. I never could. I'll never meet a nice young man and have a big Catholic wedding. I don't want to be a doctor or a lawyer or anything worthy like that. I just want to play music."

"You never said." Dad sounds bemused. "As far as we were aware, you saw your music as a hobby, like my golf."

"Why didn't you tell us you were interested in pursuing it more seriously?" Mum asks.

I sag against the cushions, worn out with emotion and too many revelations. "Because I knew you'd think it was a bad idea. You've always stressed how important it is to have a stable career."

"We do believe that," Dad says, "but that doesn't mean we can't have a conversation, if it's what you truly want."

I raise my head. "Really? You'd consider letting me come to Dukes to study?"

"I'm not saying we wouldn't have reservations," Mum warns. "Of course we would. Music's a hard business to break into, but we'd never stop you following your dream."

A smile teases the corner of my mouth. "And...and you're honestly OK with me...me being—"

Before I can finish, Mum and Dad converge on me, wrapping me in their arms. How could I ever have doubted them? It seems ridiculous now, confronted with their unconditional support. I lean into their hug, holding on to them. There's an ache inside me, a jagged hole where Georgie should be, but my parents' love makes it easier to bear.

The door to the student centre bursts open, crashing against the wall. All three of us break apart and round to face the newcomer.

"Zeph?" I gape at him. He looks nothing like his usual impassive self, eyes wild, face damp with sweat.

"Thank Christ. I've been hunting all over for you." Zephan's gasping so hard he can barely speak. "You have to come. Now. Or it'll be too late."

87. GEORGIE

"Y OU'RE NEXT, GEORGIE," Dutch calls. His words are an electric shock, jolting me to my feet. When did my legs turn to Plasticine? They shudder beneath me and I almost flop back onto the sofa. When I stoop to unpack my guitar, my head swims. Am I going to faint? Maybe that wouldn't be a bad thing. Would get me out of performing, at least.

"You cool?" Dutch asks, coming over.

I straighten with my Fender and manage a nod. Cool, that's me. Cool, calm and collected. Definitely not about to melt into a blob of jelly on the carpet.

"No need to look so terrified." Dutch presses my shoulder. "It's just a bit of fun."

But it isn't. I have to show Mina she didn't toss her heart out there for nothing, that I'm here to catch it for her and keep it safe. Except, I don't even know if she'll be watching.

Dutch steers me over to the door and opens it for me. "Can you find your way OK?"

"Yeah," I force out, voice jagged. "Thanks."

"No probs. When Calypso introduces you, just step out on stage and she'll help you to where you need to be." He gives my shoulder a last squeeze. Then I'm standing in the corridor, the door to the performers' lounge closing behind me.

I hesitate, guitar cradled awkwardly under one arm. This feels unreal. It's like I've walked into an anxiety dream, the one where I'm about to go on stage only to realise I've forgotten to rehearse. Every movement is sluggish, the air thick as Dad's turkey soup. My heart thuds against my ribs, too loud, too fast. *Come on, George, get a grip.* In a daze, I cross the width of the corridor and trail the opposite wall until my fingers brush the stage door. One final gulping breath and I pull on the handle.

A classic rock track — Deep Purple, I think — blasts my eardrums. It's a wild meshing of Art's powerful vocals and flawless drumming, Andre on electric guitar. The whole feel is different from Art's usual style. It's darker, grittier, obviously designed to impress his dad. As I climb the stairs, the boards pulsate beneath my feet. I steady myself against the banister. *Great.* I'm woozy enough without the floor threatening to shatter under me.

When I reach the wings, I prop my back against the nearest wall. My hand grips the neck of my Fender like a crutch. I screw my eyes shut, nerves jangling in sync with the music. I can't do this. No way I can step out in front of a hall full of strangers and sing. Christ, I couldn't even do it for a handful of judges. Too late to back out now, though. I'm committed.

I inhale. *Don't hyperventilate.* Where can Zephan have got to? Has he tracked Mina down, or is she already miles away? What if she isn't in the audience? I can't exactly perform the song I wrote for her. I'll have to sing something else, but what? 'Girl Like You'? God, not again. I made such a hash of that last time. Still, given how much I've practised it this week, it's my best bet.

Too soon, Art finishes his song and the hall erupts. Below me, the stage door opens and shuts with a stifled thump. Footsteps hurry up the stairs, and my heart flings itself against my larynx.

Then Zeph grunts in my ear. "Found her. She's coming."

"What? Really?"

"Yup. Had a hell of a job tracking her down, so it bloody well better be worth it."

Before I can thank him, he's gone again, the door whooshing shut on his retreating footsteps. Mina's still here. She's on her way, and all this won't be for nothing. The relief has scarcely sunk in when the applause fades and Calypso's once more at the microphone.

"And now," she says, her words reverberating in my skull, "please put your hands together and welcome the amazing Georgie Wilde."

88. MINA

"WHAT'S GOING ON?" I run to keep up with Zephan, but his legs cover the ground far quicker than my shorter ones.

He glowers over his shoulder. "Georgie. She has something she wants you to watch."

"Georgie? But she went home ages ago. Blair told me she saw her about to leave."

Zephan snorts, which is probably all the response this deserves. Perhaps I shouldn't have accepted Blair's word so readily, although what reason would she have to lie? True, she's a top-class cow, but she wouldn't make something up purely to upset me, would she? Unless she was simply mistaken.

Mum hurries to draw level with me. The fact that both she and Dad are regular visitors to the gym means they have no trouble keeping up.

"Georgie," she says, barely even out of breath, "she's someone special to you? As more than a friend?"

I nod. "But I messed up. That's why I sang the song I did. To say sorry."

But Georgie hadn't heard it…or had she? If Blair was wrong about her leaving, maybe Georgie had been there the whole time. Maybe my performance wasn't for nothing, after all. But then, why hadn't she sought me out during the interval?

My brain's still spinning with unanswered questions when we reach the paved area outside the concert hall.

"Get in there." Zephan jabs a finger towards the nearest set of French windows.

I open my mouth to demand what we're doing here, but he's already sprinting towards the entrance to the Dukes Building. Then he disappears, the main doors swinging shut behind him. The three of us are left looking at each other, perplexed. From the hall, the final wail of an electric guitar melds into a storm of whoops and clapping.

"Interesting young man," Dad says, surprising a laugh out of me. I'm not sure how I'd describe Zephan Oduro, but interesting doesn't do him justice.

The applause recedes. I'm about to suggest we go inside, since that's clearly what Zephan intended, and then I hear it. *Oh my gosh*. My body goes utterly still. A guitar intro, wistful and sweet in a way that seizes my heart. And her voice, soft and yelping with a dusting of sand—a voice I'd recognise anywhere.

> *I was proud,*
> *I closed my ears to all you tried to say,*
> *I slammed the door and let you walk away,*
> *Oh, I was proud.*

Dad touches my shoulder. "Is that her? Georgie?"

Too choked to speak, I can only nod. In a haze, I move towards the open French windows and slip inside. I'm at the very back of the hall, rows and rows of seats separating me from the stage, but even from this distance, I can see her—Georgie—hair tawny and wild as a lion's mane under the spotlight. Oh, my brave, wonderful girl.

Mum and Dad move to flank me, but I can't tear my eyes from the figure on stage. She's clearly terrified, muscles rigid, every note trembling with nerves. Yet she also has the look of a warrior, someone prepared to fight for what she believes in. Georgie clutches her guitar to her as though it's a shield, jaw set with the determination to go through with this. For me. She's braved her performance anxiety, has gone up there in front of hundreds of people, and all for me, to prove something she never needed to prove in the first place. I can't help it. For the countless time that afternoon, tears overflow and pour down my face.

89. GEORGIE

"SORRY I MISSED your song," I tell Mina later. "I'm totally gutted."

"Don't be silly. Star wasn't well. Were you, girl?" In the hallway outside her room, Mina stoops to pet Star, who wags enthusiastically.

"Yeah," I mutter. "Came down with a case of greedyitis."

Mina laughs. She straightens, sliding her key into the lock.

The concert's finished, thank Christ. Much as I'm proud of myself for getting up there and doing my thing, I'm in no rush to do it again. Not on my own, anyway. We left everyone back in the reception room, campers saying their goodbyes while friends and families raved about the performances.

Mina claimed she needed to have a last scout around, make doubly sure she'd packed everything. It was an obvious ploy for the two of us to snatch some alone time. Still, either her mum and dad didn't mind or they were too busy nattering with my parents to notice.

As soon as we're inside with the door shut, we reach for each other. I hold her close, bury my face in her neck. God, I've missed this. I've missed her body nestled against mine, the tickle of her hair, her bright, lemony scent.

"I'm such a prat," I mumble. "We could've had this whole weekend together, but I wasted it."

Mina runs her fingers through my curls. "What about me? I threw away a whole week to be with you because I was worried what my parents would think, and it turns out that was for nothing."

"They're really OK with it?"

"I can't quite believe it, but they are. I always knew they wouldn't disown me or anything, but this is more than I ever hoped for. I'm...well, I'm just so happy I don't have to hide this from them."

And she sounds happy. It bubbles beneath her words like the fizz in a glass of Sprite.

I slide my hands over the planes and ridges of her back, skin warm through her dress. "You think they'll be all right with us visiting each other then? Like, for the weekend or whatever?"

"Are you serious?" Mina's laugh grazes my ear. "If Mum weren't allergic, Dad would beg you and Star to come and live with us."

I grin. When Mina introduced me to her parents, they both greeted me like a long-lost daughter. The fuss her dad made of Star, I had the strong suspicion he was considering how to stow her in the boot with the luggage.

"I like your mum and dad," Mina says. "And your brother's lovely. Definitely not as scary as he looks."

"Yeah, Jake couldn't be less scary if he tried." I squeeze her tighter, don't want to let go. Not ever.

My feelings must show on my stupid face, as Mina's lips brush mine and she whispers, "We'll sort out a visit soon, I promise."

I'm so lucky. Is it weird to feel like this? I lost out on the scholarship, after all. Probably, but I do. Getting to explore the renowned Dukes academy, to mix with stars like Calypso and Dutch. Making what I hope will be lifelong friends in Zephan and Gareth, maybe even Art. And most of all? Finding someone as special as Mina, someone who wants to be with me as much as I want her. Compared with that, what does a silly competition matter?

90. MINA

FOR AN INDETERMINATE time, there's only Georgie. Every one of my senses is attuned to her nearness—her sturdy body moulded to mine, the springy softness of her curls, her mouth, searching and gentle. I thought I'd never get to do this again, never get to kiss her or watch the emotions shift like shadows over her face. That makes it all the more precious.

A knock bursts our private bubble. We wrench ourselves apart, Georgie's expression mirroring my own dismay. Surely, it can't be Mum and Dad come to whisk me home already?

"It's only us," Gareth calls. "Zeph and me."

"Oh." I hurry to fling open the bedroom door. "Was worried you might've left."

Gareth grimaces. "Dad wants to hit the road soon, and Zeph's parents need to get back for his sister's recital, like, but we couldn't go without saying goodbye. Right, Zeph?"

Zephan replies with a curious sort of half nod, half shrug. He looks supremely awkward, the way he always does when confronted with the threat of intimacy. The temptation to tease him is too much even for me.

I take my place at Georgie's side and slide an arm around her, extending the other to Zeph with my coyest smile. "Group hug?"

"Oh, no. No, not again." He edges backwards towards the door.

"Whoa there." Gareth grabs his shoulder. "You really think we're letting you go without a proper send-off? No way, hun."

He propels Zephan further into the room, and the three of us converge on him until we're in a huddle, Gareth and me sandwiching him between us. The entire time, Zephan's muttering under his breath, "This isn't happening. This isn't happening. This. Isn't. Happening."

Gareth ignores him, his smile encompassing Georgie and me. "Glad you two sorted things out."

"Yeah. Us, too." Georgie leans her head against mine, her hair caressing my cheek.

"And your parents." Gareth's gaze rests on me, bright with wonder. "All that agonising over how to tell them, and they're completely fine with it."

Happiness floods my belly like molten toffee, and I can't stop smiling. "I know. Maybe… Maybe your parents won't mind as much as you think they will, either."

"Yeah, maybe." Some of the light fades from Gareth's eyes and he looks down. "Maybe I'll be brave like you one day and tell them."

I'm about to reassure him, to explain that it has nothing to do with courage or cowardice, only about feeling ready. Before I can say anything, though, there's another tap at the door. *Please don't let it be my parents, not yet.* Clutching Georgie tighter, I call for whoever it is to come in.

The door handle turns and Art appears on the threshold— the unfamiliar Art with his undyed hair and plain clothes. He offers a cautious smile. "Um, is this a ticket-only event or can anyone join in?"

Zephan's scowl says quite clearly that he'd like to slam the door in Art's face, but it has to be Gareth's decision. I glance over at my friend, prepared to turn Art away if he seems upset. Instead, Gareth's returning Art's smile and has moved to make space for him between himself and Georgie. Art slots into the circle, and the members of Wildest Dreams are complete.

I consider each of my bandmates in turn—Zephan, whose rigid stoicism suggests he's enduring some terrible ordeal; Gareth, his gentle features etched with both the pain and triumph of the past month; Art, a diminished version of his true self, about to return home to his oppressive father; Georgie, solid and beautiful, her expression veering from elation to sadness with the swiftness of a cloud passing across the sun.

And me.

I barely recognise the girl I was at the start of the summer. It's hard to believe how much I've changed, how I've grown in confidence. It doesn't matter that I didn't win the scholarship, because what I've gained is far more important.

There's no predicting what might happen during the following year, how many of us will find ourselves at Dukes next September. Gaz is guaranteed his place, of course, and Zeph's musical family will surely send him if they can. From what Georgie's told me, like my parents, her mum is at least coming round to the idea. And Art? My heart cracks for him, this boy whose father is determined to beat the individuality out of him, who would rather see him break his back on a building site than fulfil his God-given talent.

I nuzzle into Georgie, savouring the feel of her, the luxury of having her close. *Dear Lord, please help the five of us come back here next September, to be together again.* It won't be the same, I accept that. Perhaps things will never be wholly easy between Gareth and Art, and I doubt Zephan will ever forgive him. Still, whatever mistakes we've made this summer, Dukes is where we belong. We should be allowed to pursue our dreams, to try for the future we want. Scholarship or not, we deserve that chance.

THE END

CLAIM YOUR FREE STORY

Thank you so much for reading. If you enjoyed this book, you can join my readers' club to get a free and exclusive short story in my *Boys on the Brink* series. Simply go to

https://jamiedeacon.com/readersclub

and enter your email address. You'll then receive a welcome email from me with links to download your story in your preferred format.

You'll also be signed up to my newsletter where I share updates on my writing, post giveaways, and generally indulge my passion for the world of YA LGBTQ+ fiction. You can unsubscribe at any time and your data will be kept safe and secure.

Happy reading and I look forward to connecting with you!

Jamie

PLEASE LEAVE A REVIEW

It's no exaggeration to say that, to authors, reviews are invaluable. Just a line or two expressing your thoughts can be such a help in spreading the word to like-minded readers. So, if you enjoyed this book, please consider leaving a review on Amazon or your online bookstore of choice. It would mean more to me than I can say.

ABOUT THE AUTHOR

Jamie Deacon is an award-winning author of young adult LGBTQ+ fiction with a passion for weaving stories about friendship, falling in love and finding the courage to be true to yourself. Their debut novel, *Caught Inside*, won two Rainbow Awards and was nominated for a Lambda Literary Award, a Bisexual Book Award and a Next Generation Indie Book Award.

Jamie was born with Retinitis Pigmentosa, a degenerative eye condition that left them registered blind by their mid-teens. Now only able to view their surroundings in light and shadow, Jamie creates vivid settings inside their head and brings them to life through the magic of words.

Jamie lives with their childhood sweetheart close to the River Thames in Berkshire, England. When not curled under a blanket with a book, they enjoy British comedy, are a huge dog lover, and get way too competitive at family games nights.

To find out more about Jamie and their books, you can visit https://jamiedeacon.com

BOOKS BY JAMIE DEACON

BOYS ON THE BRINK SERIES

Caught Inside
https://jamiedeacon.com/caught-inside

Forbidden Steps
https://jamiedeacon.com/forbidden-steps

Defensive Play (Novella)
https://jamiedeacon.com/defensive-play

Off Course (Short Story)
https://jamiedeacon.com/off-course

STANDALONE TITLES

The Music of Unexpected Things
https://jamiedeacon.com/the-music-of-unexpected-things

Ink Lane
Publishing